The Strangeness of Losing Things and Finding Things

A Collection of Stories

By

Nicholas Callis

Cover design by Christopher Copeland
Cover copyright © 2025 by Nicholas Callis

Self-published by Nicholas Callis

1st edition 2025

ISBN: 979-8-9928041-1-9 (Paperback)

This book is dedicated to all those people who read on through to the end.
Thank you.

Contents

The New Mirror

Robert tightened the final screw supporting the new mirror in his children's bathroom and wiped the sweat from his brow. Even though he was wearing boxers and a t-shirt, even though the AC was blasting — he was drenched.

Probably had something to do with his thick wool socks. Wool socks in the middle of spring. They trapped the heat. Summoned the sweat.

Bad plan. Sweaty wool socks made it tough to stand on smooth bathroom counter.

Needed doing, though. The old mirror had nearly crushed the kids when it toppled off the wall. Wife wouldn't have liked that. Didn't like most things Robert did, but crushed kids would've been a whole *thing*.

He left a tiny bit of wiggle in the last screw, same as the other three corners. Something from a half-remembered HGTV show. Something about leaving the screws a little loose. Robert's wife recorded those kinds of shows for him all the time. Handyman shows and shows about flipping houses and shows with people hunting dream homes and shows about manly men succeeding at manly projects. Instruction manuals for how she wanted him to be.

One had definitely mentioned loose screws. Probably.

Though, Robert couldn't really tell the difference between a *little* wiggle and *too much* wiggle. He was an insurance analyst, not a carpenter. But he figured even *he* couldn't screw up screwing in a mirror.

At least until his wife found something wrong with it.

As if called by the fear in that thought, Kathy shrieked from downstairs, "Robert, hurry up and come eat! The breakfast I made for you is getting cold!"

The shriek forced Robert's body to convulse, his muscles to contract. One sweat-soaked wool sock slipped off the edge of the counter. Found nothing but air. Nobody was there to catch him. Robert started to fall.

But he didn't finish his fall. Robert felt a hard tug under his arm. The tug led him through an awkward, one-footed swivel on the counter. Then he slammed butt-first onto the hard ceramic. His cheeks ached, but a sore rump beat a snapped neck.

"That was pretty close," a familiar voice said.

Robert plopped off the bathroom counter and looked at the mirror. There, staring at him, was his reflection. Actually looking at him, not just reflecting back. Another Robert.

An Other-Robert.

"You almost had a bad spill there," this Other-Robert said.

"No kidding, friend." Robert rubbed his neck — the spot that would have wedged against the wall, had he finished his fall. His muscles sent phantom signals of pain and disaster to his brain. "Would've been an insurance hike for that hospital stay for sure. Wife wouldn't like that."

Robert tried to hide the shakiness in his voice, but his fear poked through, more noticeable than wool socks in spring. Other-Robert didn't seem to notice.

"Well, you're safe now," the double reassured. "I'm just glad I was working on my kids' mirror at the same time as you."

The kids. School.

Robert groaned. "Oh no. I need to make sure the kids are getting dressed or Kathy'll-"

"-Kill me." Other-Robert's eyes went wide like a deer in headlights.

Getting chewed out by Kathy was probably a close second to getting hit by a car. At least the car-crash scenario would only be a one-time occurrence. Lucky deer.

"I'll be right back," Robert said. He left the bathroom to check on Allen and Jill.

He found them immediately.

The children were sprinting down the hall, badgering each other as usual. Allen had his favorite dragon toy held aloft, as if in flight, with his little sister screaming behind him. Something about returning her hairbrush.

No time for Robert to react. No time to brace.

The boy ducked between Robert's legs as he fled from his sister. Not low enough, though.

The plastic dragon's wingtip clipped Robert's testicles. Shockwaves of pain rippled through his abdomen. He heard church bells ringing for some reason.

Robert crumpled to the floor as his kids rounded the hall. Neither looked back to check on him. At least they were dressed.

"Kids, don't…" Robert's lungs refused to work under these conditions. "Please… kids… no run."

His voice wheezed out, small and raspy and too weak to puncture his children's screams as they ran downstairs. So Robert just sat there in the hall in his wool socks and boxers, coddling his testicles, wishing that everything around him was pretend.

Robert struggled to his feet and waddled back to the kids' bathroom. His double was there again, doubled over just like him. The pain pulsating through his groin dared Robert to throw up. He saw the same desperation to hold back vomit in Other-Robert's eyes.

"Did…?" Robert gestured down.

A tear rolled down Other-Robert's cheek. "Did Allen hit me in the balls with a dragon?"

"Yeah," Robert said.

"Yeah," Other-Robert replied.

Both Roberts sighed. Both Roberts tried not to puke.

"The rest of our day *has* to get better from here," Robert proclaimed.

"Are you eating Hamburger Helper for breakfast?" Other-Robert parried.

Robert sniffed in deep — deep as the pain coiled inside his abdomen would allow.

And there it was. The scent of grease and beef and fake cheese and heart disease. The odors fought for dominance, clogging up the air like backed-up interstate traffic.

The smell coated the inside of Robert's nose like sealant. Refused him any other odors. He could feel it seep into his pores and latch onto his hair follicles. All his coworkers would know exactly what he ate for his morning meal.

"Unfortunately... yes," Robert sighed out.

"I guess we're in the same boat, then." Other-Robert tried to stand up straight. Made it to about sixty-three degrees. "Hope it doesn't sink. I can't swim."

"Me neither," Robert said.

The two men smiled.

When had Robert last seen that smile? His smile. When was the last time he felt good enough to smile?

Then Robert noticed Other-Robert's teeth. His teeth.

"That's not fair." Robert pulled his lips apart, like a horse being appraised for the races — or the glue factory. His double did the same.

Their teeth looked yellowed. Not horribly rotted or anything of that sort. In fact, Robert had never allowed a single cavity to take root in his mouth. Brushed three times a day. Never ate sweets. Always used mouthwash. Always flossed.

That just made Robert all the more frustrated with existence. At the *very* least, the universe could have given him teeth that looked as healthy as they actually were. But no, the universe colored them an off-putting off-white instead. Robert practiced smiling with his lips pursed. Other-Robert did the same.

"Come eat this damn food!" Kathy blared from downstairs. "I spent my time making this food, and you're letting it get cold. Why you chose a morning on a school day to put that mirror up, I can't even fathom."

Robert had already come close to losing a testicle to a *toy* dragon this morning — he didn't want to fight a *real* dragon before breakfast. He hurried off to dress.

All his work clothes sat neat and tidy on his bed, ready to cloak him in the unassuming mediocrity that cloaked all insurance analysts. He slipped into his trousers and shirt. He slid on his shoes. He grabbed his glasses. He swung his tie around his neck.

Then Robert decided to finish dressing in the kids' bathroom. In front of the new mirror. Maybe Other-Robert was still around.

He was, indeed.

Other-Robert stood there, struggling with his tie, trapped in the same middling work-prep ritual.

"Eggs seem easier to cook for breakfast," Robert mused as he tied his tie. "And... they're *for* breakfast. Who even *thinks* of cooking Hamburger Helper for breakfast?"

Robert was pleasantly surprised to see his double agree with a nod and a tie tug. No chance Robert would say that to Kathy. Other-Robert's agreement helped, though.

"They're not hard to cook," Other-Robert added. "I almost never burn them. I like them scrambled."

Robert's mouth filled with saliva at the thought of steaming scrambled eggs. Pavlov and his dogs would've been proud.

Robert grumbled, "I'd restart my *entire life* if it meant I got to eat scrambled eggs for breakfast instead of Hamburger Helper."

"NOW!" Kathy roared.

No. Not Kathy. Not Robert's. The Other-Robert's Other-Kathy.

Robert felt the vibrations of her voice pass through the mirror. Through his very being. The Other-Kathy screamed just like his own.

"Sorry," Other-Robert whispered as he adjusted his glasses. "Kathy's mad."

"My Kathy's mad, too," Robert replied. Nothing new there. He reached out and shook his double's hand. "Thanks for saving me."

The double nodded and took off, out of sight from beyond the mirror.

Robert wasn't shocked at his double's misery. Why would even an alternate *him* have it any better? Didn't seem fair. Other people's doubles were probably billionaires or superheroes. Or white-teethed, at least.

Other-Robert was just another Robert.

Robert went downstairs to eat his breakfast before work. His burger paste was room temperature by the time he reached the dinner table.

***

Knowing that a parallel version of himself — his entire universe — was waiting back home in his children's bathroom mirror made Robert's workday difficult.

Not that Robert's workdays were ever *not* difficult. Though, this brand of difficult came from tedious, unending monotony. From spreadsheeting away his day in a sea of cubicles. From talking to people over the phone who would never remember that he existed. Would never care that he existed.

The potted plant beside the elevator was the only sign of life in the office. Besides the workers. If they counted. Robert was relatively sure the plant wasn't fake. Someone had thrown up outside his cubicle a year ago. The smell never left. Still, he always managed to trudge through everything. Always got his paperwork filed. Always closed his accounts.

Today, Robert could barely open up Excel.

"Hello," he whispered to the reflection smeared across his computer's screen.

No answer.

Maybe the reflection in the water cooler? He walked over for a cup.

"How's the testicle?" he asked.

Still no response. Just water-cooler bubbles.

Robert considered jamming a pen to the back of his throat. Throwing up all over the floor. Puking was as good of an excuse for adults to go home as it was for kids. He just wanted to go see if Other-Robert was in the new mirror again.

"Robert!" Mr. Burkins barked an inch from Robert's head.

Robert flinched. Good thing he wasn't standing on a bathroom counter. Definitely would've fallen to his death. He turned around to face his boss. His Dungeon Master.

Mr. Burkins stood there, short and squat as a tree stump, and smiled out an unfriendly smile. Robert was at least six inches taller than Mr. Burkins. Still, Robert had to fight off the urge to look up whenever they spoke. Like his boss was big. Like his boss was more important than a middle manager actually was.

"He- hello, sir," Robert sputtered out. "I was just taking a little break. Got thirsty. I'll be back to work in no time."

Why did Robert feel the need to say that? He always finished his assignments. Always took on extra duties. He never missed work. Never took off. Robert didn't need to defend his value to anyone.

Yes, he did. Nobody noticed anything about Robert. He needed to remind people that he did good work, or they'd look right over him. Through him. His neck muscles pulled his head upward.

Mr. Burkins gripped Robert's shoulder and squeezed — that little boss-squeeze to assert that little extra bit of dominance and humiliation. A dull aftershock of testicle pain traveled up Robert's lower back.

"Oh, Robert. Robert, Robert, Robert. You keep this up and you'll be filling my shoes in no time. Just make sure you stay valuable!"

Mr. Burkins laughed like that was a joke and walked away, but not before sniffing the air and side-eyeing Robert. Must've smelled Hamburger Helper.

Robert crushed his water cup and returned to his cubicle.

"Four '*Roberts*'," he muttered. "Four."

Robert wished his boss would call him '*Rob*'. Wished *anyone* would.

Robert had met Mr. Burkins at a company picnic years ago. He worked at a different branch back then, farther west. Needed to move to a more suburban setting for his new family — just Kathy and a baby Allen at the time. He introduced himself as '*Rob*', but Kathy told Mr. Burkins that it was, "'*Robert*', *actually*."

Robert had said that, right? Said he preferred '*Rob*'? '*Rob*' felt cooler than '*Robert*'. Better than '*Robert*'. He was '*Rob*' in grade school. College.

Robert wanted to be '*Rob*' again.

Robert finished his work and headed home. None of the reflections in his car mirrors said anything along the way.

***

Robert had developed a strategy over the years. A method of talking to an enraged Kathy. It involved looking at the space between her eyebrows so it *seemed* like he was looking into her eyes — without *actually* looking into her eyes. Eye contact with Kathy made him far too uncomfortable.

"How did you not remember the milk?" Kathy chastised. She had been right there the second Robert opened the door. "I texted you *three times* about getting milk."

Robert concentrated really hard on Kathy's brow and tried to find an answer. An out. He found nothing — save for a single eyebrow hair tangled with one of its neighbors.

"That's the *one* thing I asked you to get on the way home." Kathy stormed into the kitchen and riffled through a small dish on the counter. "The *one* thing." She found her keys and headed out the door. "I'll be back. Maybe."

She didn't close the door. Robert had to do that.

15

Kathy was long gone by the time Robert mustered up the courage to mumble, "I don't think you texted me," to an empty room. He didn't want to check his phone. Confirm his ineptitude.

Maybe Other-Robert knew.

Robert went to check the new mirror.

Robert's double was there.

Robert's double looked just as bad as Robert felt.

"Can I ask you something?" Robert asked.

"Okay," Other-Robert groaned.

"Did your Kathy text you to…?"

"Get milk?"

A weighty dread pulled Robert's stomach into his shoes. He slumped down and sighed. No need to check his phone.

"I just messed up as usual," Other-Robert moused out. A kitchen cabinet slammed somewhere across the mirror, in the Other-house. "Kathy's looking for her keys. I hope she leaves soon. The longer we talk, the higher the chances are of her yelling at me about looking at her eyebrows."

"Alone time is always nice." Robert had the house to himself. A rarity. His kids were at a birthday party and Kathy would be anger-shopping for at least the next four hours. Still, the Other-Kathy's cabinet-slamming in the Other-house tarnished his peace and quiet. Made it difficult to think. To focus.

Other-Robert began to cry.

Robert hated it when people saw him cry. Hard to hide yellowed teeth during a crying session. He looked away. Studied the new mirror. Gave Other-Robert a moment to compose himself.

Was the new mirror seventy-eight by sixty-six inches, or seventy-six by sixty-eight inches? Robert just knew that it was big.

The mirror's hickory frame — carved into sand dunes and prickly pear and jackrabbits and all manner of desert-adjacent things — dredged up Mojave memories. The gold-painted accents bestowed the mirror with an ancient, regal quality.

It was beautiful. It was a nightmare getting it up there, but it was beautiful. Robert felt proud.

Then he felt concerned. What if Other-Robert's mirror wasn't screwed in loose enough?

Robert asked without thinking, "Do you want to trade places for a bit? Kathy's already gone over here."

Other-Robert gasped. "You'd do that?"

"Sure. I want to help. You deserve a break." Robert didn't really want to help, but he needed to know what his Other's mirror looked like. His Other's world.

"Thank you *so* much." Other-Robert clasped his hands together. "You're a real lifesaver."

Robert climbed onto the counter. Other-Robert did the same. They grabbed each other's shoulders, performed an awkward turn-around, and ducked under the mirror's top frame.

Other-Robert climbed down with a grunt and some popping knees, but made it all right.

Robert did not make it all right.

His heel slipped on the edge of the sink and he tumbled face-first onto the floor.

The bathroom mat seemed *off*, smooshed up against Robert's chin and cheek. Same color as the mat in Robert's real world. Same texture. But *off*. The fibers pushed in a slightly different direction, maybe.

"Did you just hurt yourself?" Other-Kathy yelled up from the first floor of this Other-house. "I swear if you hurt yourself, we're getting milk before we go to the hospital."

Robert forgot he even wanted to inspect Other-Robert's mirror.

"Maybe this isn't such a good idea," Robert said as he stood.

But Other-Robert was already gone — and Other-Kathy was stomping up the stairs. Robert braced himself. Prepared to be yelled at. Again. Over milk.

Other-Kathy stopped in the doorway and snapped, "You better not have hurt yourself."

"I didn't." Robert stared at the center of her eyebrows. Identical to the real Kathy's.

"Well, at least there's that," Other-Kathy growled. "Now I get to go buy milk. On my day off. Milk *you* were supposed to get. I'll be back. Maybe." She turned to leave.

"Wait a second," Robert said. One of Other-Kathy's pores seemed different. A big one, off to the inner edge of her left eyebrow. Slightly smaller than it should be, maybe.

Other-Kathy turned back and glared at Robert. "Well, *what*?" she snarled. "Spit it out. I have to get the milk you forgot." She turned to leave again.

"I said wait a second." The slightest force tinged Robert's words. That pore was definitely smaller.

Other-Kathy turned back again, stunned and silent. She looked Robert in the eye before he could zero in on her brow.

"I can get it," he blurted. "You just stay here."

"All right," she grumbled, "but don't mess up and get whole. Get two percent."

"Got it."

Robert repeated '*two percent*' ten thousand times over in his head, then left.

But leaving was easier said than done.

Moving through this Other-world mirrored the flowings of a dream. Robert's shoe caught the edge of the front door's frame, forcing him to take three stork-like stumbles into the yard before steadying himself. The doorframe seemed different. A millimeter higher? A hair's width farther out? No telling which. But definitely different. Off. Off like the bathroom mat.

His brain chewed over doorframes as he climbed into his Other's car and cranked it.

The car felt as off as the doorframe.

Robert usually shifted in his seat twice before he was comfortable enough to drive. He needed five shifts in this Other-car.

Maybe it was just nerves, being in a parallel universe and all. Understandable to be a bit nervous. But he needed to focus on getting milk for Kathy. Other-Kathy.

Robert's stomach didn't tense up quite as much at the thought of talking to this Other-Kathy. His fight-or-flight didn't trigger quite as fast.

Maybe because she wasn't real. Not *really* real. Not to him.

He made it to the Other-grocery store. The lights shone a little brighter here. A little warmer. Flickered at a slightly different rhythm.

Robert picked up the milk. Two percent.

Instead of going straight home like he would have done in his world, Robert drove around a bit to see if he noticed any other differences.

From what he could tell, everything was the same.

But everything also wasn't the same.

The supply store two miles from home sported the same blue fencing in both realities. This reality also had a tree at the corner of Smith Lane and Dove Wing Way. A tree that bore a scar on its trunk. A scar from a wreck that had killed two people, five years ago.

But this fence's blue was a bit bluer. This tree's scar cut into its trunk a bit deeper.

Robert felt disconnected. Like matter bumbling around in a sea of dark matter. He wasn't sure if it was a good feeling or a bad one.

Comic Cave came up on Robert's right, in a little strip mall. He passed the little comic shop all the time in his world. He never dared to go in.

Comic Cave held D&D campaigns every few weeks. The Comic Cave in Robert's real world did, at least. Flyers advertising the campaigns found their way out into the community. They showed up taped to park benches, or blowing down the sidewalk on Jasper Street, or pinned to noticeboards outside the community center, or tacked onto power poles along Spearman Boulevard. Their upper-right corners usually had mustard stains on them. The owner must've favored mustard.

Robert was so desperate to go in. Years had passed since his last campaign. Maybe he could start up again, after a rules refresher. Maybe he could even take this Other-Allen and Other-Jill.

No. They weren't his kids, and he didn't want to get Other-Robert in trouble. Robert turned away from Comic Cave. He drove back to his street — his Other's street — and entered the Other-house with milk.

***

That disconnected feeling stayed for dinner, swirling around Robert like a fog. It kept everything at arm's length — a shield held up to fend off this photocopy reality.

21

Other-Allen sat to Robert's left, moving peas around with a spoon. Other-Jill rocked around in a high chair to his right, more interested in making elephant noises than eating. Other-Kathy sat across from him, chewing her food harder than necessary. Everything seemed normal.

But it wasn't.

Robert's lifetime of studying the minute intricacies of eyebrows highlighted every difference. Every alteration. All the microscopic changes that coalesced into an uncanny sheen.

Other-Allen separated his peas by greenness, unlike Robert's real Allen who separated them by size. Other-Jill's nose-pick-to-food-chew ratio leaned slightly more in favor of nose picks. Other-Kathy favored a rolling chew compared to the real Kathy's straight up-and-down chomp.

Robert recalled his towering barbarian, Rathgrar, from his D&D sessions way back in college. Odd thought to have.

"How was everyone's day?" he asked without thinking.

The utensil-clanking stopped. The pea-sorting and nose-picking and hard-chewing stopped. Robert gulped. Hearing his voice at the table was as alien to him as it was to everyone else.

D&D wasn't real. Just a game. Robert always ended up in foggy swamps in his campaigns.

Robert looked at Other-Allen. "How was school… umm… son?"

"It was okay, I guess." Other-Allen didn't look up from his peas.

Robert cleared his throat and nudged this Other-son. "Just okay? What did you do?"

"Well... me and Jerry, we got in trouble for taking Mrs. Hedge's frog out of his tankrarium thing, but everybody laughed. He peed on Jerry!"

"You peed on me and your mom quite a bit when you were a baby," Robert joked. "Are you a frog, too?"

Other-Allen smiled. He had gotten so big. Was Robert's real Allen the same size?

Robert turned to Other-Jill. She stared at him, wide-eyed.

"And how was kindergarten for you, Jill?"

"Good! I drew some elephants." She waved her hands by her head to make big elephant ears, then made a surprisingly authentic elephant noise.

"I knew you had elephants on the brain, Jilly-Bean."

"I'm elephant girl!" she half-screamed, half-giggled.

"I can tell." Robert smiled and patted Other-Jill's head.

Robert waited until the Other-kids returned to their meals, then he looked across the table. "So, what did you do on your day off..." The name would have stuck in his throat in the real world, but this wasn't the real world. "...Kathy?"

His Other's wife stared at the remainder of her food. When the real Kathy was frustrated, her mouth coiled into a hook shape on the left side. The hook was there now, on

Other-Kathy, but it wavered. Didn't cut as deep into her cheek as usual.

"Not much," she sighed into her plate. "Just some chores. Some shopping."

"Oh, come on," Robert teased. "You can do better than that."

That might've been too much, but the fog made Robert feel like anything mean this Other-Kathy threw at him would simply roll off — a sword strike bouncing off barbarian chainmail.

Other-Kathy didn't say anything mean, though.

"Well, I went to that antique store off May Avenue and got a little dresser I've been eyeing. It's a bit beat up, but it was cheap."

Robert nodded. "Maybe I can fix it up."

Other-Kathy half-smiled. "You did do a pretty okay job on that mirror."

"Yeah. Yeah, I did." Robert half-smiled back. He forgot that his teeth were a bit yellowed.

***

Robert didn't smile when he noticed Other-Robert in the new mirror later that night.

"What's wrong?" Robert asked.

Robert's double looked even worse than usual, over there in Robert's real world. His double's eyes were puffed up from crying and his back hunched with more of a slump than usual. Buffalo-like.

"It's just been… a long day." Other-Robert breathed out all the words at once.

Robert gulped. "What happened?"

"I just… wanted to make sure I didn't mess up anything in your life. So I was… I pulled back more than usual. So I wouldn't draw attention."

Robert didn't think his double *could* pull back more than Robert already did. The conversations at the dinner table with his Other-family had been *so* easy. *So* basic. How could Other-Robert do *less* than that? Surely Robert's double felt the same disconnectedness from being in an Other-world. Felt the same power.

"Did anything really bad happen?" Robert's neck ached for some reason.

Other-Robert sniffled. "Your Kathy yelled at me for not talking to your kids enough. I just want to come home. This was a bad idea."

Other-Robert reached through the mirror and waited for Robert to help him onto the counter.

And Robert left his Other there, reaching and confused, for one second. Two seconds. Five. Eleven.

"Maybe it'll get better," Robert reasoned. "I had a hard time at first, too. Maybe we can just stay in each other's worlds a bit longer? Just to see if we can get a handle on things."

Other-Robert's arm receded. "I don't know about-"

"I think it's a pretty good idea." Robert looked right into his Other's eyes. He noticed Other-Robert's gaze tilt up, ever-so-slightly. Up to Robert's brow.

Other-Robert groaned. "Well… I guess-"

"Great. Have fun." Robert turned off the lights and walked out of the Other-children's bathroom.

Robert didn't care if Other-Robert enjoyed the break from reality or not. His Other's problems fled his thoughts the second he lay in his bed. No. This bed wasn't his bed. The mattress was firmer than his own. This pillow wasn't his pillow. It compressed more than his own. But lying there felt good. Felt better.

Robert even dreamed better that night.

In his dreams, Robert strode through Comic Cave. Not as Robert, though. As Rathgrar. The barbarian had died in a campaign in Robert's college days. Swamp of Forlorn Hopelessness. Wight ambush.

Robert always followed the rules. Never reused a dead character, no matter how special they were. But those rules didn't matter in this Other-world. He could role-play whatever he wanted.

He wanted to be Rathgrar the barbarian.

Rathgrar turned over rows of comics with his tree-trunk arms. He snatched away the owner's mustard-slathered sandwich and ate it in one bite. The owner protested, but Rathgrar swung his axe around and bellowed and bared his yellowed teeth and reduced the man to a quivering puddle.

Rob smiled in his sleep.

Rob smiled constantly over the next few days. His teeth didn't bother him at all, whether he was Rob in the waking Other-world or Rathgrar in his dreams.

They didn't bother anybody else, either.

Other-Kathy enjoyed seeing his smile. She made time to be with him quite regularly now. Their time together became dates. Dates became evenings out. Evenings out eventually led to Rob making love to Other-Kathy for the first time in years — even though she wasn't his real Kathy.

For the first time in a lifetime, Rob remembered what it felt like to feel *good*.

But every time Rob checked the new mirror, Other-Robert reminded him that none of this was real. That none of this would last.

Rob's double pleaded to switch back whenever Rob entered his Other-kids' bathroom to clean the counter or gather up towels or click toothbrushes back into their chargers. All Other-Robert did was complain about how much extra work he had taken on, out of fear of making Mr. Burkins angry with the real Rob.

Did his Other think *that* would make Rob switch back? An even heavier workload? That was his Other's problem, not his.

Rob would simply persuade his double to stay put whenever Other-Robert tried to come through the mirror. He almost felt embarrassed at how easy it was. Just a few halfhearted assurances guaranteed Rob another day in the Other-world.

The better world.

But Other-Robert *did* almost show some spine a few times — like the time he threatened to sleep with Rob's real Kathy.

Rob knew his double wouldn't. Couldn't. Rob let Other-Robert know that. Rob *didn't* let Other-Robert know that he had already slept with Other-Kathy.

Other-Robert even tried to climb back through the mirror once, when the pressures of Rob's real world became unbearable.

And Rob had just held Other-Robert back — pressed his hand to his double's forehead until Other-Robert tuckered himself out. Rob was simply too strong. He shouldn't have been. They were duplicates. Mirrors. But Other-Robert submitted before Rob even broke a sweat.

The Other-world must have enhanced Rob. Better air, maybe. Better food. Other-Kathy had started cooking eggs for breakfast.

Other-Robert stayed in his place after that.

On Friday, Rob took his Other's kids — *his* kids — to the park. They weren't really *that* different from the real things. No need for a distinction. Not anymore.

He had no idea Jill liked climbing on the jungle gym so much. Maybe she would join the gymnastics or dance teams when she reached high school. Rob couldn't wait to be there, cheering her on. And Allen liked playing goblins-and-heroes with his friends. They ran around the playhouses and trees, shooting fake bows and casting fake spells and swinging fake swords.

The playground gravel crunching under his children's shoes sounded normal. Natural. Just gravel. Not gravel from another reality. Just gravel.

Rob decided to take Kathy and the kids to Comic Cave the next day.

***

Comic Cave's owner looked up from a ham sandwich when Rob and his family entered. The sandwich was slathered in ketchup. Mustard must've been for lesser realities. But everything else about the comic shop was just like the comic shops Rob used to feel so comfortable in. So safe. So good.

Rob breathed in the scent of comicbook ink and miniature-model paint. He laughed. Kathy gave him a weird look that would have made him feel ashamed of his happiness in the real world. Here, though, Rob just smiled back. He made sure to show his teeth.

He walked down rows of comics and action figures and trading cards with his kids until they reached the back of the store. A large table sat under a flickering panel light. Dice and character sheets littered its surface. A sign on the wall listed dates for upcoming campaigns. It even highlighted beginner campaigns for kids. Next one was next week. Saturday, at six.

Rob knelt down and looked at his children. "You two like adventures, right?"

"Yeah," they both said.

"With dragons and elves and monsters and treasure?"

"Yeah!" they both screamed.

Their excitement fed Rob. Made him feel invincible.

"Well, I think I'm just gonna have to bring you two with me next week when I start my old hobby back up. Want to go on an adventure with Dad?"

His kids jumped and laughed and clapped. Rob bought them a few comics, then took his family out for ice cream.

Rob found Kathy in the kitchen later that day. She wasn't *really* Kathy, but Rob spun her around and kissed her more passionately than he had ever kissed anyone in any universe — real or not.

"What on Earth's gotten into you lately, Rob?"

It had been so long since Kathy used that name. That better name.

"Oh? Something's wrong then," he teased.

"Not at all." She kissed him back. "I just never remember feeling like this. Or, I don't know… feeling like *you* felt like this. Like you feel good. Not for years."

"Just feeling at home."

Rob made love to Kathy twice that night.

***

Rob woke up, stretched, dressed, and decided to take another day off from work. Day four.

He had plenty of vacation days built up. Why not use them to figure some things out? Figure out what his new family liked. Figure out who he would be in this new world.

Why not give 'handyman' a try?

He headed down into the basement and started rummaging through an old tool chest. Rob thought about what he could do around the house. What he could fix. What he could create.

The gutters were getting clogged. Maybe install some leaf guards? Why not build a fence for the backyard? The kids would love to have a dog.

Rob grabbed a hammer.

And thought of the new mirror.

Sweat welled up in his palm. The hammer nearly slipped out of his hand, but Rob tightened his grip until his knuckles went white. He tried to think of anything he hated about this new life as he tossed the hammer from one hand to the other.

Not one thing came to mind.

Rob walked up the stairs. He entered the kids' bathroom. He was glad to see Other-Robert slink in just as he entered.

"Oh, hey," the double mumbled. "I was wondering when we were going to-"

"I've got a question for you," Rob stated.

"Oh. Okay."

"What makes you think you deserve to come back over here?" Rob kept his face still.

Other-Robert just stood there and quivered while his mouth opened and closed like a fish.

Rob didn't give Other-Robert a chance to defend himself, not that his Other would try. "What have you done over there, besides be even *more* pathetic than usual?"

"I… I just… didn't want you to get in trouble."

Rob dropped the hammer onto the counter so his Other could see it. Figure it all out.

"All you do is roll over," Rob growled. "Roll over and whimper and hunch over and look between people's eyebrows!" He picked up the hammer. Twirled it around.

"Please let me come home!" Other-Robert's voice cracked.

"Why?" Rob snarled. "You'll just ruin everything I've built over here. You'll do what you *always* do. Give and give and give. And it'll all be gone, all over again! All this work!"

Rob pulled back the hammer, ready to shatter the mirror. Claim his Other's world. Restart his entire life.

Rob swung.

And Other-Robert shrieked.

Rob froze, mid-swing. He watched his double cower there — shivering, mumbling something, clasping his hands over his mouth.

"What?" Rob lowered the hammer. Leaned in. Tried to make out anything in Other-Robert's mumblings. "Move your hands. I can't understand you. Why are you…"

Teeth. Rob's Other was covering up his teeth.

32

Rob had ignored Kathy's first mention of his yellowed teeth. Wrote it off as some passive-aggressive jab that didn't really mean anything. But it festered. Grew for years like a mouth ulcer that turned out to be cancer. It dug into his brain, chittering over and over until only his reflection was allowed to see his teeth.

Now, he didn't even have that.

Rob climbed onto the counter, passed through the mirror, and stepped onto his real counter. He jumped down to the floor. His double stumbled back into the corner. Rob followed his Other's gaze to his own hand.

Rob had brought the hammer with him.

The double's eyes went wide. Grew terrified.

That terror made Rob sick to his stomach. Made him want to bash his own face in. He let go of the hammer. It thudded to the floor, the impact muffled by the bathroom mat.

Rob rushed to his double and pulled him close. Other-Robert struggled for a moment before embracing him back.

They both cried.

"Here." Rob stepped back and pulled some paper out of his pocket — the crumpled receipt from Comic Cave. He wrote down the time of the next D&D night. Allen and Jill needed to get there a bit before six. "I promised to take the kids to this. You need it, too." He folded up the receipt and shoved it into Other-Robert's shirt pocket. "Do you remember Rathgrar?"

33

Other-Robert's eyes lit up. "Yeah."

Rob smiled. "Good."

In one fluid motion, Rob pushed his Other onto the counter and through the mirror. Other-Robert tumbled to the floor in the correct universe.

When his double stood, Rob said, "Pretend it's all fake. You deserve it."

It felt wrong to say. That was Other-Robert's real world. But unreal felt *so* good. Unreal eventually became real. When it did, it still felt good.

"I'll… try." Other-Robert began to walk off.

"Wait," Rob said. He bent down and picked up the hammer. "This is yours."

He handed it through to his double.

Other-Robert looked at the hammer, then back at Rob. "What do I do with this?"

Rob shrugged. "Just try to make something."

"I don't think that's a good idea." Other-Robert looked away. "What if Kathy doesn't like what I make?"

"It doesn't matter. Pretend she likes it until she does. Pretend *you* like it until you do." A tear rolled down Rob's cheek. "Thanks for saving me."

Other-Robert smiled without covering his mouth, then left.

Rob stood there, alone, in his real world. It didn't feel like his real world anymore. This real world had a slight difference in the air. An unhealthy quality. Grease. Hamburger meat. Over-processed cheese.

The mirror was right there. Maybe two *hims* could coexist in one world. Maybe they could take turns living one life.

Rob peeked out of his real kids' real bathroom, into his real house. An alien house.

A cold sweat broke out on his forehead. He hiked one leg onto the counter.

"There you are!" Kathy appeared in the doorway, mouth in a hook shape. "I thought you finished putting in that damn mirror. What's wrong with it now? Did you damage the wall?"

Rob looked at the mirror. He met his own eyes. Not his double's. Just a reflection.

"No." He stumbled back from the counter. "I was just checking the screws."

Allen and Jill popped up at their mother's side. Allen was holding that damned dragon toy. Rob covered his groin on instinct.

"Hey, everybody," Rob forced out, "how about we all go out for breakfast and ice cream?" He smiled through pursed lips.

No. Rob's teeth were fine the way they were. He smiled wide and showed them off. "I can take off work and we can all go have some fun."

"*Really?*" his kids screamed simultaneously. They laughed and clapped. They jumped up and down and tugged on Kathy's shirt.

Rob squatted down and smiled at them. "Yes, really. Maybe we can even stop by Comic Cave and-"

"Robert!" Kathy lashed. "Are you *crazy*? They have to be ready for school in twenty minutes. Stop filling their heads with nonsense. And come eat your breakfast before it gets cold."

"We can let them skip a day," Rob managed, "can't we?"

Kathy ignored him and looked down at Allen and Jill. "Sorry, kids. Daddy's wrong. He can't take you to get ice cream. Now, both of you go and get your backpacks ready for school."

The kids grumbled and headed off to their room.

Kathy turned to leave.

Rob clenched his jaw. Pretended to be a barbarian. "Kathy, just relax."

Kathy froze. Turned back. Looked Rob in the eye. She didn't speak for a moment. Two moments. Three.

"What did you say to me?" Kathy's angry expression cracked. Confusion pushed up through the cracks. She looked more like the Other-Kathy now. Stunned by Rob's assertiveness. Primed.

It was enough to pretend.

"Just relax." Rob glanced at his reflection. He imagined how broad Rathgrar would be in real life. How tall. The barbarian could hurl Kathy like a pebble. "Don't make it more than it is. The kids won't miss much from one day of school, and some ice cream would definitely help with your crankiness."

Rob popped his back and stood up straight.

"Are you. Fucking. Stupid?" Kathy's tone didn't invite a response. "Do you think *I'm* stupid?"

The pitch was perfect. Deadly. An arrow. An arrow dipped in a poison specifically brewed to kill barbarians and insurance analysts.

"N- no. No, not at all," Rob stuttered. "I just thought that..."

His spine curled back into a hunch. His gaze drifted to Kathy's eyebrows. An angry mountain range formed in the folds of skin between them. Rob wanted to look Kathy in the eyes, but he couldn't. Her eyes would show how angry she was. He could tell it was because of his teeth.

Robert pursed his lips.

"You think you can just contradict *my* parenting in front of the kids? *Right* in front of them? Un-*fucking*-believable!" Kathy turned and stormed out.

But she'd be back.

Robert turned around and climbed onto the counter and threw himself into the mirror.

He didn't go through.

Robert's face met the mirror's surface. His nose cracked. His glasses crushed up against his eyes as their frames bent. He toppled backward and crashed to the floor.

"Oh Jesus Christ, Robert!"

The disgust in Kathy's tone conjured up the flavor of Hamburger Helper. Nausea tickled the back of Robert's throat.

Kathy yelled, "If you fell off that counter, I'm *not* helping you get to the doctor."

Robert groaned. He must've missed something. Done something wrong. Made a lousy roll somewhere, maybe. He rushed out of the bathroom. He ran to his kids' room before he knew what he was doing. He grabbed their wrists.

"Come on, kids." Robert dragged them out.

He just needed to level up. Kathy was stronger here. Real. He just needed a rules refresher.

"Let's go get ice cream." Robert pulled his kids down the hallway. They began to struggle.

"Dad, let go!" Allen yelled. "I need to get ready for school. You'll make me late!"

Jill shrieked, "You're hurting my hand!"

"Ice cream," was all Robert could whimper. His wool socks squished with each step. The sweat. Bad fashion call for spring.

"I *hate* you," Jill stung. "Mommy hates you and *I* hate you. Let *go*!"

Robert started to cry.

He looked at his children. They looked so real. He squeezed their hands harder. Their skin felt so real. Their little muscles pulling away from him felt so real.

He bit his tongue. Pushed the tears back.

"Daddy loves both of you very much."

Rob pulled his children down the stairs while he pretended they weren't real.

Insects and Leftovers

Eric opened his eyes early Friday morning, facing his bedside dresser as usual. His dresser was bare, save for a dusty framed photograph, a pair of glasses, and a lamp purchased from a yard sale many years ago. It was a lovely lamp. An impressive lamp. Victorian-looking with copper trim around white-and-blue porcelain.

Then Eric noticed that he was *also* looking back at his wife. Looking at her with eyes in the back of his head.

Odd. Most people didn't have eyes in the backs of their heads. But Eric did. He saw a thousand copies of Susan, each trapped within a little geometric bubble. He reached his hand back and felt around.

His fingers found two large half-spheres jutting from his scalp, right where his bald spot had started showing

40

fifteen years ago. The spheres' texture alluded to golf-ball dimples. They were cool to the touch, like metal. Pressing them shifted the images of his wife. Made the thousand Susans distort and twirl. The twirling Susans reminded Eric of looking through a kaleidoscope.

But through the back of his head.

So, not *exactly* like looking through a kaleidoscope.

"Susan," Eric whispered, still facing away from her, "you awake?"

No, still sleeping.

If she had been awake, Susan would have put on a smile to make Eric feel better. Lied to him out of faded love. Eric rarely looked back at Susan anymore. Didn't want to burden her with putting on an act.

Fortunately, the new eyes didn't spot a fake smile.

Eric sat up and fumbled for his glasses in front of the framed photo. The photo captured Susan, Sarah, and Stephen, all enjoying a camping trip to the beach — way back when the kids were still in elementary school.

Eric looked at the photo. He considered picking it up to examine the details. Considered comparing the kids *back then* to the kids *now*, now that they were in college. Considered wiping off the dust.

He got up and walked his well-worn path to the bathroom instead. The new eyes watched Susan until she disappeared from view.

The new eyes — their thousand perspectives — were hard to get used to. Alien. Processing it all made Eric's head spin, like watching TV over a weak antenna signal — half actors acting, half staticky images bleeding into one another.

Eric used to watch shitty French romances with Susan back in college. The picture quality in his dorm room was ninety-percent static, but it didn't matter. Not then.

Now, he preferred the clearest picture a TV screen could provide.

The more these new eyes focused on the bathroom wall, the harder it was for Eric to focus on brushing his teeth. He closed his old eyes and rubbed them. He tried to close the new ones, but they didn't have eyelids.

Eric looked at himself in the bathroom mirror. Attempted to set his old eyes as '*default*' in his brain. Didn't work. Just gave him a good look at his saggy skin, stubble, wrinkles, and green eyes long-turned grey. And these new eyes — did they look as tired? As aged?

He turned around. Tried to see the new eyes *with* the new eyes in the mirror. No use. Eric saw a thousand tiny copies of himself, but in each copy, the new eyes were barely more than pinpoints on the barely-more-than-specks that were his thousand balding heads.

He prodded the strange spheres again.

Had they grown larger? Something had eyes like that, but Eric couldn't place them. Too early to think.

"Hello," he whispered. Eric wasn't sure how these new eyes worked. He wanted to make sure they didn't have a mind of their own. "You… alive back there?"

No response. No new brains. None that showed, at least. Eric reached back and felt for a mouth at the base of his skull. Nothing. He finished up and walked out of the bathroom with a mind for breakfast.

But a cloud parted beyond the bedroom window right as Eric reached the bed — and the new eyes saw the sunlight.

Eric grew nauseous. His head buzzed. The skin on his scalp tightened. He nearly stumbled back into bed. The new eyes seemed awake. Invigorated. Hungry for the light.

That light. Too bright for Eric's old eyes this early in the morning.

He shrugged off the vertigo and headed out of the bedroom, into the hall. The new eyes looked at Susan one more time as she lay there in bed. She smiled with her eyes closed.

How long had Susan's smile looked so staged?

Eric sighed and shuffled on. His feet transitioned from the scratchy hallway carpet in front of the kids' abandoned rooms, to rough wood stairs, to cold kitchen laminate. Those transitions always irked him. Warm to cold. Comfortable to jarring. A divergence. A change.

He fumbled for the kitchen light switches. Flicked them on.

It didn't get bright, not immediately. The lights in the kitchen were cheap. Needed time to warm up. But Eric knew his way around in the dimness. He walked through the half-dark to the pantry and retrieved his oatmeal mix, still thinking of Susan's placebo smile.

Then he felt a tiny sting on his heel as he went to get a bowl.

The kitchen floor sported a few peeled-up sections of laminate — just here and there. Not that many spots. Ten, maybe. Eric had meant to fix them. Had meant to remodel the whole kitchen. It wasn't *that* bad, though. Not really. Just some little pricks and winces — just here and there. Eric had built up enough callouses on his feet to ignore the pain, usually. No need to change. Not yet.

He walked to the sink and poured water into his oatmeal.

The dim lights grew a bit brighter, and the new eyes saw a glint on the sharp tip Eric had stepped on.

Eric went back to the sharp tip. Bent down.

Blood.

Then Eric noticed *more* sharp tips.

All the tips were painted in red, all through the kitchen. Those other tips, though — their blood was dark, dry, and dull compared to Eric's shiny spot of new blood.

Had he really cut his feet — *let* himself cut his feet — so many times? There were more peeled-up places than he realized. Thirty, at least. Fifty?

But Eric only ever walked in specific paths through the kitchen. Only ever did anything in specific paths. Walk to kitchen. Eat oatmeal. Get in car. Drive to paint plant. Mix paint vats. Leave work. Watch crystal-clear TV while Susan fake-smiled.

Susan used different paths — tried to, at least — to make the days blend together less. She used to dance and sing and hug him in the kitchen when they were younger. Freer. Unbound. Now, Susan would sigh whenever she had to move out of Eric's way as he traveled down his path.

Too much blood on all those sharp tips to just be his.

It took years for laminate to get that bad. Years of ignoring it to get that bad. Eric didn't want to see the sharp tips — their blood — anymore. He returned to the counter and started stirring up his watery oatmeal.

But the new eyes refocused on the blood's shine. Their obsession grew and grew.

"Stop," Eric told them.

They didn't stop.

Eric spilled some oatmeal as he slid the bowl into the microwave. His hands felt clumsy, like the new eyes were using up bandwidth in his brain to admire the blood. No, the glint in the blood. The light. Their insistence chewed at him until he couldn't take it.

"*What*?" he asked the new eyes. "What are you looking at?"

The new eyes didn't answer. Silent, like before. They just *wanted*.

"Fine, then." Eric walked over to the blood and wiped it up with a napkin.

No more bloody glint. Just laminate in need of fixing. The new eyes relaxed.

The microwave dinged. Eric pulled out the hot bowl and began shoveling oatmeal into his mouth.

No sugar. No cinnamon. No raisins or bananas. No time for that good stuff.

Then the kitchen lights gave a final flicker and shifted to full brightness. The new eyes zeroed in on the store-brand bulbs like a shark smelling blood.

The nausea returned. The buzzing. The feeling of wanting. Of pushing through.

Eric's shoulders tensed. His shirt collar tightened, almost like his neck had thickened. His sleep shirt pulled snug around his chest. Had he put on some pounds? He reached back and covered the new eyes. Tried to settle them.

"Ow!"

A sharp pain zapped Eric's hand. He jerked it away. Blood puddled up in his palm.

The new eyes focused right back onto the light, obsessed. Moths did something like that. Beetles, too. Flies. Probably most bugs. Flew into candle flames and died, or those blue bug zappers. Eric recalled Sarah's high school softball games. Recalled the insects that would swarm the big lights around the field once night came.

That's what the new eyes reminded Eric of. Insects. Bugs.

Stupid bugs. These new insect eyes seemed stupid. They loved the light.

Eric bandaged his hand and forced down some more oatmeal — and all the while, the insect eyes grew more and more entranced by the discount bulbs.

Then Eric felt a pull. Like a new gravity had found him. It took him a moment to comprehend the sudden weightlessness. Eric looked at his feet.

The insect eyes had willed him up, toward the light, until only his tiptoes scratched at the floor.

"Stop it." Eric gripped the counter and pulled himself back down for one last spoonful. When the insect eyes tried to pull up again, he reached back and flicked one of them. He heard an angry clacking as he sank back to the floor.

Eric scraped up the last bit of oatmeal. He used to love French toast with a side of diced strawberries in the morning. No, loved that Susan loved it. He stopped making French toast a long time ago. Oatmeal was easier. '*Pre-chewed*', he would joke.

Susan would always fake-smile at that.

Eric walked out of the kitchen, back to the staircase. He peered up the stairs. He called out, "Susan, are you hungry?" He waited.

No response. Just a muted shifting of sheets.

Eric didn't blame her. No French toast or diced strawberries waiting down here.

Sunlight trickled through the den windows across from the kitchen. Eight o'clock — that's what den-window sun meant at this time of year. Eric didn't know why he had abandoned French toast and staticky French movies. Or when. But he knew this.

Eight o'clock. Time for work.

Eric headed over to a little closet in the den. Susan had filled their bedroom closet with her own things, but that was fine. Eric had the barest wardrobe possible. He never went out anymore. No need for flashy fashion.

He picked out a standard work outfit and laid the clothes on the couch in front of his giant TV. 4K resolution. Very clear.

"Stephen and Sarah should be getting into town in a bit," Susan called down from the floor above.

Eric paused. Looked up. "Oh. Yeah, that sounds about right." Spring Break. Now he remembered. "Is Sarah's car still acting up?"

Susan responded, "I'm meeting them at the mall for an early lunch. You should come with me. The kids would like to do more than just watch TV with you."

Eric's muscles went rigid.

"I have work," he sputtered back.

Susan always met the kids whenever they came home for breaks. Holidays. The three would always stay out the entire day. Visit the newest restaurant or bakery or clothing store. Some place Susan had discovered and saved in the back of her mind. Some place to *be* with the kids when they visited. A chance to learn how they'd grown. Changed.

Susan always brought back leftovers for Eric. Eric assumed the leftovers were for him. Susan never ate them. Those leftovers were always better than oatmeal.

The floor creaked somewhere above Eric as Susan moved to her closet.

"You always work when they're here." Her voice punctured down through the ceiling to Eric. Through Eric. "Take the day off. It's just paint, and you never take off. It'll be fun. You need to come with us."

Her tone — she already knew what Eric would say.

"I…" Eric wanted to surprise Susan. Give her an answer she wasn't expecting. "…have to work today."

"Take off, Eric," she repeated. No life in the words. No emotion. No flavor. Like oatmeal.

"I can't," Eric replied. No one could mix grey paint like him. Grey was his specialty.

"All right," Susan said, still riffling through hangers. "I offered."

Eric tried to dress quietly so Susan could pretend he was gone.

"I can't go," he whispered back to the insect eyes as he pulled up his pants and laced up his boots. "I'll see the kids later when they come over, and we can… watch some movies. It's no big deal. Movies are just as good as going out with them. No need to change it up now."

The insect eyes ignored his excuses.

"What would you know about it, anyway," Eric grumbled. He tugged off his sleep shirt and slipped on his flannel. Weird. Tighter than usual.

Then the insect eyes noticed something — a dress draped over the recliner in the corner of the den.

Susan must've thrown it there. Probably what she was hunting for in her closet upstairs. Looked new. Eric couldn't recall seeing Susan wear it.

It was a beautiful dress. Black mostly, with swirls of white spiraling from the left shoulder on down. Little flecks of silver shimmered near the bottom. The trim? Eric didn't know what that part was called. The dress reminded him of fancy breakfasts and French romances. His bedside lamp seemed less impressive than he remembered.

But the insect eyes only cared about the silver — the silver and its light.

That buzzing returned. That pull. That weightlessness.

Eric barely had time to grab onto the couch as the insect eyes forced him backward, dead-set on the dress and its silvery light and the sun pouring through the window.

The couch slid four inches. Four more. A foot.

Eric's shirt shifted. He heard fabric rip. Heard angry clacking and strange creaking. Something whipped through the air and tickled his ear. Why was his back so itchy?

The insect eyes pulled him and the couch five feet closer to the dress before tiring.

"Eric, are you okay?" Susan called down.

"It's nothing," Eric yelled. He slapped the back of his head. Something akin to a power cord brushed up against his wrist. He heard more of that angry clacking.

Eric collected himself and checked the den-window sun again.

It was getting late. No time to go kiss Susan goodbye. No time to ask her where she and the kids would be visiting without him. No time to worry her with the insect eyes. Just time to travel his path down to the paint plant.

These new insect eyes, though — they might be a little distracting for Eric's coworkers. He threw on a baseball cap to hide them and hurried out the front door.

Before he could find the right key to lock up, Eric noticed Greg Rodgers out of the corner of his eye — his old eye. The young man was packing some folding chairs and coolers into his SUV. Eric looked away, like always.

But a strong gust caught the lip of his cap. Tugged fast and hard. Tore it off of his head. The cap landed up in the Rodgers' elm tree.

"Oh no."

The insect eyes looked at Greg. Greg noticed them looking, too.

"Oh, hey there, Eric. Wow. Uh, *wow*." Greg scratched his full head of hair. "How's... how's it going?"

"Oh... you know," Eric said as he spun around to face Greg. "It's going."

Eric felt off-balance. Like a third grader struggling with a backpack full of books.

Greg closed the back of his SUV and smiled at Eric. A genuine smile. The Rodgers always seemed genuinely happy.

"Good to hear," the young man said as he waved Eric over. "Haven't talked in a while. Almost thought you decided to become a mime or something."

"Nope. No mimes here."

"How's Susan? Kids coming in for Break?"

"Susan's fine," Eric answered, as if he *could* answer that. "And yes. We're- she's meeting them in a bit. I can't go, though. Because paint."

Greg's smile quivered just a bit. Eric wanted to look away.

Greg scratched his chin. "So how'd, uh," he motioned to the back of his head, "how'd *that* happen?"

"I'm... not sure," Eric managed. "My father told me once that he made it through World War II thanks to the eyes in the back of his head, but I never thought he was serious."

"Why does it look so... you know." Greg winced.

A knot twisted up in Eric's stomach. Or maybe that was just his shirt tugging. Tightening.

"So... *what*?" he asked.

Eric should've inspected the insect eyes more closely in the bathroom. Found a hand mirror to hold up and look at them or something. No. That would've meant asking Susan where she kept one. She might have gotten up. Seen his predicament. Worried. Pushed him down some new path before he could run off to work.

"Turn around for a sec." Greg fished around in his pocket. "It'll be easier to just show you."

Eric turned and heard the *click-click* of a cellphone camera. He turned back and squinted down at the little screen — and nearly puked up his oatmeal.

"Oh no."

The eyes were insect eyes. Eric knew they would be, but he hadn't counted on them being so *huge* — each half-a-softball in size. They shimmered dull grey, like pencil lead.

And there was *more*. More insect to go along with those insect eyes. A massive beetle head, armored in dark-grey exoskeleton, jutted from the back of Eric's head.

Eric used to take his family on camping trips to the beach whenever he got the chance. Little Stephen and Sarah would flip over driftwood logs to pass the time. Beetles always fled onto the sand when their driftwood homes were disturbed.

Sarah would know what kind of beetle this was. She was majoring in biology. Stephen would want to squash it.

Eric couldn't remember the last time he visited the beach with his kids. With Susan. Those beach trips were never planned. Always spur of the moment. Those beach-trip beetles were nice and small and laced with good memory — unlike *this* beetle.

This beetle sported scissor-like mandibles and long antennae that draped down to Eric's rear. The back of Eric's shirt bulged in the photo. Emerging legs, maybe, kicking to

53

be free. He spotted a rip in his shirt. A hooked claw poked through.

No blood, though — unlike Eric's ignored kitchen laminate. No mutilated flesh where chitin met human. The beetle seemed to be rising out of him. Breaching the surface of a pool of water. A pool of Eric.

Eric missed his bald spot.

Greg looked into his garage and yelled, "Babe, did you pack the twins' Ghibli towels?" He looked back at Eric. "Those kids love that Japanese stuff."

Eric noticed that Greg didn't have a hitchhiker on the back of his head. If Greg did, it probably would've been a tiger or a wolf. Not that anyone could've seen anything through that full head of hair.

Lindsay Rodgers walked out of the garage, bags upon bags in her arms.

"You really think they'd let me forget those, you big dummy?" She piled everything into the SUV and walked over.

"Easy there, cowgirl. Just checking." Greg pulled Lindsay close and kissed her forehead.

"All right there, cowboy." Lindsay fit so perfectly in Greg's arms. Smiled so genuinely in them. She looked at Eric and gave him a little wave. "Hey, neighbor. Headed off to work, I see."

"Are you taking a trip?" Eric blurted.

"Yep," Lindsay chirped, "heading down to the beach for a week. Haven't felt sand between our toes in a while.

Figured it was time for a refresher. Spur-of-the-moment thing."

"Not a fan of the beach myself," Eric lied. He wanted to see the ocean again. The beetle agreed. It seemed invigorated by the thought of a cloudless sky over the waves.

Why had he lied?

"Well, I guess we all have our own places," Lindsay mused.

Eric couldn't think of his own places. Only his paths. The beetle *knew* its place was up in the sky. Up in the light. It knew what it wanted after a single morning of existence.

Eric jingled his keys a little. Let the Rodgers know they could go. "I hope you have a nice trip. Oh, and watch out for riptides."

Greg shook Eric's hand. "We'll keep careful. You have a safe one to work, old fella. No drag racing now, you hear?"

"Oh shut up, honey." Lindsay slapped her husband's stomach and laughed. "Bye, Eric."

Before Eric could rebuke the '*old fella*' title, the two little Rodgers girls, Nancy and Jackie, ran out of the garage. They smiled and giggled as they smacked each other with pool noodles.

Lindsay helped the girls into the SUV and strapped them in. The girls looked out the open window and waved at Eric.

Then the beetle forced Eric's head around so it could get a good look at the sun reflecting off the SUV's door.

"Oh my Gosh, Mister Eric!" Nancy shouted.

"What's *that*?" Jackie shouted.

"Oh, nothing." Eric whipped his head back around. Scratched at his bald spot out of habit. Almost got bit again. "Just a weird mole or something."

"His name is Totoro!" the girls yelled simultaneously. Greg started the SUV.

"Uh… sure, I guess," Eric uttered. One of Totoro's antennae whipped around and struck him in the nose.

The children laughed as the Rodgers backed out of their driveway. Greg gave Eric a smile and a salute.

Eric smiled like Greg back then. Thought he did. That was a while ago. His kids laughed like Nancy and Jackie back then. Thought they did. That was a while ago.

Time flew. Pulled like a beetle.

Eric watched the Rodgers drive away.

He walked back to his front door to lock up.

He looked back inside instead.

So dark, not at all like outside. Eric's old eyes could still pick out things in the dimness. He took a step back inside. Totoro compelled him to stop before he could take another. The beetle threatened to rip Eric in half just so it could keep gazing up at the bright spring sky.

"Honeybear?" Eric called into the house. When was the last time he had called Susan '*Honeybear*'? Not since those beach trips ended. "I'm going now. Have a good day. Tell the kids I love them."

Susan didn't respond.

It was at least eight twenty-five, but Eric waited.

Susan didn't respond.

Eric waited some more.

Totoro watched the sunlight cut through leaves in the Rodgers' elm tree. A blue jay perched beside Eric's baseball cap. The bird chirped. The beetle clacked its mandibles and forced an entire leg through the back of Eric's shirt. The leg wrapped around to Eric's front and jabbed his chest with those hooked claws.

And Susan still didn't respond.

"Well… have a good day." Eric locked the front door and walked over to his grey car. Next to Susan's pink VW Beetle, his car looked even duller than usual.

He unlocked his car. He grabbed the handle. He opened his car door.

Then the front door opened. Susan came out. She was wearing that pretty dress that made Eric's lamp look so dull. Its silver trim caught the sunlight as Susan locked up.

Totoro clacked its mandibles and chittered. The beetle willed Eric backward, dead-set on Susan and her shining silver dress.

Eric barely had time to steer Totoro away from his wife. He strained with his mind and muscles, disrupted the beetle's trajectory *just* enough, and slammed back-first into the front door. He slid to the ground, exhausted and lightheaded.

"Oh my God, Eric!" Susan knelt down. "Are you all right?"

"Oh yeah," Eric said as he stood. He pushed his back against the front door, pinning the beetle's legs. "Never been better. Must've tripped."

Totoro tried to force Eric around. It *needed* to see the dress again. Eric pressed back harder.

Good thing Susan hadn't noticed the bug. Or maybe she just ignored it.

Susan sighed and shrugged and fished her keys out of her purse. "Well, be careful, please. We aren't young anymore. That time's long gone. Aren't you headed to work? You'll be late if you don't hurry."

"Are you going to see the kids now?" Eric asked.

"Yes, Sarah called. They made it to the mall earlier than planned. We're going to shop a little before we get some food." Susan jingled her keys.

"Oh, that's good. Are you eating somewhere new?"

"You could find out." Susan's tone didn't hide much hope. "You can still call in."

Probably fifteen steps to Eric's closet from here. Probably five minutes to slip into something more comfortable to meet the kids in. Two minutes to call work, max.

Instead, he said, "The boss really needs me today and I-"

"I'll bring back leftovers," Susan interrupted.

"Oh. Good." Eric looked away. "I always… love those leftovers."

Susan walked away. "I'll tell the kids they'll see you when they see you." She got into her car without looking back and drove off.

Eric waited until she was out of sight. Then he got into his car. Then he put his key into the ignition.

But he didn't crank the engine.

"Why don't I just go with her?"

Eric didn't know who he was asking. Totoro clearly didn't care. He could hear the beetle's legs — its claws — tearing through his shirt. Tearing at the car seat. Its mandibles picking apart the headrest.

There were so many photos in Eric's house. So many glass-cased memories. So many genuine smiles. When had those genuine smiles become pretend? The deeper Eric dug, the greyer everything became. Grey, like his paint.

The door-ajar *beep* pulled Eric out of that grey. He was standing halfway out of his car. Had Totoro done that? Pulled him out of the car? Or was that all Eric?

Eric looked down the road. Imagined Susan returning. Asking him to join her, *one* more time. His breath caught in his chest.

Two cars came down the road. Neither pink.

It was getting late. Eric needed to get to work.

Totoro didn't want to go, though.

Eric tried to get back into his car, but all six of the beetle's legs tore free. One leg slammed the door shut while the others pushed out against the car. Then Eric felt a strange sensation. An *emergence* all down his spine. His shirt ripped

59

in half, down the back. Something — some*things* — slapped against his back. Hard. As if someone was trying to beat him to death with a pair of boat paddles. He heard a near-deafening buzz.

Then Eric's feet left the ground.

"No!" he shouted.

Eric reached back and struck the insect's eyes. The conjoined pair crumpled back down to the driveway. Eric looked into his side mirror as the remains of his shirt fell off.

The beetle was near-fully emerged now — only the backs of their heads linked the pair together — and the beetle was *gargantuan.*

Totoro's thorax nearly reached Eric's ankles. The shell coverings over the beetle's wings slapped against Eric's back, bum, and thighs while the translucent wings beneath struggled to fly. Too awkward an angle, though, stuck up against Eric like that.

Eric flung the door open and crawled back into the car, dragging Totoro with him. The seatbelt barely fit around him as he smashed the beetle back against the seat.

"We're going to mix paint!" Eric yelled. He cranked the car as Totoro tore half the headrest off with its mandibles.

The car pulled away and headed down Maple Street.

Totoro squirmed. Thrashed. Pressed its legs into the car seat. Crushed Eric up against the steering wheel. Eric could barely breathe.

"Just *go* with her," Eric wheezed out. It would be so easy. The ease made it so much worse. It would just take a right turn onto Crestridge instead of a left.

Totoro pressed harder. Eric's chest laid on the horn.

The stop sign where Maple crossed Crestridge came up. Eric braked and looked left on instinct. Left to the paint plant. He could make it there blindfolded. Autopilot down his path dug into that route. Like his kitchen path.

It was so hot in the car. Stifling. The sun cut through the clouds. Shined off the dash. The beetle sensed it. Wanted it.

The car seat snapped as Totoro forced it back. The beetle curled its body upward and sank all six of its hooked appendages into the car's roof. It clacked its wing shells together and started chewing through the roof to reach the sky. The sun. The light.

"Please just *stop*," Eric begged.

Totoro didn't stop. Insects always found a way — a path — to wherever they wanted to go. Or they made one. Forced their way past any obstacle. Totoro kept chewing.

Eric gripped his chest. His pulse raced. A heart attack?

He pulled out his cellphone and fumbled through the contacts.

Stephen's number came up.

The phone rang four times before the voicemail kicked on.

"*Yo, it's Stephen. I'm either busy, or dead, or I don't like you. Leave a message!*"

BEEP.

"Stephen, it's Dad. I just wanted…" Eric tried to pin down why he had called, "…I wanted… to check up and see how everything at school was going. Freshman year is… it can be scary. I wanted to come see you with your mother. I did. I don't know why I didn't. I'm… in a trench."

He hung up and rolled down the windows. So hot. So bright.

Maybe Sarah was free. Eric looked left and almost cried. Totoro didn't cry. The beetle threw its appendages out the windows. Bent the doorframes inward.

Sarah's phone only rang twice before sending Eric to voicemail.

"*This is Sarah. I can't talk right now, but leave a message and I'll get back to you.*"

BEEP.

"Sarah, it's Dad. I just… I don't want to go left. I want to see you and Stephen. I swear I do. I told your mother I had to work, but I didn't have to. I want your mother to be happy. And you and Stephen, too. I want to be happy *with* you. But I can't climb out! I'm in so deep now." He was going to scare her. He sounded crazy. "It's all right. Don't worry. I'm all right. Goodbye."

The car idled at the stop sign, rocking back and forth as Totoro continued to chew.

Maybe Susan had her phone on her. She forgot it sometimes. Said she did. Eric wouldn't blame her if she just chose not to answer him.

Susan's number rolled into view — right as Totoro's mandibles cut through the roof.

Eric hit the call button — right as Totoro's front legs slid into the roof's impromptu opening.

The beetle rolled the metal down as easily as a sardine tin's lid. Then it lurched upward, pulling Eric tight against the seatbelt.

Eric dropped his phone.

"Leave me alone!" Eric reached back and clawed at the beetle's head. Jabbed at its eyes. Pulled at its antennae. "You want to go? Burn up if you want! Fly into the sun! *Go*!"

Totoro took his advice.

The beetle ripped Eric out of the car.

It spread its wings as wide as Eric's in-the-way body would allow.

It took flight.

Eric rose twenty feet into the air. Thirty. Fifty. Higher. Up and up and up, gaining speed all the while. Impressive, given that Totoro was flying upside down with an Eric-shaped skin tag dangling off the back of its head.

Eric saw his — their — shadow on the asphalt below. Saw it getting smaller. He pictured the beetle dragging him into space, into the sun, to burn up into nothing. Eric could never want anything as badly as Totoro wanted the light.

Could never want anyplace as badly as Totoro wanted the sky.

No. Eric had things besides oatmeal and 4K TVs. He had places, not just paths. He *had* to.

He shut his eyes. Dug through the grey. Dug through all that time spent on his paths. In his trenches.

And he finally dug something out of that grey. A spur-of-the-moment beach trip from a lifetime ago. So far back that he remembered calling Susan '*Honeybear*'.

Sarah had been sucked out by a riptide. Eric had never swum like that before. That fast. That fluidly. That purposefully. He had never been stronger than those few moments heading out into the ocean. Heading out to save his child. Heading out with no path or plan. Just a desire.

An insect paled in comparison to an ocean.

Eric started swimming. Awkwardly at first, dog-paddling in the sky, flailing like a fish being pulled into a boat to be scaled and gutted. The beetle's wingbeats overpowered his strokes.

But Eric became stronger and stronger. Totoro's ascent slowed and slowed.

Eric stroked around in the air until he was facing right, toward the mall. Then Eric forced Totoro onward, in *his* direction, as if the insect was an unwilling paraglider. They both sailed over the street, over the neighborhood, over the city.

Susan would be so surprised to see him, so happy to be so surprised. So would the kids.

Eric smiled as he swam through the air. He passed over houses and neighborhoods. People peered up at him from yards and sidewalks. They gawked and pointed and cried out.

Eric just swam faster.

The highway snaked around below him now. He was so high up. The wind stung Eric's skin and made him miss his shirt.

The cars below looked like lines of ants. Sometimes, Eric found lines of ants on the kitchen counter. He wondered if any of those drivers had ant antennae sticking out the backs of their heads.

It took another thirty minutes of flying-swimming to reach the mall. Eric yanked Totoro's antennae and forced the bug lower so he could read the surrounding restaurant signs.

Eric recalled eating leftovers from all of them. Recalled living vicariously through their doggie bags and take-home Styrofoam boxes.

Susan and the kids would be somewhere new. Somewhere inside the mall proper, maybe?

Eric flew down. He passed through the mall's giant double doors. He glided through the atrium air until he saw a huge banner outside one of the storefronts.

'STRAGATORI'S ITALIAN EATERY. GRAND OPENING. FREE DESSERT.'

He forced Totoro down low and peered through the restaurant's front window. Susan and the kids sat off to the right, enjoying a pizza. Eric picked Susan out instantly. It was the dress. She looked so beautiful in it.

"Honeybear!" Eric flew over to the door and tried for the handle, but Totoro jerked about too violently for him to grab on. He flew back to the window. "Kids, it's me! Come open the door."

They didn't seem to hear him. The couple at the window tried to ignore his presence.

"I made it! Come let me in!" Eric banged on the glass, more by accident than on purpose. More with his entire body than just his hand.

"Somebody!" He kicked at the window. "Just let me in!"

A waiter came out, armed with a broom.

"Sir," the waiter clipped, "we have a *very* strict no-shirt, no-service policy, as well as a no… *pets* policy. Leave!"

The waiter tried to shoo Eric and Totoro away, but all Eric saw was the open door.

"Move, please," Eric shouted. He pushed off the window and steered the beetle around the waiter.

As Eric slipped through the door, one of Totoro's legs snapped out and bashed the waiter square in the jaw. The waiter crashed to the floor.

"That wasn't me," Eric yelled.

The waiter clutched his face and glared at Eric through the closing door.

Patrons scattered as Eric flew through the restaurant. His feet dangled down into plates and kicked over wineglasses. The fury gusted up by Totoro's wings knocked down every picture frame hung along every wall. The insect's buzzing drowned out all other sounds, as if someone had cranked up a portable generator in the middle of the restaurant. Stragatori's became a war zone, blood and guts replaced with pasta sauce and spaghetti noodles.

But Eric's family was *right* there.

He flew over.

"Kids! Kids, it's so good to see you! I'm sorry I didn't take off work. I-"

"*Dad*?" Sarah screamed out over Totoro's wingbeats. "What *is* that? Why is there a woodcutter beetle stuck to your head?" She gagged.

"That's Totoro." Eric knew Sarah would know what kind of bug Totoro was.

Stephen stood up — dinner knife in one hand, pizza cutter in the other. "Holy shit, Dad! That's gross as fuck!"

"I know. I'm sorry-" Eric was jerked sideways. His thigh hit a table and knocked it over. An expensive-looking pasta dish spilled onto the floor. "Stop moving!" He strained down, grabbed a fork off another table, and blindly thrust it backward. The utensil found a gap in Totoro's chitin and stuck in deep. The bug hissed like it was cursing at him.

Eric steered Totoro back to his family. "Just ignore it. I'm here now. What are you three having? Is that sausage pizza? Looks great. I-"

Susan slammed her hands down onto the table. "Eric, we're trying to eat here. This is too much."

The waiter came and stood to Eric's left — broom raised and ready, jaw bruised and swollen.

"But…" Eric sensed the grey returning. The trenches deepening. "But I'm here now. I didn't go to work."

Sarah wiped some tears away. "Dad, I think you need to go to a doctor, like *now*."

"My dorm had a cockroach problem," Stephen said. He had gathered up all the utensils on the table. It looked like he had Swiss army knives for hands. "They had to fumigate the whole building. I bet we could hose you down with a bug bomb if we got you one of those paint masks so you wouldn't suffocate. You have those at work, right?"

Eric blurted, "Now, let's not do anything rash-"

Totoro pulled Eric straight up. The insect latched onto the ceiling. Chunks of ceiling tile rained down as the beetle tore about in a panic.

"Dear Lord, this is so un*couth*," an older woman huffed.

A chubby man leaned toward his wife and muttered, "We're not eating here again, I can tell you that."

Susan dropped her head into her hands. "Eric, please leave."

"But y- you *invited* me!" Eric blubbered as he dangled helplessly.

"I did. And you refused the offer." Susan looked at him, and Eric looked away. "So just wait at home and I'll bring you leftovers."

Sarah added, "But go to the doctor first."

"We can take care of that bug later," Stephen suggested. "Sarah, did you bring your softball bats with you?"

"Kids, why didn't you answer your phones?" When Eric spoke, the insect stopped thrashing around. Stopped moving. Both of his children looked away. "Stephen?"

"I mean... my phone dies a lot," Stephen stammered. "Bad battery or something." Then Stephen's phone rang. He dropped his silverware weaponry as he fumbled through his pockets.

"Sarah?" Eric held his hands out. "Sarah?"

Sarah started to reach for him, but lowered her hand and played with a napkin instead. "Dad, we love you," she tore the napkin, "but we were out with Mom. You never show up. We just end up, like, crossing paths eventually. I was just busy enjoying a break from classes. I guess I didn't notice your call."

"But... I made it. I'm *here*." Eric looked at his wife. "I love you, Susan. I don't know why I stopped making French toast or stopped our bad-movie date nights or stopped... *everything*. I just got stuck. I don't know how or when or- or where, but I *did*. But I love you. I love your dress. It's so pretty on you."

Susan smiled. Maybe fake, maybe not.

"I love you, too," she sighed, "but we're trying to have family time, Eric. Time we made that you *didn't* make with us. We'll see you at home." Susan pushed back her chair and stood. "Please, go. You're making people uncomfortable."

Eric looked down. Someone's order of fettuccine Alfredo clung to the sole of his left shoe.

"I'm sorry, I…" Eric couldn't find the words he wanted. It all receded back into the grey.

For some reason, Totoro detached its hooked claws from the ceiling. Eric dropped down to the floor. He headed for the door, hunched over so the beetle could rest against his back.

He made it to the door. He reached for the handle.

Then a light — a distilled reflection of sunlight — flashed from somewhere. A cook near the kitchen. The polished metal tray they were holding. The tray threw the light onto Susan. Her dress' trim cast out a thousand rays of silver.

The light burned *so* bright in Totoro's compound eyes — so bright that Eric saw stars in his own.

Totoro pulled Eric back, toward Susan.

The beetle hissed. Drew closer to her. Inches from her. It reached out its claws. Opened its mandibles wide.

Then the waiter struck Eric and the insect in the head with his broom.

Then again.

And again.

One of the waiter's swipes hit the fork stuck in Totoro's side. The beetle shivered and screeched and took flight.

It fled toward the restaurant's storefront window and crashed through. Then it bulldozed through one of the mall's giant ceiling windows.

Then it was free.

Eric screamed as he soared into the clouds with the bug. He kicked out. Jerked around. Tried to swim against the current.

Then he imagined the leftovers he'd find at home later.

Eric stopped struggling and just cried.

He cried until all his tears were gone.

Totoro dragged Eric around the sky for a while — but the beetle eventually slowed to an awkward, upside-down hover, about fifteen miles east of the mall. It clacked its mandibles. Not angrily, though. Slower than its earlier clackings. Calmer. Like a question asked in insectoid.

Maybe the beetle was concerned. Maybe it pitied Eric.

Eric let out a weak laugh. How lost was he if insects could pity him?

He looked out across the city.

Nowhere felt right. Not his house. Not the paint plant. Not the mall. Not anywhere he could see for miles and miles around.

"Where would you go?" Eric asked Totoro.

The insect didn't answer. Maybe that *was* its answer. Maybe Totoro was lost, too. Maybe that's why the insect paused.

Getting lost sounded like a plan. Comfortably lost. Away from any little paths carved into the ground. Bugs never seemed to know *exactly* where they were going — and still, they seemed happy enough bumping into big lights at high school softball games along their way.

"You pick, then," Eric said.

The insect took him everywhere. Flew in all directions. Hours passed by. The sun eventually dimmed to twilight. Eric didn't recognize the streets below. The buildings. He guessed he was in another city entirely.

The pair finally landed in front of a restaurant named Frank's Fish Market. Eric figured Totoro had picked this place for the sign — a hulking mass of white-and-blue neon tubing shaped into a swordfish. Same colors as Eric's lamp.

Eric had never heard of this place. Never eaten leftovers from this place.

He had found it before Susan.

Eric reached back and pulled the fork out of Totoro's side. "I'm sorry for stabbing you."

The beetle clacked its mandibles.

Then Eric felt a strange sensation prickle the back of his head. He felt lighter. Better. He remembered breathing in beach air. He reached back and felt at his scalp. No human-sized woodcutter beetle. Just a bald spot.

A loud *bang* drew Eric's attention up to the neon swordfish.

Totoro was perched up there. The beetle tore the fish's tail off. The glass fell to the ground and shattered.

"Wow," Eric gasped.

Totoro's carapace shimmered a beautiful metallic silver in the neon light. Just like a dress with silver trim.

Eric waved at the bug as it gnawed on the swordfish. Totoro ignored him. Eric headed into the restaurant alone.

He decided that he would order far too much food to eat by himself. Enough to merit five or six take-home boxes, minimum. Good thing Totoro hadn't ripped Eric's pants off along with his shirt. He fished around in his pocket and pulled out his wallet.

The swordfish's head crashed down to the asphalt outside as Eric asked a confused waiter for a menu — and directions to the nearest clothing store.

Lessons from Top Hat Benjamin

Would a twenty-foot drop snap a neck?

That's what it looked to be, not that Jim had any way of really knowing. He had been homeless for so long. He had dumpster-dived all that time. Crawled through muck and shit all that time. Scavenged through abandoned buildings and wallowed in trap houses all that time.

And not once had he come across a tape measurer.

The closest thing he owned was a rope.

Seemed like something to just avoid, anyway. How to *not* snap a neck from a twenty-foot drop — much better question. No need to measure a deadly fall if he wasn't falling, right?

"Oh, right." Jim's confusion cleared up.

Jim needed to know if a twenty-foot drop would snap a neck because Jim was about to hang himself.

Odd, forgetting that.

Jim had made his way to the most-wretched tract of the most-barren stretch of old downtown to find the perfect suicide spot. The buildings here had grown older and weaker the farther he wandered — until they ceased to be buildings at all. Clean windows transitioned to filmy windows, to broken and boarded-up windows, to broken windows simply left open. Foundations slumped, ruined and listing. More rot than structure. More rat hive than home. The roads sported holes deep enough for Jim to bury himself in.

A perfect place for trash to end up. And end.

The living section of the city — with its skyscrapers and cars and people and country clubs and traitor brokerage firms that fired people named '*Jim*' — was a far-off streak of watercolor paint on the horizon.

Jim looked toward that living city from the ruined bridge he now stood on. Hated it. Wished for it.

Then he climbed past the bridge's crisscross of flaking iron support beams and guardrails. This bridge probably saw conga lines of cars in its heyday. Now, its concrete crumbled under the weight of one pathetic, malnourished, heroin-addicted *former* wealth management advisor.

Jim shuffled to the bridge's edge, where weather and neglect had eaten the concrete away from a rusty girder. He walked out onto the girder. It whined but didn't break. Then

Jim sat down on his girder and dangled his feet off and over the sides. Off and over a deep, deep culvert.

Jim laughed into the culvert. His echo laughed back. Forgetting his own suicide in the end run of his own suicide. He should've scrounged up a burger wrapper to write down an itinerary.

"Must be the shock," he reassured himself.

Jim remembered seeing videos about going into shock when he walked past his son's room. Garrett was always watching medical videos on his computer while his little sister, Tabitha, sat in his lap. Tabitha would ask Garrett a million questions. Garrett wanted to be a doctor.

Maybe if Jim had lingered in that doorway a moment longer — asked Garrett some questions — he could've built some sort of bridge back to his old life. Could've proven he gave some semblance of a shit about Garrett. Tabitha. Could've at least learned how to tell if this was shock or not.

"Yeah, yeah, definitely shock."

Or maybe it was just the drugs.

Jim always knew his firm *could* suss out his number-fudging. His account-shifting. His extra extravagancies. His little bags of special powder. He knew they wouldn't, though. They *did*. Then he knew it would be easy to find another position at another brokerage firm. It *wasn't*.

The cocaine had helped at first, way back when the money was dwindling but still there. The coke kept him energized on his search — his search that never amounted to anything.

But cocaine was expensive.

Heroin helped later on, after the cocaine became unobtainable. Heroin numbed the ache of failing. Nice and affordable, too. If belonging to the world of stocks and bonds was worth anything in the end, it at least prepped Jim for keeping track of the figures as the drugs and late car payments and bills and foreclosures and lawsuits and lawyer fees rotted his savings — his life — away.

Stocks and bonds didn't help at all now, and all his drugs were gone.

"You fucked up your brain synapsations with that stuff." Jim spoke without wanting to speak. "Now you're all scrambled up."

Even Jim's subconscious knew what he was now. Its uninvited truths made his skin feel unclean. More unclean than usual. It made him feel dirty underneath the skin.

But it was absolutely right, that little voice. Drugs made more sense than shock. Jim wasn't a doctor. That's what Garrett wanted to be.

Jim took a deep breath, then looked *down there*. Down into the culvert. Down into his final destination.

Down there wasn't filled with calm, clean water. More refuse than water *down there*. The only water *down there* sat about in stagnant puddles where the concrete had collapsed in on itself.

Jim looked between his legs at his girder-perch. Hoped the bridge's exposed rib bone could handle the snap he would make at the end of his rope.

Right. His rope.

He reached into his plastic sack of belongings. Riffled through empty food cans and empty needles and empty dime bags. He found his rope near the bottom, coiled up like a snake.

Jim pulled the rope out. Felt it. So greasy. So prickly. He tied one end around the girder while he imagined the drop waiting at the other.

The girder rained down rust. Filled his nose with a metallic scent that conjured up memories of childhood nosebleeds. And cocaine nosebleeds.

Jim strained until the rope felt hot in his hands.

It would have wounded his soft stockbroker hands, but he didn't have soft stockbroker hands anymore. His hands were rough as sandpaper now. The rope felt like satin now. He used to sleep on satin sheets.

Jim tugged once more and looked up. Hoped to see God.

No God. Just smog from the paper mill, up a ways from his suicide bridge. The mill's smokestack clouds tinged his last breaths with chemical rank. The poison caked his tongue and drained down his throat. The fumes muddled the sunlight and sky into shades of hopeless.

Then an ember of color sparked in all that hopeless grey and brown.

Birds. Two birds. A black one and a blue one.

They flew down into the culvert and started picking through some trash. Tabitha would have known what kinds they were. Rebecca, too.

Rebecca would always take Tabitha bird-watching whenever Jim decided to stay late at the office. Rebecca would always quiz Garrett on his medical knowledge whenever Jim decided to take an extra conference call. Rebecca would always ask Jim to take her out on the town whenever Jim had ignored her for a bit too long.

And Jim always decided to triple-check *one* more account *one* more time instead. Rebecca never complained. Rebecca loved sleeping on satin sheets. Jim loved seeing Rebecca lying on satin sheets.

Rebecca.

Jim screamed into the culvert, frightening the birds away. He fought hard to forget. Scratched at his temples until his nails came away bloody. But his mind wouldn't let go of Rebecca, now that he had summoned his wife up from the depths.

Her thin lips.

Her brown eyes.

Her pale skin.

Her black hair.

Her narrow shoulders.

Her odd-angled neck, hooked through that noose, in that dingy shower, in that dingy motel room.

Jim tied the free end of his rope into a noose. Maybe a noose. The only knot he knew how to tie was for a necktie. Hopefully, this knot would do the job.

He slipped the maybe-noose around his neck. Fit nicely, just like a tie. Scratchier, though. Heavier.

Jim looked back down, into the culvert, into a puddle.

And Rebecca looked back up at him.

She climbed out of the puddle like it was the fancy pool at the fancy country club they used to frequent. She loved doing laps in front of all those fancy people. She swam competitively in college.

Rebecca got to her feet, soaking wet and naked and beautiful — even with that red rash ringed around her neck and vomit smeared down her chin. She smiled up at Jim as she clutched an ugly teddy bear to her chest.

"I'm sorry," Jim managed with all the strength of a corpse.

Rebecca just kept smiling and squeezing that ugly teddy bear.

"You can fix it," she soothed. "Just finish." She pointed to the rope around Jim's neck and giggled. "Is it the right size? You always did buy clothes that were just one size too big."

Jim suddenly remembered that he was afraid of heights.

"I don't... I don't want to?" He ground the rope between his sandpaper palms. Soaked it with sweat.

"I didn't either," Rebecca cooed. Her voice was so soft. Like satin. "I had to work up to it. You helped me do that."

Jim started to cry, but Rebecca gently shushed him and continued.

"I felt so bad that I couldn't help you. I tried, but you just…" Rebecca hugged herself. Jim should've hugged her more. "…left me after you lost it all. Left me… even more than before, when we had money. I didn't know how to help you, but I couldn't leave you. So I just… left. But you can fix it now. You're almost done now. Almost."

"You destroyed *everything*," Jim moaned.

Rebecca didn't work. Left her litigation position at a reputable law firm after Jim made Partner. After Jim told her it was pointless to keep pursuing her career. So she had no way to help after he failed — and failed and failed and failed. All she could do was sit by and watch their lives crumble. Like Jim's bridge.

Jim eventually started hitting Rebecca to cope with it all. Hitting her helped like a drug. Cheaper than coke. Cheaper than heroin, even.

The kids left after the hitting started. Went to live with Bobby. Rebecca's brother. Cousin? Jim forgot which. Forgot Bobby's address, too. Even forgot which state Bobby lived in. Had to be the drugs.

Rebecca could've gone with them. She could've stayed with the kids. Stayed with Bobby. Her side of the family. Why'd she have to pick Jim over them?

Even through Jim's tears and the paper mill's chemical haze, Rebecca looked beautiful down by that puddle.

Rebecca smiled. "You can do this. This is the best thing to do. Once it's done, you can be with me. We can go back and try again. Try the past out all over again. You can do *anything* down here. I'll show you *everything* once you're down here."

Jim stood up on the girder. Let the rope hang. He saw the happiness in Rebecca's eyes, deep as a country-club pool. Deep as a culvert puddle.

He breathed, closed his eyes, and put his foot out.

"HEY!" a strange voice rasped.

Jim wheeled around. Lost his footing. He crumpled down to his girder, wrapped his limbs around its rusty girth, and whimpered. He looked up after what seemed like a lifetime. Or a twenty-foot drop.

Near the end of the bridge leading to the paper mill, stood a man — a giant man next to a buggy piled high with a mountain of trash. No, not a giant man. The corpse of a giant man. Mummified. Nothing but weathered skin and visible bone and half-rotted clothes and matted hair reaching down to a sunken belly. God, his limbs were *so* long. How were they so long?

The man wore a trench coat that wore its own coat of filth. His sweatpants were more duct tape and twine and safety pins than fabric. He sported a combat boot on his left foot — on his right, a sandal with one of the straps missing, replaced with three zip ties.

"Wh- who are you?" Jim squeaked after his heart stopped pounding in his ears. He hadn't seen a single living thing all day in this waste land. Excluding rats and roaches and feral cats. And the two birds. And his Rebecca, but she was dead.

The strange man sauntered over, leaving his shoplifted shopping cart at the end of the bridge, safe from all the holes in its crumbling concrete. It only took him a few steps to reach Jim with those Granddaddy long legs.

"Name's Top Hat Benjamin," the man said at the safe-ish end of Jim's girder. "And *you*, my druggy jumpin' friend, don't gotta go and do this crazy death-dive shit."

Benjamin's voice was gravel. Or tar. Gurgled up like crude oil. His greasy beard shimmered like glass. His matted-up hair ended in a dozen mishmash ponytails. Little skulls hung from the ends of them. Some were crow skulls. Others, rat and possum skulls. Two were donated by cats. One ponytail was pulled through a doll's head. The dead decorations clacked together like wind chimes as the man swayed to a song Jim couldn't hear.

Ben said, "I can help you outta this bind your mind's got you all briared up in, all right? It's T. H. Ben's spesh-eel-tee. Helping the helped-less-fortunate outta their misfortunes. Used to be a shepherd. It's true, trust me. Ask any little sheep you see 'round here."

"I don't want help," Jim meeked out.

His brain couldn't parse this Ben. So tall. So wrong. This Ben was more spider than person. More horror-movie tree than human.

"I came out here to do… *this*," Jim admitted. "Just this. There's nothing else to do."

Top Hat Benjamin snorted. "Course there's nothin' else to do out *here*." He spread his too-long arms and knelt down. "That's why you should come with me, to where there *is* somethin' else. Some place you'll love, or my name ain't '*Top Hat Benjamin*'. A place for lost ones to form a big, nice flock, all their own. Take off that one-way necktie and let's vamoose, partner!"

"That… doesn't sound bad." Jim chewed his lip and looked down at Rebecca.

Rebecca shook her head and clawed at her neck. She screamed, but she made no sound at all.

"I'm sorry," Jim called down. "I swear I'll come back. I *swear*. I remember when you were alive. I swear I'll come back and jump, and we can go back and try again." He turned away from Rebecca and her brown eyes — and met Ben's warning-red gaze. "I'll go with you, but I'm… going to leave this here. My rope." Jim slipped off his noose.

Top Hat Ben smiled like that was a joke. "Cool, friend-buddy, cool. Cool as ice. The chilly kind, not the trailer-park-party kind. Don't think anyone's gonna steal that neck-stretcher up from you no-ways!" Ben laughed. If a radiator could laugh, Ben's laugh was an exact match. "Now let Ben show you a few things about surviving through our ol' man-eat-man world that'll have you forget all about this last hoo-rah you planned out here all by your lonesome." Ben extended his hand. "Deal, little sheepy-boy?"

Ben's nails were long. Sharp. Hooked. Vulture-like. And his hand was *so* filthy. More dirt and grease than hand. Was it just bone under all that grime?

But Jim's hands were just as unclean.

"Just for now." Jim offered his own.

"Right, right, *right*!" Top Hat Benjamin gripped Jim's hand tighter than a bear trap and shook it like a crocodile. "Good, good, *good*!" The man ripped Jim off the girder as if he were weightless, up and away from the edge. Away from Rebecca.

Ben shot Jim a giant, toothy grin — minus half a full set of teeth — and near-carried Jim back to his trash cart. The handful of teeth left in Ben's black-gummed maw couldn't stop the stench of rotten meat from pouring out.

Jim hated missing teeth. They reminded him of how much he had taken dentists for granted. He scrubbed his tongue around in his mouth until he tasted blood.

Jim had lost five teeth since Rebecca.

"Let's get this lil pilgrimage on the move!" Ben started pushing his cart toward the paper mill's smokestacks stabbing into the sky.

"We have to go *there*?" Jim asked, pointing to the stacks as he followed.

Top Hat Benjamin nodded, rattling his ponytail skulls. "Yes sir-ree. To the castle! To the keep! To *Casa de*

Sobrevivir! You'll dig it, friend-bud. You'll dig it, or my name ain't my name."

Jim sniffed. Covered his nose. "Okay."

They kept walking.

Jim looked back. He couldn't see the bridge anymore.

Just dead, empty city all around. Dead, empty houses. Dead, empty businesses. Dead, empty lives. Top Hat Ben didn't seem to care about the ghost-lives all around. The man just pushed his cart onward while he hummed and whistled and stank.

After thirty minutes of wandering, Jim wondered what had become of his house. It was such a nice house. So big. So unmissable. So unmistakable. Now, he couldn't even recall how many rooms there were. But he could recall the *exact* placement of *every* spot on that polkadot shower curtain in that motel bathroom. That didn't seem fair.

After thirty more minutes of wandering, Jim wondered why someone named '*Top Hat Benjamin*' didn't wear a top hat.

He felt stupid for just noticing. Had to be the drugs.

"Why do they call you '*Top Hat Benjamin*'?" Jim asked.

Ben turned. "'*They*' bein' who, '*they*'?"

"People, I guess?"

"Only *I* call me '*Top Hat Benjamin*'," Ben gurgled out as he grinned, "just like only *you* call *you* '*failed-stocky-*

boy Jimothy'. How dumb are you, failed-stocky-boy Jimothy, asking dumb shit like that?"

Jim stopped. "How do you know my name?"

No, that wasn't Jim's name. Jim's name was '*Jim*'. He was sure of it. Almost. Did he call himself '*Jimothy*' now? Would it even matter if he did or didn't?

But Jim stopped caring about his name when Top Hat Ben grabbed his arm and dug those predator-sharp nails into his skin. Jim's cries got no sympathy from the man. Just laughs.

Ben abandoned his shopping cart and pulled Jim into a forest of overgrown weeds and brambles. They eventually came to a rusted and ruined chainlink fence. Ben tore back a section of metal and dragged Jim through to the paper mill's loading lot, where trains would dump off their tree-cargo for the factory to eat.

"Looks like these heroin-holes are leakin' out more than rot-blood," Ben teased as he ripped off Jim's sleeve. The man's dirty fingers pressed into Jim's track marks until the wounds oozed. "Grey matter bubblin' up from 'em like rain outta clogged gutters. I dub thee… let's see… Sir Noose-neck, the *holey* knight!"

Ben's head fell back impossibly far as he howled out a laugh. His laugh echoed all through the empty lot.

Jim thought of those two birds. Wondered if Bobby was treating his kids well. He tried to pull away from Ben.

"Get it?" Ben grinned at Jim. "Do ya? *Holey*! Like the holes in these druggy trash arms!" Ben squeezed until Jim nearly lost himself in the pain.

Jim screeched, "Please let me go *back*!"

Top Hat Ben just laughed louder and squeezed harder.

"Don't you worry now, Jim'borine-tamborine. I know I can rub off as a wee-bit wily, but I *really* do love the dumbshits and the druggies out here. Reminds me of my sheep, and I'd never hurt my sheep… unless I got a little hankerin' for some smack-glazed mutton!" Ben's head fell back even farther with his second laugh.

Then Ben stopped laughing.

The man's head dangled there, upside down, devoid of expression. Jim thought Ben was recalibrating. Jim's computer used to do that sometimes. Jim used to have a computer and a corner office.

Top Hat Ben's head snapped back into place. A yearning began to build in the man's eyes. A focus. The anticipation of a cat looking at some little creature it wanted to kill for no reason. He let go of Jim's arm and sniffed the air. He licked his finger to feel the wind's direction.

"A dog's nearby," Ben growled. "A big, juicy, meaty dog."

'*Dog*' chased all the pain out of Jim's brain. He panicked. Looked around for high ground. There were no train cars on any of the tracks in the lot. No storage crates.

No stacks of trees waiting to be paper. No safety. Just an old Toyota Camry sitting on flats.

A big street dog could climb its way up there. Jim had learned to be scared of street dogs. They had teeth. Claws. Numbers. Jim had nothing but whatever little stock-market factoids the dope hadn't cooked out of his skull.

And dogs always wanted to survive. Did everything they could to survive. Never hung nooses off bridges. Never gave up on life.

"We need to go." Jim tugged on Ben's coat, but his hand slipped off the grime. He grabbed on again. Tugged harder. "We need to *go!*"

Top Hat Ben wasn't going anywhere. He splayed his legs out wide. He dropped onto all fours.

"The key," Ben explained, "is to get 'em on their backs. Like turtles. That's when you got 'em good and split'er'ated. That's when you got yourself a banquet!"

A midnight-black dog lumbered out of the paper mill's loading dock, two hundred yards out. Was something *that* big even a dog? Was it a wolf at that point?

The beast looked at them. Sniffed the air. It walked toward them. Then it began to run. Charge.

Only a wolf could run like that, tearing chunks of asphalt up with its claws. Only a wolf could snarl and snap its bone-crack jaws like that, foaming saliva all over. Only a wolf could rage and roar like that, louder than a motorcycle engine.

And only Top Hat Benjamin could run at a wolf like that.

Jim would watch crabs run from the surf when he took his family to their beach house — back when he owned a beach house. A strange sideways run, with all their appendages flicking like gears in an old-fashioned machine. He spent most of those beach trips on business calls. Or calls to hide certain business.

Ben ran like those crabs.

The crabs were cute. Ben was not.

Ben and the wolf collided.

Jim almost saw '*This isn't right*' flash in the wolf's eyes when Ben flipped it over. There wasn't anything in its eyes after Ben tore everything out from down below.

Ben's spidery fingers ripped the beast's chest open as easily as a trash bag. Gore sprayed out in three-hundred-sixty degrees. Blood. Guts. Undigested food. Shit. Half a rib flew off into the distance like a boomerang. Some mystery organ soared high up into the air. It came down onto the Camry's hood and exploded.

Ben was absolutely right. Flip them like turtles.

Jim retched.

"Wooooooo boy!" Ben bellowed. "Now *that's* what I'm talkin' about! Grade-A protein, hot and savory!"

Ben looked like a thing out of a nightmare — all that red dripping off his face, all that meat caught under his nails. The man hunched over the wolf and sniffed in deep as steam bubbled up from the animal's carcass.

Jim inched over and looked down at the poor wolf. Ben had split it right down the middle, from the throat to the jewels. Hollowed it out in a single moment of violence. It reminded Jim of watching his housekeeper prepare roast duck for Christmas dinner.

Jim retched again.

With the flick of a wrist, Ben snapped off both of the wolf's front legs.

"Here ya go, stocky-boy." The man handed Jim one serving of wolf leg. Much heavier than a roast duck. "This is whatcha want, this right here. That good, good marrow."

Ben wrapped his lips around his wolf-leg meal and sucked at the cracked bone. His wiry-haired cheeks shot inward. His eyes rolled back in his head like a shark's.

Rebecca got out of the Camry with that ugly teddy bear in her hand. "Do you remember Gregory's Diner?"

Jim dropped his wolf leg. "What are you doing here?"

"Do you remember?" Rebecca repeated.

Seeing her made Jim nauseous — even more nauseous than seeing Ben tear out the wolf's tongue and gulp it down like an oyster.

But Jim remembered. "I took you there on our first date."

Rebecca smiled. "You looked so dorky in your oversized business suit. Dorky... but cute. I didn't think you'd wear it so often after we married, though."

Jim grabbed at his neck. Checked for a rope. "I'm sorry I stopped taking you there."

"It's okay, love. You had work. You had a family. You had to provide. I understood." Rebecca looked over at Ben as the man drained wolf leg number-two. "I liked Gregory's strawberry milkshakes the best."

Based on Top Hat Ben's sucking face, Jim wagered that Gregory's strawberry milkshakes were about the same consistency as bone marrow. He turned back to Rebecca. "Please tell me what to do."

Rebecca smiled. "Go back to your bridge and hang yourself."

Jim looked down and whimpered. Ben's slurps drowned him out.

Rebecca walked over and held Jim's hand. "I know it's scary, but we can go back and try again. Do better this time. Time isn't important when you're dead." She kissed his hand. Left a little vomit on his knuckle. "Isn't a little fear worth fixing the past?"

The two birds from the culvert flew by overhead. Jim wanted to ask his kids how fast the average bird flew. Where were the kids, again? Right. Bobby's. Jim tried to remember Bobby's address. He could only remember that Bobby lived in South Carolina.

"Don't look at those," Rebecca urged. "Look at *me*. You can look at me all you want after you jump. I'll lie on satin sheets for you. I'm just dirt now because of you, but I'll be *me* again once you jump. I can tell you all about me. We never talked enough, but we can talk forever once you jump. Talk and laugh and make love and visit Gregory's every day. But you have to jump first."

Before Jim could answer, Ben forced his way between the two. The man placed his blood-soaked hands on Jim's shoulders. Jim lost sight of Rebecca for a moment, behind Ben's bulk. She was gone when Jim peered around the man.

"Go on and-" Ben belched. The smell made Jim yearn for paper-mill smog. "-eat up. Gotta build up them strong bones with bones!" Ben pushed a severed wolf leg to Jim's chest. "Ain't no little sheep gonna follow no banshee-siren bitch to the Great Behind on *my* watch. Not gonna follow a pair of fucking birds, either, with their lies up there in the skies. Now eat!"

Jim didn't want to eat, but he didn't want to be rude. That kill looked pretty tough to pull off, after all. Bone marrow would taste like Gregory's strawberry milkshakes, maybe. It would — if he thought about milkshakes hard enough.

Jim sucked up through the broken bone.

Bone marrow didn't taste like Gregory's strawberry milkshakes at all. Jim threw up.

"Awww, don't you worry," Ben babied. "Just too weak and worthless to keep it down right now. Weak and worthless like those nasty birdies. Hollow bones, that's all they got under those fancy'fied feathers. Flimsy bones, no good for runnin' around in the gunk and the mud and the beautiful concrete and steel and trash. Lyin' bones for that shitty sky, to fly high, high, high. Bones that aren't even there, almost! What's there to suck out if they're hollow from the get-goin'?"

Ben scratched at his beard and toyed with his ponytail skulls. Then he slapped his knee and howled out his radiator laugh. "The fuck was I thinkin'? Water comes first, not food! Water's the more important of the two when you got nothin' left but *survive*. That's all you need. A refreshmenty glass of water."

Before Jim could wipe the vomit off his chin, Ben wrapped one of those horror-movie tree-branch arms around his waist. Then the man hoisted Jim over his shoulder and took off across the loading lot.

Jim almost screamed out that he was being kidnapped, but then he remembered he had agreed to come. No one would care about a thing like Jim, anyway.

The wolf's loading-dock entrance came and went overhead, and the two entered the paper mill proper. The floors were scuffed from countless work boots toiling for countless years. Jim used to laugh at people who wore work boots.

Jim wanted some work boots now. Work boots would be worth a thousand of the ruined Birkenstocks he wore now.

Machines churned everywhere, fed by a million humming cables. Jim hallucinated little patterns in the cables' tangles as Ben carried him through door after door, room after room, hall after hall.

Ben finally stopped. The man tore a stairwell door off its hinges and stepped through — and the two entered another world. A worse world. A world of groaning metal and thick shadows and red emergency lighting and chemical vapors and choking smog.

Ben breathed in and shivered. Jim could tell that Ben was home.

Jim tried to wriggle free, but Ben squeezed him hard enough to move around organs before starting down a flight of grated stairs.

Then it was down, down, down.

They descended into a rat maze of tunnels with walls coated in vibrating iron pipes. The pipes screamed and spat hot steam onto Jim's face. The steam burned at first, then cooled into chilly dew.

"Rebecca?" Jim mumbled. Rebecca would kiss Jim when he returned to the motel, after a long day of failed job hunting. Her little kisses helped soothe those failure-burns — like chilly dew. He'd still hit her, though.

"Rebecca, is that you?"

No answer.

"Rebecca? Take me back to the bridge."

Still nothing. Nobody.

Where was everybody? Jim figured there had to be workers, but there weren't. None in the stairwells, the rooms, the halls. No hands tending the machinery or switchboards or levers.

Just Ben, who took him down, down, down.

Maybe all those workers got fired. Maybe they were all homeless. Or maybe it was just that nobody wanted to stop Top Hat Ben from saving a life. Jim would pull his car onto the shoulder to make way for ambulances — back when he had a car. Same concept.

Ben shifted his shoulder and dropped Jim onto the concrete floor. Jim rose from the rough foundation, his clothes now soaked with that slimy, lukewarm water that always found its way to the bottoms of places.

Then Jim followed Ben down a hallway lined with yellow industrial lights, all buzzing like angry insects. He followed until the two came to a giant room built around a just-as-giant iron boiler.

Ben slapped the boiler and motioned for Jim. "Come on over, Jimmy-jam. Come on over and take a bite outta ol' Rebecca's belly and gorge up that delicious aqua de life'a!"

That *name*. Jim wanted to go back to his bridge. Did Ben know Rebecca? Maybe Ben had been a guest at their wedding.

"'*Rebecca*' was my wife's name," Jim mumbled out. "My ex-wife's name. No, no. No. Rebecca was my wife. Is. *Is*?"

They never divorced. Not technically. Not unless suicide counted.

"That cadaver got the same name as good ol' Rebecca, here? What a teeny-weeny world we survive in!" Ben's gritty laugh fused with Rebecca's rumbles and the chamber's echoes.

The sounds congealed into a churning bass so powerful that it hurt Jim's bones.

"Ever bite her belly?" Ben asked. "Bite her belly and gorge up the water?"

Before Jim could answer, Top Hat Benjamin bit into Rebecca's belly.

Ben didn't need too many teeth to cut a hole in iron, apparently. All he needed to do was unhinge his jaw, latch on, and give his head a few turns. Like a cookie cutter. Must've been another secret trick. Like flipping dogs.

Ben pulled away and spat the iron plug onto the floor — a chunk as big as a sewer cover. Then he started gorging up the limy water that gushed out over his face.

As Top Hat Benjamin's stomach ballooned like a tick, Jim's Rebecca came around the boiler-named-Rebecca and pressed her skin to its iron surface.

"Don't worry. We're still married." Rebecca smiled and cuddled that ugly teddy bear up to her vomit-covered chin. "I know you found the divorce papers... after you found me in that shower. I never signed them. I had them ready, but I never signed them." She pulled away from the boiler, red blistered down her cheek. "Don't you want to go back to when I never even thought about divorce papers? We'll do everything right this time. We can go back and fix it *all*... if you just jump."

"Yes," Jim said. He could barely hear himself over the boiler-room cacophony. Did he really say '*yes*'? Or did he just imagine it?

It didn't matter. He still had his wife. There she was. Even if she was only a shade. Only still his wife on a technicality.

"Yes," Jim said again. "I want to go back. I'll do it this time."

Rebecca smiled, turned, and ran down a shadowy hallway.

Jim followed Rebecca through the dark until he found her at the end of an iron catwalk. The catwalk stretched out to the center of a massive, siloed room. Jim walked to Rebecca and looked down, past the catwalk's edge, into a death-dark pit. Then he looked up. Chains dangled down from the ceiling like jungle vines, swaying just within reach.

Rebecca grabbed the closest chain and passed it to Jim. "It's not a rope, but it will do. Anything to get you back to me... get you out of this present. You've suffered enough. Survived enough."

The cold of the chain metal crept into Jim's hand, up his arm, through his chest. He looked around the giant room. The grated walls made him feel caged. Birds probably hated cages.

Jim struggled out, "I should get back to Ben..."

Rebecca grabbed Jim's face and kissed him. Jim tasted stomach acid on her lips.

"You can't keep stalling." Rebecca took the chain and wrapped it around Jim's neck. "You need to do this for me. I did it because of you, remember? So you need to do it for me." She pulled at the chain. "I started painting. Did you know that? Watercolors. I started after you lost everything. It was all I could do to keep myself sane. You never even noticed my paintings in our bedroom before we had to move out. Jump, and I'll teach you how to paint."

Jim peered into the endless dark below. Thought of that culvert under his bridge. He put one foot out.

Then he heard a chirp.

"Did you hear that?" Jim pulled back from the edge.

"No." Rebecca tugged the chain. "Jump."

There it was again. And again. Two distinct chirps.

Jim slipped the chain off his neck and looked up. Those two birds circled overhead, playing with each other. Must've found a way in through a busted window. They looked so happy, diving through the chains together. His kids used to play like that in the backyard. Garrett would chase Tabitha around her playhouse and swing her about in his arms when he caught her.

What city did Bobby live in, again?

The birds flew down and passed overhead. The wind from their wings caressed Jim's face. Cooled his skin. Cleared his head.

"Jim, *please*!" Rebecca dropped that ugly teddy bear. It fell into the pit.

Jim turned. Looked back down the shadowy hallway. The birds must've flown through there. Tight hall. They'd hate it. Maybe he could help them find a way out.

Jim abandoned Rebecca at the end of that catwalk and headed back to the hallway. To find those birds.

He was *almost* there when Ben writhed out of the shadow, bulbous and jiggling, belly full of boiler water.

"There you are!" Ben reached out and caged Jim in his arms. "Thought I lost you. Wouldn't be much of a shepherd if I lost my sheep! Come on now, the water's a'waiting. You'll need some of its vy-toe-mines if you wanna grow a thick wool coat for winter." Ben started dragging Jim back down the hall.

"Did you see those birds fly by?" Jim asked.

Ben snarled and hocked a tar-black wad of phlegm onto the wall. "Fucking sky rats. No, rats are *good*. Nice and juicy. Pop in your mouth like grapes. No, no, no, you ignore those birds soaring up high, flying off into the distance the way they do. And forget that ghosty bitch with her lies about that easy retirement in the back-past. Focus on the *now*. On the *ground*. The *low*-low. That's where you need to point your peepers if you want to go on survivin'. Aren't you thirsty?"

They made it back to the boiler, its iron wound still hemorrhaging water onto the concrete.

Jim wasn't thirsty. That didn't matter. Ben shoved him under the boiler's hole.

The hot, piss-colored water forced its way down Jim's throat. His stomach filled up. His air ran out. He breathed in the water. He tried to pull away from Ben's hand.

Ben's hand stayed locked onto Jim's shoulder. Kept him under.

Jim struggled and thrashed and squirmed. It did him as much good as the wolf. His head began to pound. Black blobs blotted out his vision.

Then Jim felt Rebecca's hand grab his own.

Jim remembered rushing to Rebecca as she hung in that motel shower. Remembered grabbing onto her satin-soft hand. Remembered how cold her satin-soft hand felt. Remembered that ugly teddy bear soaking up water and vomit and half-digested pills on the shower floor.

Rebecca squeezed his hand and whispered through the boiler water, "Remember when we'd go to the country club in the summer? Before you lost our life? That pool was so lovely. I loved swimming. Now I can swim all the time. Water isn't a rope, but it will do."

Rebecca pecked Jim's cheek. She let go of Jim's hand.

And Jim started to die.

When there was almost nothing left of him in the dark, Jim heard the chirps again. He saw those birds in the blackness of his vision. The black bird wasn't completely black. Red stripes streaked across its chest and wings. Garrett always made black-and-red the color scheme for all the cars in all his videogames. And Tabitha always loved blue. Always dressed in blue. Colored pictures with blue. The blue bird was as blue as blue could be.

Summerville. That's where Bobby lived. Summerville, South Carolina.

Jim tore free from Ben's grip and crashed down to the concrete.

"Whoops!" Ben rolled Jim onto his stomach. "Looks like you *can* have too much of a good thing!" The man chuckled and slapped Jim's back.

Jim's teeth rattled. He coughed up a lungful of Rebecca's water as his insides died a little.

"Bet that hit the spot, though, huh?" Top Hat Ben joked. "Better'n any fucking high-up bird or long-gone'd ghost. Just some tasty refreshingment, right *now*. No past. No future. Just good, good boiler water and *now*." Ben lifted Jim up and licked his face. The man's tongue left behind a trail of saliva that burned like battery acid. "But we gotta move on along, partner. There's uppers to ride… lessons to learn-o-fy… caged sheep to caged fight!"

Ben grabbed Jim's nape and dragged him back through the rat tunnels, then up flight after flight of steep, iron stairs. Top Hat Benjamin whistled along with the clanking metal and whirring machinery as the water inside his belly boiled away and cloaked him in steam.

Jim's brain finally cleared enough to tell up from down. Where was he? Somewhere small and cramped and loud. An elevator? An elevator. An elevator grinding its way up through the paper mill's innards.

Oil scent spiced the air. Electric sparks leapt from the elevator's button panel. The sparks rained down onto Jim. Stung his skin.

"This… isn't safe." Jim yelped as the elevator jerked violently, clacking against cement and steel. His eardrums fluttered under the power of the din. "We… we need to get out of here! It's going to fall!" He hit the '*halt*' button. The button plopped out and rolled across the elevator floor. "We're going to die!"

Top Hat Benjamin added his laugh to the clangs and screeches. Hard to tell which sounded worse.

"That little factoid don't weigh a whole helluva lot, *'specially* comin' from someone who was ready to go full-body fishin' off a bridge before ol' Top Hat Ben came along." Ben pulled Jim close and cradled him tight. "But don't you worry. Everything's gonna be fine-dandy. Top Hat Benjamin wouldn't let his *widdle wamb* get butchered without teaching him all there is to teach about survivin' first. And the best way to learn how to survive… is by gettin' a little skin ripped off in the game."

The elevator stopped. The doors heaved themselves open. Jim stumbled out and fell to his knees. He breathed in. Let his lungs feast on the paper-mill breeze. It was so much fresher than Top Hat Ben's elevator air.

And the sun. That hazed-over sun and dirtied sky. A sight worthy of watercolor paintings.

Jim looked around after his fill of smog and semi-sunshine. He was on the mill's sun-baked roof, surrounded by a wrought-iron forest of smokestacks and scaffolding and pipes. Sheer drop-off threatened him from the edges, nothing but thousand-foot drops beyond.

Maybe just twenty-foot drops.

Jim's blood rushed from his skin to his muscles as the adrenaline flowed. It made him feel cold. Maybe that was just a side effect of Rebecca's poisoned water. Jim didn't know. But he shouldn't be here — that, he knew. And where were the birds? Free? Or still trapped in that nightmare?

Then Ben was upon him again.

The man dragged Jim toward the largest of the smokestacks. A door-sized hole had been chiseled into its base, jagged around the edges like animal jaws. Yells and screams and loud bangs and copper smells belched out of the impromptu doorway as smoke rose from the stack's top, high above.

"What's in there?" Jim tried to dig his heels into the roof. He'd be safer on his bridge than he would be in there. Safer on his girder. Safer *anywhere* else.

Ben leaned in. Let his ponytail skulls bonk against Jim's own. "The cree'shindo-finale lesson, buck-a-roo-nee-o. Life boiled down, pure and ready to shoot up." Then Ben forced Jim through the opening — into a sea of filthy, sickly, angry people.

Ben pushed the people aside as if they were weightless. They reformed after Ben and Jim passed, like a slime mold with a single consciousness. The people screamed and danced and fucked and seized. They banged on the sides of the smokestack with pipes and planks and bare fists, creating a horrible kind of music.

Jim couldn't tell if the people were on drugs, or if the people were making the drugs up in their heads.

But Jim *could* tell that his feet were warmer than they should be. He looked down.

A net of woven rebar formed the floor beneath his Birkenstocks. The net dangled Jim and the others over the mill's stomach — a great cistern filled with boiling muck, far below. The rebar warped and whined and threatened to fail as the crowd undulated.

Jim tried to slip away, but Ben's grip was iron. All Jim could do was allow his shepherd to guide him toward the core of the human mass.

Ben looked into Jim's eyes when they reached that core. The man kissed Jim's forehead. Then he bit down on the corner of Jim's ear. Then he ripped a chunk off. Chewed it. Smiled as Jim screamed. "You gotta get down in the mud and the blood and fight for your right to be alive *now*, stocky-boy!"

Ben threw Jim down onto the rebar.

Heat billowed up from below and seared a checkerboard pattern onto Jim's cheek. He rose up and wailed and tried to run back to the birds, but there was no way through the crowd.

Ben crawled up a skeletal tower forged from bent steel beams and rusty scrap metal and discarded tires, held steady amidst the crowd atop the broken backs of chained-up dopeheads. The man plopped into the garbage-heap throne crowning the tower and surveyed the crowd. The chaos. Then he laughed and bellowed, "All right, you shits and stains! It's time to... *Sheer*! *That*! *Sheep*!"

The crowd exploded.

Everyone screamed at Jim. Snapped their teeth at him. Jabbed at him with broken bottles and box cutters and shanks.

The mass shouted so many things at Jim. All at once. All while they hurt him.

"Do it! Just do it!"

"Fuck him up!"

"Break those pretty teeth out!"

"Make him puke up blood!"

"Do it!"

"Fucking do it, pussy!"

"DO IT!"

Jim didn't know what to do. Somebody else did.

Jim didn't hear the man approach from behind — couldn't, not through the crowd's jeering. He definitely heard the board hit his head, though. The strike sounded just like the *boink* from Saturday morning cartoons — that noise when the rabbit hit the duck with a mallet. Tabitha loved cartoons. Garrett would watch them with her. Jim never had time.

Jim fell down.

The shouts reversed. Distorted. The black blobs revisited Jim's eyes, but no birds. There was nothing now but the conglomerate, "*BOOOOOO*!" from his cagemates.

"Get on up now, stocky-boy," Ben whispered in Jim's ear.

How had Ben gotten off that throne so fast? It was the legs. So long. Jim could almost feel the stench of Ben's breath burn his skin. Burn worse than the rebar.

"You beat down this fella here," Ben gurgled, "pop his head like a fucking zit, and you win a trash bag full of Ben-Bucks! Think roundabout that. Enough to buy you fifty hooker gals that look *just* like Rebecca so you can fuck 'em 'til your pecker rots off. Enough to buy all the smack needles in the world and turn them holey arms into arm'y holes. Enough to really, *really* enjoy the fuck outta your *Now*! Enough to forget ever wanting anything else at all! Now... FIGHT!"

Jim's blood boiled. He rose and roared and flung his fist sideways through the air and struck the board-wielding man in the jaw. The man fell down. Jim smelled burning flesh — the man's back cooking on the rebar. Or maybe that smell was his own face.

Jim's hand flared with pain. Jim's hands weren't made for this. They were made for typing and enjoying cocktails and making money and stealing money and getting caught stealing money and getting fired and wringing out every drop of goodness in his world.

Jim crawled on top of the man. He recognized the man's face. Almost. The man had Jim's face. Almost.

Jim started beating the man's face in.

He kept beating that face in, over and over, until his hands felt like bursting open.

After a few minutes, Jim couldn't feel his hands. After a few more minutes, the man's face was nothing but a ruin of pulpy meat. Jim rolled off the man, exhausted. He didn't care about the burning rebar. He could see up through the top of the smokestack. The sky looked oddly clear.

Jim breathed in deep and stood up.

The crowd cheered and lavished Jim with shrieks and spit. But he didn't care about their admiration.

"Where's my prize?" Jim yelled. "I want my prize!"

"Your prize, *sheep*," Ben snarled out as he parted the crowd with an iron shepherd's crook, "is right under your fancy-schmancy matchin' shoes."

Top Hat Benjamin reached down in front of Jim. The man coiled his long fingers through the rebar over and over like octopus tentacles. Then Ben peeled back a section of the metal as easily as Jim had peeled open his firm's termination letter.

Ben smiled. Steam billowed out of the gaps in his teeth. "Just gotta get your lil self on *down there*."

Down there was a million miles away.

Down there was that boiling muck.

Down there was a swamp churning with used needles and satin sheets and divorce papers and polkadot shower curtains.

Then, as all those dirty things roiled around in the smoke and tar, a rope sprouted from the mire and began climbing up toward Jim.

A rope tied into a noose.

And something worse than a noose rose up with it.

Rebecca bubbled up from the mill's stomach, her grime-caked hands gripping the rope as it vined its way higher and higher. Boiling sludge clung to her body and replaced her beauty with ruin. But her gaze was so much worse than that ruin. So hateful. So scathing.

So justified.

Jim fell back and screamed.

"You don't get to scream at me!" Rebecca wasn't smiling anymore. Wasn't cuddling that ugly teddy bear anymore. "You don't get to scream when you caused *all* of this! The least you can do is this one *single* thing!" She shook the rope. "Come *down here*! Come *down* to me! *Now*!"

Jim couldn't go *down there*.

But Top Hat Benjamin insisted.

Ben's iron crook hooked around Jim's neck. It ground Jim's skin away. It forced him down. Pushed him farther and farther through the opening.

Jim clung to the edges of the rebar-hole with all his strength, but Ben laughed at his strength.

"I don't want this!" Jim cried out. "I want *home*!"

"Everywhere's home when you got no home, ya nut-bag!" Ben laughed and pushed harder. "Get on *down there* and kill that cunt! Rip those Ben-Bucks out of her trash-bag guts! You already merked her once. Do it *one* more time and you'll be free... just like me!"

Top Hat Benjamin was absolutely right. Everywhere was Jim's home now. Everywhere, except for any and every place Jim would ever want to live — not just *exist. Survive.* He didn't have a home anymore. He didn't have anywhere. Anyone. Anything.

And Ben was absolutely right about Rebecca, too. It didn't matter that she had hung that noose in that motel shower herself. Or that she had slipped it around her neck herself. Or that she had taken all those pills to make sure she couldn't go back on herself. None of that mattered. Because Jim had guaranteed all of it.

Jim had killed Rebecca with his own two sandpaper hands.

Jim had destroyed everything.

Jim looked *down there*, down at his wife. Felt her wrath pulse out like radiation. He deserved to bake in that radiation. His grip on the rebar loosened. He began to fall.

He began to let himself fall.

Then the birds chirped somewhere high above.

The chirps reverberated down, into the smokestack. The walls trapped the birdsongs. Amplified their melodies. The songs overpowered the crowd's howls, Ben's chuckles.

The notes swirled around Jim's head and swept everything else away. And Jim finally remembered.

Skylark Street. Bobby's street. 1437 Skylark Street.

Jim ripped loose from Ben's crook. Left some meat and blood behind.

He turned his back on Rebecca, just as she reached one ruined hand up through the rebar.

Then Jim ran for his life, pushing and clawing and biting and striking the people all around him until he reached the exit.

Jim ran out of the smokestack boxing ring and sprinted across the sun-baked roof. Top Hat Ben crawled out after him, moving on all fours like those beach crabs. No person should move like that.

Jim stumbled into the elevator and hit every button that remained in the ruined panel. The doors closed right before Top Hat Ben could reach in and grab him with those horrid claws.

Jim pictured the birds a million times over as he rode the elevator down. Imagined their chirps a million times more as he ran through the paper-mill maze with all those industrial lights and hissing pipes.

Nothing looked like it had before. Everything was different. All a new nightmare, shifted and warped. But Jim kept running.

The burning steam didn't matter. The morphing maze of rooms and hallways didn't matter. The boot-and-sandal *thump-clop* close behind didn't matter. Only the birds mattered.

Jim made it outside and ran through the empty loading lot. He jumped over the hollowed-out wolf and hoped Top Hat Ben would want seconds. He dared to look back.

Ben didn't want another serving. The man slapped the wolf carcass out of the way and kept crawling after Jim, his mouth wide open, primed to eat Jim alive.

But Jim would never find those birds if he got eaten alive. He screamed Bobby's address over and over as he ran and ran — ran for the only place he could think of.

Jim passed dozens of abandoned buildings — all identical to buildings he had squatted in and smoked in and shot up in, ever since he had destroyed everything good in his life — until he finally made it back to his bridge. He squeezed between the rusty supports and stepped onto his girder with Ben's thump-clops right behind.

Jim walked out. Reached the end.

"HEY!" Ben rasped from the safety of the bridge. "I said you don't gotta be doin' nothing crazy like that! Come on back from there. Let Top Hat Benjamin save your trash life!"

Ben sneered out a smile and slammed his combat-booted foot down onto the girder. "Them birds got you all temptation'd, huh? Lil sheep wants to fly? Maybe I just gotta *kill* 'em, then. Eat those birds up so they aren't flying through your noggin no more."

No.

Jim yelled as loud as he could. He remembered to yell really loud if a bear ever charged at him. That's what the park rangers had said, way back when Jim and his family visited Yellowstone — way back when he could afford things like that.

He didn't want to go on that trip at first. Said he was too busy. No wifi out there. No business calls out there. But his kids had begged and begged. Rebecca had begged and begged. Good that Jim caved.

No wifi at all. No business calls at all. Jim talked with his kids *so* much over those seven days. It was a good trip. A good trip capped off with a quick pitstop at a Yellowstone gift shop — and the purchase of an ugly, overpriced teddy bear for Rebecca.

And Jim never even saw any bears to yell at.

Top Hat Benjamin wasn't a bear. If a bear wandered across Top Hat Ben's path, it would probably just end up like that wolf. But Jim yelled all the same. He yelled until Ben stopped smiling.

Jim moved forward. Kept yelling. Forced Ben back. Jim stepped off his girder, onto the bridge. He picked up the biggest chunk of concrete he could lift. He yelled one last time, yelled so loud that his throat tore itself apart.

Then Jim hurled the concrete through the air.

It struck Top Hat Benjamin's cheekbone and exploded into gravel and dust.

Jim thought Ben's blood would be a different color. A monstrous color.

Ben's blood was just red.

"Jesus F. Christ! What's your deal, friendo?" Ben winced as he held his dirty coattail up to his dirtier cheek. "Fine then, shit-stick. Go wherever. Do whatever! *Ahhhhhhh*! See? I can scream like a damnation'd psycho junkie, too." Ben backed away. "Fuckin' freak. Last prick I try to helping-hand off a ledge."

Ben reached the far end of the bridge, then turned back and gave Jim one last smile. "No sheep's *ever* gonna catch a bird," he shouted.

Then Top Hat Benjamin walked off toward the paper mill, humming and whistling and stinking while his ponytail skulls rattled together.

The sounds and stench faded, and everything was still again. Like before.

Jim looked back to the end of the girder. His rope was still there. Top Hat Benjamin was absolutely right — no one wanted to steal a noose. Jim walked to it and looked down into the culvert.

Rebecca was down there, back in her puddle. She looked up at him with wide eyes and screamed something Jim couldn't hear.

Jim blinked.

Just a muddy puddle now.

Then something moved near a pile of trash.

Jim eased down and grabbed onto his rope. He climbed down, nice and slow. He didn't want to spook them.

They had come back. The black bird with the red stripes. The little blue bird. They jumped about and picked through the trash together, oblivious to Jim's presence.

Presents were always a surefire way of getting back on kids' good sides. Jim remembered that, at least. Birds would make good presents. Not as good as ugly teddy bears, but still good. He needed to find a burger wrapper. Write down Bobby's address before it flew out of his head.

Birds first, though.

Jim inched forward, really slow and really steady, as he thought up a plan to catch those birds.

Skin

It was a Sunday. Mother was preparing to take me and my brother away today. Again. My dad was failing to stop her. Again. But that didn't matter because I had just seen our neighbor, Mr. Wilkshire, pull his head off.

I saw it through my bedroom window. I was sure of it. My eyesight was perfect.

My mother threw a suitcase into the back of our van. Easy to tell by the bang. Bang number-eleven. She yelled something at Dad somewhere in the front yard. Even though I couldn't see their battle from my bedroom, I could hear all the yelling and blaming and dysfunction just fine. Dad had left the front door open, so all that noise wafted into the house on the summer breeze.

Not that I needed the breeze to inform me that Mother was melting down again. It happened frequently enough for me to anticipate the motions. Spot the setups.

At least she stopped at eleven suitcases this time. Remembered that she needed to leave enough room in the van for me and Derrick. Mother usually stuffed both of us into one seat, squished together. Definitely wasn't legal, definitely wasn't safe. But who could know? It wasn't like anyone could see us through the dirt on the van windows.

I had bigger things on my mind than car safety and broken family dynamics, anyway.

Like my headless neighbor.

I peered, wide-eyed, into Mr. Wilkshire's kitchen window — well, what I assumed was his kitchen window. No way to be sure, but sometimes I saw chicken feathers flying around in that window. Where else would chicken feathers be flying around, besides a kitchen?

Mr. Wilkshire had pulled hard at his hair, like Dad sometimes did when he thought no one was watching. But Mr. Wilkshire's head just kept coming up with his hands until it popped off. Slid off, more like. No grossness or blood or guts. Like his head was a flimsy Halloween mask. There was nothing underneath the mask — just empty space.

I heard Mother yell something about not being able to see through the van windows.

Mother refused to clean the van herself. She preferred carwashes. She especially loved carwashes that *weren't* automatic. The ones with actual people cleaning cars by hand. Like servants. We rarely had the spare cash for that, so the dirt just built up. She hated dirt. Called it the "*poor man's paint.*"

I liked drawing squiggly lines in the dirt with my fingers.

Mother did not like my squiggles. She discussed them with Dad. *At* Dad. She'd mention other things, too. Things my seven-year-old brain couldn't puzzle out. Things like '*rut*', '*stagnant*', and '*resignation*'.

Teachers never went over those things in school, and I never worked up the nerve to ask about them. Not with all those other kids around me, ready to look at me.

Still, I knew people shouldn't pull their heads off, even though I never asked questions in class.

Mr. Wilkshire's headless body started to shake. Vibrate.

I thought about getting Derrick. Turning off his too-loud stereo. Dragging him out of his stinky room. Making him come look. He was thirteen. That automatically made him infinitely smarter and wiser than me.

But I didn't. He'd just call me a loser.

I thought about getting my parents.

But I didn't. They would never pause an argument for me.

Then something broke against the front door. Veered my brain away from picking out potential witnesses. Probably a little flowerpot. Probably busted close to Dad's head. He always stood in the doorway during these fights.

Half-in, half-out. Quieter than Mother. Yeah, probably a flowerpot.

Mother lined the walkway with those flowerpots to "*spruce up this eyesore*." She always made sure to say that loud enough for Dad to hear. The look on his face always made me want to leave the room. It made me prefer my bedroom — and I hated my bedroom. It was the pink walls. A gross shade, dull and faded. Orange would've been my choice. Pumpkin orange.

I opened my grimy window to get a better view of Mr. Wilkshire. I hung out so far that I almost toppled into the side lawn.

Mr. Wilkshire always looked normal to me. Normal-ish. He was a bit lanky and nearly as tall as the young tree in our backyard. His skin looked too loose for his bones. His walk seemed *off*, like he was trying to convince people that his walk was a normal walk. He always wore one of those Russian ushankas that I renamed the '*dog-ear hat*'. He kept chickens — a lot of chickens — in coops that rested up against a little shed in his backyard. Despite all that, I never thought of him as *ab*normal.

Suddenly, Mr. Wilkshire had a head again.

It wasn't a person's head.

A gigantic, coppery-colored snake erupted up from his button-up shirt collar. The real Mr. Wilkshire hung in the air, looked down at his person-costume, and flicked out his forked tongue. The reptile was so thick that his person-costume's top two shirt buttons popped off. They struck his window like BB pellets.

Without his person-costume, Mr. Wilkshire looked more normal than ever. Maybe not normal. Correct, though. Natural.

The real Mr. Wilkshire flowed up and out of his person-costume. His serpentine body dipped out of view as more and more slithered free.

The way he emerged sort of reminded me of soft-serve ice cream coming out of the dispensers at the mall. Dad used to take me and Derrick to the mall for soft-serve sometimes, if Mother went shopping or something. She found out once. Complained about that waste of money — money that should've gone toward carwashings — for days. Weeks. Months. I hadn't tasted soft-serve in a year.

Mr. Wilkshire kept pouring out of himself. There must have been sixty feet of him. I wasn't sure how his arms and legs worked or how all that snake fit inside that skinny person-costume, but he managed somehow.

Mr. Wilkshire finally finished slithering out of his person-costume. Then the empty shell collapsed.

Then nothing. Stillness.

Maybe it was a trick of the light?

No, I was sure of what I saw. My eyesight was too good to mistake a weird, lanky man for a sixty-foot snake.

My parents continued to argue outside. My brother continued to drown them out with music in his room. I continued to snap my head from one window of Mr.

Wilkshire's house to another, desperate to see what snakes did in the privacy of their homes.

Then Mother stormed inside, stomping through the house so much harder than she needed to. I knew what that meant after Mother had been packing up the van.

"Well, Michael," my mother scolded, "maybe you should have considered that before making such a *stupid* financial decision."

She had on her kitten heels, the black ones with a fancy brand name on the back. I could tell she was wearing those based on their sound. One of their heel tips had worn down. They made a strange, mismatched *clip-clack* now.

My dad's shoe-falls followed Mother's. His sounded like regular work boots on our fake-wood floors. He always wore those work boots, almost like he wanted the plastics plant to call him in.

"All I did was sell off some drawers we weren't using." Dad sounded like a boxer burned out in round six, flailing against the heavyweight champ.

Mother huffed out a breath. "It was a cabinet, not a set of drawers. *My* cabinet. Mine. Cohnen & Locke. Made in nineteen thirty-two. Nineteen thirty-two! And you pawn it off for a handful of change."

Her pace quickened. She would get Derrick first. I was always second. I didn't mind. It would give me more time to look for Mr. Wilkshire.

And there he was.

He stood up — well, rose up, since snakes couldn't stand — in the window farther back in his house, right at the corner. I always figured that room was his bedroom. Would a snake-person sleep on a regular bed? Or coil up on a giant rock, maybe? I liked being warm. A warm rock would've been my choice.

Our houses were really close together — only a few lawnmower passes between them. Every detail of Mr. Wilkshire's snakey body was clear as crystal in my perfect eyes.

Most of his body shimmered a deep copper, but there were zigzags of mahogany in there as well. The mahogany started on his snout and twirled down his back, forming a repeating diamond pattern. Those diamonds were filled in with milky gold. His underside scales mimicked cool pearl. The sapphires-that-were-his-eyes never blinked.

He lunged down, out of view, and came back up with a struggling chicken half-hidden in his mouth. I understood why I sometimes saw feathers flying around now.

Mr. Wilkshire's jaws unhinged. They worked back and forth. Walked the chicken down his throat. One of the chicken's legs twitched before disappearing.

"I needed cash to pay the gas bill," Dad groaned, "and that cabinet's been sitting in the garage for nearly six years. You didn't seem to care about-"

"Michael," Mother bit back, "I will *not* continue this discussion." She knocked on my brother's door. "Derrick?

Derrick, honey, we're going on a trip to see your aunt. Come on out, now."

"Melanie," Dad sighed, "don't do this again. Please. This is ridiculous."

Dad always said it was ridiculous. It was. Trying to stop it with a word was just as ridiculous.

Mr. Wilkshire gulped, and the lump-that-was-the-chicken slid down his throat, out of view, to be digested. Then he turned. Then he saw me. His mouth opened a bit, revealing countless hooked teeth, each large enough to puncture a tire. Was he weighing the pros and cons of eating me? Or was he just shocked that I wasn't screaming?

He ducked down right as Mother opened my door.

I turned and caught a glimpse of Derrick heading for the van, lost in whatever CD he was listening to in his player. My brother's face was scrunched up. His face always did that when he was trying to ignore the world.

Mother walked into my bedroom. She grabbed my arm with one jewelry-covered hand and snatched up my bag with the other. My bag contained almost all the clothes I owned. Even then, it was barely half-full — I never cared for having too much crap to clutter up my already-tiny living space.

"Cynthia, quickly," Mother half-hummed as she pulled me out of my bedroom. "Hurry, now." She always sounded too happy to go on these trips.

"I saw the neighbor-" I started.

"That's nice, now come along." She tugged me down the hallway.

Our hallway was only wide enough for one person at a time to use. Comfortably, at least. Mother always complained about that. It seemed like she tried to catch Dad in the hall just to prove her point. I wasn't sure what he could've done about it. Pushed the walls really hard to move them out?

Mother pulled me into the living room. Dad stood in the front doorway.

"Melanie, please," was all Dad could say. He took off his coke-bottle glasses and rubbed his eyes. The left shoulder of his jacket was covered in dirt. Yep. Flowerpot.

I should've felt bad for him. I didn't, though. I was too concerned with getting back to my bedroom. My window. I wouldn't even mind my dull-pink walls if it meant I got to watch a giant snake — pretending to be a weird man in a weird hat — eat chickens.

Mother ignored Dad's barely-there pleas. "Come along now, Cynthia. It's time to see your aunt." She pushed past Dad and yanked me out of the house.

"But Mr. Wilkshire's a snake!" I tried to pull loose, break free, go back. I needed to see if Mr. Wilkshire had started on chicken number-two. Needed it more than air and water and food.

Mother gave my arm a hard jerk.

"Do *not* say things like that," she snapped. "Good Lord, how embarrassing. Now come along. Aunt Velma has everything you'll need."

That was partially true. Aunt Velma was loaded. She ran a clothing business or owned a fashion line or something. She always wore nice stuff. My mother made do with slightly damaged shoes and jewelry that always seemed to lack a few stones. I wasn't sure why my mother got hand-me-downs while Aunt Velma got the good stuff.

But I *was* sure that Aunt Velma didn't have a snake-person hidden away at her place.

"Melanie," Dad whined as he trailed behind like a tiny dog, "if you need to go and stay with Velma, fine. But please just leave the kids. They have school tomorrow. Cynthia's only eight and she's missed more school than she's gone to."

The '*school*' card. Dad's last-ditch attempt to save us. Never worked. I didn't mind. I hated school — especially group projects. I worried that I might miss a lesson on reptiles now, though.

My mother just sneered at him, her nose up in the air. She thought that was how rich people flipped undesirables off.

"See that you get my cabinet back. I don't care if it costs you more to buy it back. Just get it back!" She dragged me down the driveway.

Mr. Wilkshire popped up in his front window, between the curtains. He laid a giant coil of his body on the windowsill, rested his scaly chin on himself, belched out some chicken feathers, and scratched his snout with the tip of his tail. He probably wanted to watch our little drama.

He wasn't the only one.

All the neighbors appeared in all their windows. Dinner and a show. Well, more like lunchtime.

The Sinclairs were both on their knees, up on their couch, watching through their living room window. Kevin Drunst spied through his screen door. The entire troop of Mullens had clumped up at their little kitchen window. They looked like a clutch of eggs with faces.

All those faces made me feel like an *attraction*. A zoo animal being peered at through terrarium glass. I wasn't even the animal all those faces should be looking at.

Mr. Wilkshire wasn't trying to hide at all. Anyone could have seen him if they just followed my gaze. A giant snake that hid in a person-costume and wore a stupid hat. *Right* there. Their lives would have been changed forever.

But they all preferred watching a family implode instead. How boring.

"Look!" I screamed and twisted in my mother's grasp. "LOOK! He's a snake!" I clawed at her hand. I pointed and tried to get her — *anyone* — to look at Mr. Wilkshire. "He's a snake and I saw him eat a chicken!"

Mother struck me.

It was a solid slap across my left cheek. The slap tore my vision away from Mr. Wilkshire. Sent me to the ground. I started crying, more from reflex than fear. Mother tugged me up and shushed me. I heard her shushing, but all I could think of was snake-hissing.

Then I heard all the neighbors' doors opening. *That* got them to come outside. Maybe they were concerned. Maybe they just wanted a better view.

Mother sneered down her nose at me. "That's what happens when you act like a naughty child in public!"

Even through the tears, I could see how embarrassed she was. Not of slapping me. Of *me*.

Dad ran over. He stopped short of snatching me away. Flowerpot dirt fell off his shoulder.

"Melanie! Don't hit the child!" he yelled.

His yell seemed quiet. How was that even a thing? A quiet yell.

"Cynthia needs to learn how to fit in somehow," Mother sneered. "She needs to learn how to act normal. She isn't learning from *you*. You don't even know not to sell my cabinets!"

Mother pulled me around to the back passenger's door and shoved me into the van. Derrick was already seated, dead to the world, lost in his music. I was right. One seat, two children. I pulled the seatbelt across Derrick and buckled us both in.

We pulled away from the house. From Dad. From the voyeur neighbors.

I almost told Derrick to look at Mr. Wilkshire, but as we drove off, I saw that there wasn't a giant snake in that front window anymore. Must've gone back to eating chickens after the show ended.

So I just looked out the dirty window and watched the world pass by. Nothing else to do on the four-hour trip to Aunt Velma's. Trees and highway rails and seas of grass fused into a single brushstroke, and time flew by and stood still all at once.

Two hours burned away before Mother spoke to us.

"Listen, children," she said without looking back, "I just want you both to know that Mother loves you very mu-" Derrick made a disgusted sound, "-that Mother loves you very much, and that is precisely why I'm taking you away from that dreary place. Think of this as a tiny holiday. How fun!"

"Let's just go back," Derrick grumbled as he slid his headphones down around his neck. "We're gonna go back anyway. Let's just go back *now*."

I had almost forgotten that he had ears. Did snakes have ears?

Mother made a *tsk-tsk* sound. "Derrick, darling, please be quiet. You don't know what you're talking about."

"No!" Derrick shouted. "Don't tell me to shut up. *You* shut up!"

I covered my ears.

Mother looked back and screeched, "Derrick Rockefeller Johnson, don't you *dare* raise your voice at me!"

"Fuck you!" Derrick yelled back. "Dad probably invites ladies over when you take us away."

"I…" Mother put on a pretend-sad expression and looked away. "I don't… I can't believe this is who you are now. You used to be my little boy. You're so like your father now."

She didn't say anything to me. Mother never tried to get me on her side when she fought with Derrick. Maybe she figured there wasn't anything I could do.

I didn't feel neglected or hurt. I should have, but I never did. I had a window to look out of. It was dirty, but my eyesight was perfect. A dirty window was enough. The sun was warm. I always preferred warm to cold.

Then we drove past a snake. A fat one, slithering along the shoulder.

"Oh!" I yelped. "A snake!"

We zoomed by so fast. Maybe it wasn't even a snake. Might have been a piece of blown-out tire or a stick. I was pretty sure it was a snake, though.

Wasn't sure who I was trying to tell. Derrick had his headphones back on and Mother didn't care.

Fine by me. It was my snake, not theirs. I could probably learn a lot about snakes in school. Be a reptile scientist someday. No, a snake scientist. A snake scientist who wore an orange scientist lab coat.

I smiled and looked out the window with my perfect eyes and wondered if that snake was related to Mr. Wilkshire. A cousin or something, maybe.

***

"These glasses hurt my eyes," I explained to Mrs. Finch. "I still can't focus on stuff without getting headaches."

Mrs. Finch didn't care. She made me walk all the way up to her desk just to yell at me. Why not just let me stay at my desk if she was going to yell?

"So you think eighth-grade biology is an easy-A class. Is that it, missy?" Mrs. Finch's nose looked like a beak. It complemented her name too perfectly. "Think you can just *opt out* of assignments because of a little headache? Well, that is *not* how the world works. You were supposed to have a rough draft of your paper done *today* so your partner could proofread it. And now, your partner will have nothing to proofread at all!" Mrs. Finch paused dramatically.

She loved doing that. Pausing. Getting everyone to focus on whoever she was humiliating. I imagined nosey neighbors watching me through windows. Wasn't sure why.

"Well, Cynthia?" Mrs. Finch demanded. "What will your proofreading partner do?"

"*Not* proofread anything," I responded.

I checked out after that. Mrs. Finch went on for a good three minutes, but there was only so much of her cawing I could take in one sitting.

The left temple of my new glasses was loose at the hinge. I had called it an '*arm*' when Dad took me to the glasses store two days ago. The lady bending the nosepieces into position said those were called the '*temples*'. She never acknowledged that something was wrong with the temple or its hinge.

It had taken me an hour to settle on a pair. Dad hadn't helped at all. He just said I looked nice in whatever pair I asked his opinion on. But I finally found a pair I liked — burnt-orange metal frames all the way around the lenses. I wanted bright orange, but I couldn't find any. These frames also had the biggest space for lenses out of all the glasses I looked through. When I wore them, I looked like I had two magnifying glasses glued to my face. But, if I was going to need glasses to see from now on, I was *going* to get the ones that let me see the most. I was *going* to keep seeing, even if my eyes had decided to betray me for no reason.

I'd need to see as clearly as possible once I became a zoologist.

Mrs. Finch bawked on and on and on. Her bawks were annoying, but not even half as annoying as my mother's opinion on my new glasses. *I* was the one wearing them, but my mother was the one who seemed embarrassed by them.

"Oh, please do be a good girl and go exchange those monstrosities for a smaller pair," she had complained when she saw my glasses. Over and over and *over*.

And Dad hadn't said one single thing through all that complaining.

Things were so clear when I was little. Wherever that dull-pink paint in my bedroom was a shade duller? Saw that.

Mr. Wilkshire's coppery scales shimmering in the sunlight while his jaws crushed that chicken? Saw that, too.

Now, I needed help to see anything farther away than my outstretched hand.

Mrs. Finch slapped her desk with a ruler. "Well, Cynthia? How is that going to get resolved in my gradebook?"

I must've missed a question somewhere. "Can I sit now?"

Mrs. Finch snorted and flicked her fingers at me like I was a bug. But she made sure to give me one last nugget of parting wisdom as I turned away.

"You're going to have to get with the program," she grumbled, "or the world's going to swallow you whole, missy."

I sulked to my desk near the back. I always sat by myself. I put the absolute-bare-minimum amount of effort into remembering my school's sports mascot, the faculty members' names, and the street my school was on. But I put a *lot* of effort into being as far away from everyone as possible, as often as possible.

I sat down, opened up my biology notebook, and started doodling snakes while I tried to remember what it felt like to have crystal-clear vision — like the vision I had when I was little.

That trip to Aunt Velma's lasted longer than usual, the one just after I saw Mr. Wilkshire shed his person-costume. We stayed for about a month. Mother complained about that cabinet the entire time. By the time we got back, Mr. Wilkshire was human again. Looked human, at least.

That didn't matter, though. I was a kid. One-track mind. I was *going* to catch him. I was *going* to prove that I was right. That he was a snake.

That meant concocting elaborate plans on how to trap him — all day, every day. One scheme involved hiding two large boxes in the bushes outside his bedroom window. They would have slammed together, each strapped to a catapult-like arm tilted on its side. I would have used a cat as bait.

But catapult-building was above a seven-year-old's pay grade. So I begged for a camera for my eighth birthday. Made sure to ask Aunt Velma to guarantee I'd get a good one. The perfect lens to snap a shot of the snake. Got that camera, too.

But it was no use.

Mr. Wilkshire left. Moved out two days after my eighth birthday. He didn't say anything to anyone. His house was just empty one morning.

Eight-year-old me had almost felt betrayed.

I flipped to the back of my notebook. To a chicken feather taped to the cardboard. I peeled back the tape and picked up the feather. Twirled it between my fingers. At least I could still see things this close to my face.

I remembered sneaking into Mr. Wilkshire's abandoned house two weeks after he vanished. Broke out a window with one of Mother's flowerpots. I searched for *anything*. A big rock that he slept on, loose scales, fangs.

There was nothing.

Until the last room.

It was the room I had seen him eat the chicken in. I found a feather. No proof that he was a snake. No clues about where he went. Just a feather.

"Everyone!" Mrs. Finch clapped to get the class' attention. "Focus up. It's time for us to get into our review pairs." She clapped again and side-eyed me.

The sea of students began to move. Some kids dashed off and partnered up with friends so they could goof off the entire period. Some went slowly, assigned to work with others they'd prefer to murder. One nerdy kid got partnered up with the captain of the baseball team. Felt for that kid.

Felt for me, too.

"Hey, freak." John sat down beside me and farted. "Give me your paper so I can see how dumb it is."

John had nasty breath. Even nastier than his farts. I had told him before, but he never cared to act on that info. And his name wasn't actually '*John*', but I never cared to commit the real thing to memory.

"Didn't do it," I said.

I read over his paper after he threw it at me. It would've been a good draft if we were third graders. His paper described how bees weren't wasps, how bees weren't as cool as wasps because bees died after they stung things, and how bees "*weren't hardcore*."

The paper was supposed to be about animals interacting with other species in their environments.

How did his paper smell as bad as his breath? Did he lick it?

"Looks good." I tossed it back. "Definitely an A-plus." I went back to drawing snakes.

"What's yours on?" John asked.

"Haven't written it yet, remember?" I mulled over the prospect of taking an art elective, so I could learn how to draw textures better — reptile scales and the like. Artists didn't have to interact with people. Not a lot. Maybe '*artist*' would be a good career path. At least a good side path off the zoology main road.

"But when you *do* write it, freak." Always that added '*freak*'.

"I don't know. Snakes, probably." I didn't know why I kept talking.

"Only freaks like snakes," John snickered.

"Yep," I said as I doodled. People didn't like that, shrugging off their insults.

"You're a freak!" John shoved his stinky fingers into my face and grabbed my glasses. Got a chunk of my hair for good measure, too. "A freak in lame freak glasses!"

I was on my feet in a second. "Give them back."

"Freak!" John backed up, became fuzzy.

"John, you skid mark! Give them back. *Now*."

I slipped my feather into my pocket. I clenched my fists. I heard John gulp. He might have backed down — if everyone hadn't started chanting. Fueling him up.

"*Freak! Freak! Freak!*" went around the room like a hymn.

John started running around the classroom, laughing all the while. His laugh was so stupid. At least I could follow that laugh. Didn't need eyes to follow an idiot who couldn't shut up.

I chased him around desks and students. I tried to grab him. His arm. My glasses. But I missed. I missed over and over and over.

The chanting made my heart race. Made me sweat. Made me think of petting-zoo field trips from elementary school. Those animals always looked so miserable, being gawked at and poked and prodded by all those snotty children.

Mrs. Finch's blurry shape waddled over. "What's going on?"

I ignored her. Focused on getting my eyes back. I used to see so well. I felt something cold in my palm.

"Can't write a snake paper without your glasses, freak!" John turned back and bonked me on the head.

Enough of an opening.

Scissors were pretty standard for middle schools. No clue where the pair in my hand came from, though. Snatched off a desk, maybe. Must've been reflexive. Like a snake's strike.

John didn't see them. Mrs. Finch didn't, either. Neither did the class. Everyone was too focused on mocking me. Having fun.

Then everyone was focused on John. Everyone stopped chanting when they couldn't compete with John's screaming. Clearly, it wasn't fun after that.

I grabbed my glasses off the floor right before Mrs. Finch grabbed my wrist. It was a miracle that their loose hinge didn't break when John dropped them. It was a miracle that I picked them out from the out-of-focus splotches of the carpet.

"Oh my *Lord*," Mrs. Finch stammered. "You're a... a little *monster*!"

I slipped my glasses back on. My breathing slowed. My pulse wound down. Then I saw what I had done.

John sat there, slumped in a desk, head pointed down. His hands were gripped onto his thigh. Two puncture holes in the center of his pants leg showed off pale skin. And red. He cried and looked up at me. Then he looked back down at his leg. Then he cried some more. Big baby. The scissors hadn't even gone in deep enough to get stuck. He pissed his pants. The piss would probably make him smell a little better.

My arm almost popped out of its socket when Mrs. Finch yanked me out of the room.

"I don't know what's wrong with you," she squawked as she dragged me down the hall, "but something is *definitely* wrong with you. Something horribly, terribly wrong on the inside that can't be fixed. Perhaps some discipline can at least push you down a better road."

Heading to the principal's office should have terrified me. It would have terrified anyone else. Calls to my parents were definitely inbound. Probably suspension. But the silence of the halls was *so* nice — I didn't care if I was in trouble.

Mrs. Finch continued her lecture, but I just spaced out and wondered whether or not Mr. Wilkshire was venomous.

No. He was a constrictor. I remembered the shape of his head. Long, like a python's. Constrictors didn't produce venom. Did some snake-people have venom? Maybe they were all constrictors like Mr. Wilkshire. Or maybe he was all alone.

Mrs. Finch dropped me off outside the principal's office. I sat for twenty minutes. The aloneness was nice. The vent blasting arctic air onto my head was not nice.

The principal finally called me in.

I read the name plaque on his desk as I sat. Principal Belt.

Principal Belt tried to lecture me about assaulting people with scissors. He also tried to scare me by telling me that both of my parents were on their way. I just took my glasses off. Made him easier to ignore. Turned him into a jiggling smudge that looked sort of like an amoeba in a cheap suit.

Dad arrived ten minutes later. He sat down beside me and didn't look at me.

I slipped my glasses back on. Dad was wearing a set of brown coveralls and his work boots. A chemical smell from the plastics plant clung to him. And his glasses. *Wow.* My lenses weren't even half as thick as his.

I felt bad for Dad.

"So," Dad started, "what's the problem?"

Principal Belt put his hands together and leaned on his desk like a good administrator. "I think you know what the problem is, sir. It was explained quite thoroughly over the phone to you... *and* to your wife."

I wagered that Principal Belt would regret calling my mother.

He continued, "Cynthia, here, stabbed a fellow classmate. This is a very serious issue."

'*Stabbed*' was a bit much. More like '*barely-punctured*'.

My dad looked at me. Most kids would cower when faced with an angry parent's stare. But my dad didn't look angry. Just tired. He couldn't yell at Mother for slapping me all those years ago. He couldn't yell at me now.

I didn't cower.

"Yeah... okay," Dad managed. "Cynthia, why did you do that?"

I didn't have any reason to lie. "The kid stole my glasses. He wouldn't give them back."

"Will you do it again?" Dad asked.

"No," I answered, "I won't."

Doubted I'd need to. Nobody was going to steal glasses from the girl who stabbed — barely-punctured — John. Nobody smart, at least.

My dad rubbed his hands together and scratched at his arms. Flakey from a sunburn, maybe. Or the chemicals at the plant. "Well, I think that's settled."

Principal Belt looked confused. Couldn't tell if he was being belittled or not. "Now wait a minute, sir. We need to discuss disciplinary actions further."

Principals loved discussing disciplinary actions further.

My dad stood up. "I need to get back to work and I'd like this wrapped up before-"

Before Mother arrived. He *almost* got out in time.

Mother came in with her hand to her forehead, like an actress who thought she was way better than she actually was.

"Cynthia! What on Earth is wrong with you?" She sat down next to me and sighed loudly.

Dad sat back down and sighed quietly.

Mother shook Principal Belt's hand. "Good day, Mr. Belt. I'm positively *aghast* at all this. Did Cynthia make much of a scene?"

Principal Belt looked at me. "Your daughter decided to stab another student in the leg with a pair of scissors. In the middle of class. She made a scene, yes."

I threw my hands up. "John *started* the scene when he stole my glasses! They all started it! They were making fun of me. Yelling. I didn't know what to do. I couldn't even see! *They* did the deciding, *not* me!" Didn't seem fair to pin this on me. Not *all* of it. "And the scissors barely cut his stupid leg."

They weren't even venomous snake fangs. John should've been grateful.

"You shut your mouth," Mother barked at me. "How embarrassing. How absolutely embarrassing. Did you think about how people will talk about this? About you? About *me*?" She looked away from me and grabbed her chest. C-grade acting at best. "My God. Why can't you be more like your brother."

My brother had punched a kid in the dick a week ago just for laughing at his new haircut, but I decided not to bring that up.

"Relax, Melanie," Dad mumbled. "It's not that big of a deal."

"No. Not from you, Michael. You don't get to say *anything*." Mother's anger sounded real. No acting there.

"Why not?" Dad asked.

Principal Belt interjected, "If we could get back on track…"

Mother growled, "Because you never got my cabinet back!"

"Jesus Christ." My dad rubbed his eyes. Scratched his arms. "That was years ago."

"You're right. It was years ago." Mother's jaw clenched. "Years of *me* visiting every antique store that *you* said *you* might have sold it to. Gone, just like that. My cabinet. Cohnen & Locke. Made in nineteen thirty-two. Gone."

Dad stood up.

"I'm going back to work." Dad looked at me. "Cynthia, don't stab anyone again."

Dad walked out. Mother stood and guffawed.

Principal Belt got up and shouted, "Now *wait* a minute!"

But his shout didn't do shit. Principal Belt was probably used to being in control of situations like this. Wasn't accustomed to being overshadowed by family anti-dynamics. Poor guy.

Mother rushed after Dad. Their voices — Mother's mostly — stayed long after they disappeared from view.

It was just me and Principal Belt.

I looked at him. "I'm suspended?"

He looked at me. "…Yes."

"I'll get a ride home with one of them."

I got up and headed into the hallway. My parents' voices echoed around in the air even though they were both out of sight. Had to be the lockers. Lots of metal for the bickering to rattle off of. I reached into my pocket for my feather.

And couldn't find it.

I stopped dead and checked my other pocket. Not there, either. I checked my back pockets and the little pocket on my shirt, even though I knew I hadn't put it in any of those.

Must've missed my pocket back in Mrs. Finch's classroom.

My eyes started to water. My neck started to itch. I sprinted back to the classroom.

I started hunting for my feather the second I made it back. The classes had changed already. New faces leered at me. Mrs. Finch leered with them. But those leering faces didn't matter. Only my feather mattered.

I searched and searched. Got itchier and itchier. But I didn't find that feather. Probably on the bottom of someone's shoe in some other classroom.

It was gone. Gone like Mr. Wilkshire. Gone like my perfect eyes.

I grabbed my things and rushed out of the classroom, out of the school, before I passed out or threw up. I scratched at my neck until my skin burned.

My parents were both gone by the time I made it outside. Neither of them wanted to bother with dropping me off at the house. I didn't want to sit in a car with either of them, anyway.

I started walking home. The walk would take about an hour on foot. Whatever. Fine with me. The sun was shining bright, no clouds at all. I liked the heat. It dried my tears and soothed the itching.

143

***

My college advisor's office reminded me of a jail cell. *Just* enough room for her grade-school-sized computer desk and a few filing cabinets. *Just* enough room to guarantee that there was no room for a second person to sit comfortably. The cubicle walls were coated in posters telling whoever was reading them that they could '*do it*', whatever '*it*' was.

I'd take dull pink over those posters.

"Do you *really* want to drop out? Now? Really? Are you *sure*, Cynthia?"

They were all questions. My advisor didn't mean them as questions, though. More like warnings. Rattlesnake rattles.

"Are you *completely* sure?" my advisor asked again.

She probably thought I was spacing out. I was just trying to read the fine print on the posters. My eyes weren't very good anymore, not like they were when I was a kid. Just kept getting worse. I was on my eighth or ninth round of ever-thickening lens prescriptions since my first pair, back in middle school. My lenses' thickness rivaled Dad's now.

I pushed my glasses up and looked my advisor in the eye. "I'm sure."

My glasses slid back down. They left semi-permanent dips in the bridge of my nose. It wasn't fair that my eyes went downhill so fast.

"But… you're so close to being done," my advisor huffed. "You literally only have *half* a semester to go. And

144

you can't get your money back for this semester. You know that, right?"

"That's okay." I scratched at the rash on my neck. One of the nursing students in my dormitory said I might be allergic to something in the building.

"But you can't! There's just a few months to go."

"I said I'm okay with paying for the classes." I worked at three local diners and the college library. I had enough cash. Barely enough. But enough.

My advisor seemed relieved by that. I wasn't sure why. Wasn't like she was getting my wasted tuition or anything.

After an unnecessarily deep sigh, my advisor interlinked her fingers and looked at me for an unnecessarily long time. "But you simply *have* to finish. How will you get on in the world if you just quit? You'll regret this, Cynthia. Trust me."

This wasn't regret.

I had spent nearly four years pursuing a communications degree at my mother's insistence. Communications instead of zoology. Even after planning on zoology. Dreaming about zoology. Loving zoology. Loving it ever since I had seen that snake slither out of that person-costume as a child.

But *no*. Zoology wouldn't pay bills. At least that's what Mother told me. Over and over and *over*. Until I chose a '*paying field*' just for some peace. Maybe that's why Dad gave in so much. Just for some peace.

That was regret.

"Did you hear me, Cynthia?" My advisor sounded like she had repeated herself a few times. "I really mean it. Can you handle that regret?"

I stood up. My shoulder tore half a poster off the wall. A poster showcasing a brave kitten dangling from a clothing line. Well, half a kitten now.

"Gotta go pack." I left my advisor's cube-cell so she could start keying my regret into her spreadsheets.

As I headed down the hall, I heard her mumble, "Get ready for life to swallow you whole, honey."

I didn't care. The world was going to swallow up my communications degree — whether it was complete or not. Knew that halfway through my first semester. Should've switched back then.

That degree wasn't for me, anyway. It was destined for someone else. Destined to create someone else. Someone who actually *liked* communicating. Someone who didn't volunteer to do all the work for every group project by themselves — just to avoid interacting with classmates. Someone who didn't turn down every party invite. Someone who didn't ditch every date.

I grabbed the cardboard box I had laid on the receptionist's desk and headed out into the summer air.

The heat made me feel better. Faster. At least I got to move out of my dorm in the summer. Better now than winter, when everything moved in slow motion.

I detoured through a small park to enjoy the heat a bit longer before reaching my dorm. Not really a park. More like a field with *just* enough trees to not *technically* be a field. The detour only added a few minutes to the walk, but I hoped I'd see a snake cross my path during those few minutes.

My eyes landed on the biology building instead of a snake. It was about a block away, on the opposite end of the semi-park.

Intro to Zoology. It was *right* there.

I had it marked down my freshman year. Bought all the assigned reading materials. Watched all the suggested documentaries.

Then I dropped it at the last minute.

I crushed the empty box to my chest as I walked. Why hadn't Mother realized how important, how *vital*, that path was to me? Why hadn't Dad encouraged me to follow my dreams or whatever good parents were supposed to do?

Why had *everyone* screwed *everything* up for me?

It had been so long since I had seen Mr. Wilkshire slither out of his skin. Sometimes I half-thought I just invented it in the moment — a little girl's fantasy to escape a shit reality. Every time I saw a snake in a biology textbook or on a nature documentary, I was *almost* certain I had seen Mr. Wilkshire turn into a snake. I was *almost* certain I had seen all those details in his scales, his eyes, his teeth.

But I'd never be *absolutely* certain now, because I'd never be a zoologist now. I should have been a zoologist. It wasn't fair.

I wanted this penultimate walk through this park-that-wasn't-a-park to yield a snake so badly I could scream.

No snake slithered by. The park was too small. Too busy with feet. Too loud. Snakes didn't like all that. I understood that.

I exited the park. Reentered civilization. I crossed the street to my dorm without checking for traffic. Would've missed a car with my eyes, anyway.

I entered the first-floor lobby. My dorm was four stories. I lived on the fourth. The elevator was out.

I would have to call Mother at some point. Crush her with the news of my failure. I figured now would be as good a time as any, before the stairs wore me down. Legs were overrated.

There was an ancient payphone in the lobby. A dusty relic for homesick kids to cry into. Homesick kids with dead cellphones and no carrier pigeon. I checked my cellphone. Dead. I looked around. No carrier pigeon.

I never called my parents. Well, I did, but only enough to let them know I was alive. Two separate numbers to remember now — worst part of the divorce.

All of Mother's complaining about the cabinet — about *everything* — eventually shut Dad down. He might as well have been in a coma. Might as well have been an inanimate object. Might as well have been a cabinet.

Mother got bored without someone to defeat. She headed off to Aunt Velma's — permanently — soon after I headed off to college.

I sat and waited for a pair of freshman girls to finish up their phone call. Had to be siblings. Had to be with their folks. They screamed more than they talked. Screamed about how midterms were going to kill them and how the guys here were so cute and how they missed Scruffy.

I should've missed Derrick more than I did. I should've called more. Checked in more after he moved upstate with that girl he knocked up.

The siblings left. My turn. I dropped my box on the floor and wasted a dollar in quarters to call Mother.

The phone rang.

I felt bad for Dad. Not because Mother left, but for how much *him* she burned out of him, just to end up leaving in the end.

Mother picked up on the fourth ring.

"Hello?" She sounded strange over the wire. A little confused. "To whom may I ask is calling?"

"Cynthia."

"Oh… oh! Cynthia." Mother put on some classical music, as usual. It made these conversations feel like an elevator ride. "It's so good to hear from you. I'll have to tell your aunt you called when I see her."

That wouldn't be tough, considering it was Aunt Velma's house. Plenty of room, but still. Poor Aunt Velma.

"I'm dropping out," I said, "so I won't be reachable here anymore. I'll let you know what my new number is when I find an apartment."

"*What*?" Mother sounded as shocked as my advisor. "What do you mean? Is the semester over? Surely that's what you mean. You're graduating, yes."

"No. I mean I'm dropping out."

It was just me and the elevator music for a long time.

"Cynthia, you absolutely cannot do that! You *won't*. What an embarrassment. To think of all the money I wasted on your schooling, just to… end up like *this*. You were getting that degree for me. For me! I was going to show it off to all the ladies. Oh, God damn your difficulty, Cynthia."

I wasn't sure what my mother meant, considering that *I* had paid for all this wasted time with my own cash.

"Yep," I continued, "so I'm not going to be reachable here anymore, so-"

"You are *just* like your father. Just like him."

"*How*?" I hissed. "Explain it to me."

That was always Mother's go-to insult, no matter what, even if something had no relation to Dad. If it annoyed her, it was just like him.

"I *will* explain it!" Mother's breathing grew heavier. "He never tried. Neither do *you*. You frustrate me so much. You've always frustrated me so much with your… difficulty. You've always been so… so off. So strange, like you don't fit. No, like you don't *want* to fit! On purpose! Imagine that.

150

You're going to ruin your life, Cynthia. Mark my words. And you'll have nobody to blame but yourself!"

"How big is Aunt Velma's guest room, again?"

The receiver clicked.

That always ended it. Mother always told me to call it the '*vacation house*'. Blasphemy to hint that it was just a bedroom and a half-bathroom in another person's home.

I hung up the phone and looked out the lobby doors. A pigeon was pecking at a French fry by a trashcan. Mother would've called it a dove. Doves were her favorite bird. So proper. Pigeons were dumb, but I liked their cooing.

I thought about how fast Mr. Wilkshire could swallow a pigeon while I huffed up the four flights to my dorm room with my box. I opened the door and headed inside.

And immediately got punched in the face by the scent of sea breezes.

My roommate, Shelly, was in. She loved saying, "*It's Shelly time*," all the fucking time. I still forgot her name sometimes. I forgot names a lot, almost to the point of being concerned that I had early-onset dementia.

Shelly had only been my roommate for a few months. Nothing about her caught my attention. Like most of the people I was required to be around, I just tried to avoid her. Ignore her.

Easier said than done.

"Holy shit! It's snake-girl!" Shelly belched as she stumbled out of her bedroom. She sounded drunk. She drank

151

a lot. "Snake-girrrrl, *nana* nana nana-nana *nana* nana nana-nana snake-girrrrl!"

"Yep," I said. '*Yep*' was the easiest response to anything Shelly said.

"Get it?" Shelly asked.

"Yep."

I tapped my box. Looked around. Took stock. Wasn't tough. Just three rooms to check — my micro-bedroom, a living room big enough for one folding chair and maybe a soda can, and a kitchenette that two roaches would feel cramped in. I started in the kitchenette and began throwing belongings into my box.

"It's like that old comic show." Shelly looked up at the ceiling and searched really hard for an answer. "Uhhhhhh… Superman!"

"Yep."

"And we can give you a catchphrase! Like mine! Which is…?"

"Shelly, I don't-"

"IT'S SHELLY TIME!"

I sighed. "Yep."

I kept packing.

Toothpaste — into the box.

Ramen packs — into the box.

Notebooks filled with bullshit communications notes — *not* into the box.

"God*damn*, you're weird." Shelly hung her arms around my neck and shoulders and waddled behind me as I gathered my things. "Like, do you remember when you told me about... about that snake dude?" She squeezed tighter.

Shelly knew I wasn't a fan of people touching my neck and back. Made my allergy-rash-thing itch worse.

"Do ya remembah?" Shelly rocked back and forth. "Do ya, do ya, do ya?"

Remember it? Hard to forget. Like most mistakes. I had told Shelly about Mr. Wilkshire turning into a snake — Shelly and a group of her friends whose names I couldn't recall for any amount of money. That little mistake happened about a month ago. Worst mistake I made in college. Besides choosing communications, at least.

I had downed a few beers with them that night — just to silence all their complaining about how I never drank with them. Then I just sort of spilled the beans. Nobody listened when I was a kid. I assumed Shelly and her friends wouldn't listen, either.

I assumed wrong. Shelly never shut the fuck up about it. Ever.

"Move, please." I pushed her off and headed into my bedroom.

My bedroom here was nearly as empty as my bedroom back home. These walls were less irritating, at least. No dull pink. Just plain tan. Tan was kinda-sorta similar to orange.

I only cared about necessities. Never collected anything. No toys, no shoes, no books, no CDs, no nothing.

Didn't want to become attached like Mother with that cabinet.

I tossed all the clothes I cared to keep into the box. Didn't bother folding anything. Then I picked up my three spare pairs of glasses and gently placed them on top of all those unfolded clothes. My glasses were the closest things to cherished possessions that I owned. Not by choice. Why did my eyes have to let me down like everybody else? I left my bedroom.

And Shelly immediately wrapped her arms around my shoulders and neck again. She rubbed up on my rash. Made me itch.

"You were like, '*It really happened. I saw him eat a chicken.*' God, *classic*." She clung onto me as I shuffled back to the kitchenette.

"Heeeeey," Shelly said after burping out a tiny cloud of vodka, "what's going on? Are we moving?"

"I am."

"What?"

"I'm dropping out." I pushed her off again and started taping up my box.

"Aren't you, like, almost done?"

"Completely done now." I looked around one final time. None of the mostly-in-focus items were important enough to grab.

Shelly laughed and hiccuped and *almost* barfed. "You. You, you, you." She got behind me and wrapped her arms around me a third time. "You know, you're *so* weird.

154

You and your snakes. Why don't you ever do anything with me? You think you're better than me?" She started to ruffle my hair. "I bet you think you're better. You don't even have any friends."

"Get off, Shelly." I tried to shake her off again, but she clung on tight. She grabbed a handful of my hair and started to pull me around.

"I'm just *teeeeasing*." Shelly laughed and belched and rocked about. "Wow, your neck is all… schluffy. Is that a word? '*Schluffy*'? You need to lotion your skin better, girl." She laughed louder. Rocked around harder. I started to lose my balance.

Then Shelly rubbed her hand across my face and knocked my glasses off.

I snapped my head back. My skull connected with her nose. Shelly's arms loosened up just enough. I slipped around behind her and wrapped my arm around her neck. Put her throat in the pocket of my elbow.

"Whoa, wha- stop! W-" Shelly didn't finish.

We both crashed to the floor. I locked my legs around her waist.

If Mr. Wilkshire wanted to eat a deer or something big like that, he'd have to strangle it first. Constrict.

I slid my free arm around Shelly's chest and arms. She struggled. Knocked over the lone stool in our kitchenette. I didn't let go. Didn't even feel tired. Every time she breathed out, I squeezed in.

How long could a deer or a cow hold out with Mr. Wilkshire's coils crushing in on them? Surely longer than a person. And what about the horns?

I could've studied how snakes used their specialized muscles to constrict. I could've learned how they ate horned animals without hurting themselves. I could've started down a road I would've loved traveling for the rest of my life — if I had just taken that Intro to Zoology class.

No. If people had *let* me take it.

It wasn't fair.

It wasn't fair.

It wasn't fucking fair.

Shelly stopped wiggling.

I let go.

She lay there for a long time. Or not long. It felt longer than it was, like how most serious things feel. Probably only a few seconds in reality. I sat there, watching Shelly not move, and wondered if Mr. Wilkshire had ever eaten a person. Maybe that's where he got his person-costume to begin with.

Shelly moved. Sat up. She puked up what used to be a hamburger and convulsed into a coughing fit.

"The fuck's *wrong* with you?" Shelly struggled out. "You… you're a- a fucking *freak*!" She didn't grab onto me again.

"Yep," I said.

I slipped my glasses back on, got up, and walked out with my single box of belongings.

There was more stuff in the dorm. More stuff that was technically mine. But I didn't care. The college could toss it all in the trash. I just wanted to be somewhere else. Somewhere far away from that Intro to Zoology class I'd never get to take.

I paused in the lobby. The payphone was right there. Mother got a call. Dad deserved one, too.

No. He wouldn't care if I moved — or if I dropped out. He hadn't cared enough to pull me away when Mother slapped me. He never helped me pick out glasses, either.

As I stood there with my box hugged to my chest, I realized that Dad had never hugged me. Not once.

The payphone was all the way over there. Too much effort to walk all the way over there. Like hugs.

I walked outside.

I headed through the park one last time. There were still no snakes. Or maybe there were. My eyes got worse by the minute.

At least the heat made me less itchy.

I pushed my glasses up and headed for Parking Lot S.

***

I clipped Derrick's jeep as I pulled into our old home's driveway.

There wasn't much for it. Didn't matter how carefully I drove. How slowly.

Not with eyes like mine.

I carried around a bag of Sharpies, all different colors, to touch up scrapes and scratches on other people's

157

cars. I thought I had trouble seeing lecture notes when professors wrote on their boards back in college. Fourteen years of downhill vision had shown me that I basically possessed superhuman sight back then.

Doctors couldn't help. Couldn't prescribe me anything. Just told me I had cataracts. Told me I needed surgery. But I didn't have the time to deal with that. Or the cash. Thicker glasses would have to do.

I walked over to my brother's bumper and knelt down.

Derrick's jeep was red. I had a red Sharpie. Three, actually. All different shades. I started coloring in the damage.

Lucky I bumped his jeep and not one of the other half-dozen cars scattered about the front yard. The estate sale was winding down. Seemed like it had been pretty busy based on the scars left in the yard — courtesy of all the assholes driving onto the grass.

It was rude, parking in the yard like that. But I couldn't do anything about it now. Those dickhead drivers were gone now.

Gone like Dad.

"Cynthia," Derrick shouted from the front door.

He looked like Dad. I felt a strange urge to apologize for something. Something about a payphone?

Derrick waved me over. I made my way through the yard and up to him. He hugged me. I patted his back.

"You have a nice jeep," I noted.

Derrick had some money. More than me. Library work didn't pay much, but it let me avoid people. Some good that communications degree would have been. My eyesight was starting to make paperwork and book-filing tough, though.

"Thanks," Derrick said. He finally let me go. "Your car looks… great."

"Thanks," I said — even though Derrick was clearly lying. The shittiness of my car didn't bother me. Couldn't. One perk of being near-blind was not having to look at my P.O.S. car all that closely. And it was orange. The orange counteracted most of the dents and scratches.

"Glad you managed to get out here," Derrick said. "I hope you'll stay a little while. I got the family here. The kids would love to see you."

"Uh… yep." I couldn't tell if that was a lie. Didn't seem like it.

Me and Derrick never talked much as kids. Now wasn't much better. We both just stood there, unable to proceed with the interaction. Then an elderly couple grunted for us to move aside as they carried out Dad's favorite coffee table.

"Let's go out back." Derrick motioned through the house. "Nothing's out there for anyone to want."

Something strange tugged at my stomach as Derrick led me through our old home. Not nostalgia, but something close. Like my brain wanted to feel nostalgia, so it tried simulating what wasn't there.

I followed Derrick through the kitchen where Dad used to make us bologna sandwiches — and didn't feel anything. I followed Derrick through the little room where we used to play boardgames before he got all grungy — and didn't feel anything. I followed Derrick past the too-tight hallway that led to our old bedrooms — and didn't feel an urge to go see that dull-pink paint.

I passed the basket where Dad kept his ready-to-send-out mail. An envelope addressed to me sat in it, "*Happy Birthday*" written under my address. My thirty-seventh birthday card. Dad's glasses sat next to the basket. Their lenses weren't even half as thick as mine.

I reached for the envelope, but decided against it. Dad never wrote anything in those cards other than "*From Dad*," anyway. Let the Hallmark employees do the heavy lifting. Fair.

I followed Derrick out the back door. He lit up a cigarette and took a deep drag.

The backyard's grass was three times higher than the front's. Dad must've stopped caring about appearances for places no one would ever see after Mother left. Fair.

"It really is good to see you, sis." Derrick sucked down half his cigarette.

"You shouldn't smoke," I told him. He breathed a plume into my face. Not on purpose. Probably.

"That's what Maggie keeps telling me."

Maggie. Derrick's girlfriend. No, wife. He married her. Gary was the kid he knocked her up with. How old was he? They had Emma and Terry now, too. Wasn't sure which of the new batch of kids was older — twins. They were the size of chickens when I saw them in the hospital. Good thing none of those nurses or doctors were snake-people.

"Yep," I said. "Listen to Maggie. Please."

"All right." Derrick took another drag. "So... what are you gonna do with it?"

"With what?"

"The house, Cynthia"

"Oh... right." My spine tingled. I reached up and itched at the eczema on my neck — or whatever the rough patches all over me were. Doctors were as helpful with my itching as they were with my eyes.

I looked back into the house. Dad had left it to me. How had I almost forgotten that?

"I'm... not sure." My neck got itchier.

"Yeah, I figured you wouldn't be thinking about it." Derrick dropped his cigarette on the ground and stomped it dead. "I wouldn't want to live here. Not with all the memories I have here."

"Yeah. Memories." I remembered that snake.

"Are you sad at *all*?" Derrick asked.

His question made me itchier. I looked into his eyes, expecting to see judgement or resentment or hate. I saw pain instead.

"Because I'm not," he mumbled, "I don't think. And I feel like shit about it. I feel like shit because I don't feel like shit, you know?" Derrick scrunched up his face. All he

161

was missing was that old CD player. He fished his keys out of his pocket as he focused on the backyard's single tree. The trunk was thicker than both of us combined now. "I'm gonna go get a burger or something. Haven't eaten all day. Be back in a bit. Just make sure people pay for the stuff they take. These old farts are like vultures with dead people's shit."

Derrick headed back inside.

Before he closed the door, I blurted, "Are you happy with Maggie?" I looked away when he looked back at me. Why did I look away? "Do you feel like you... drove down the right road?"

Derrick scratched his head. "The right road?"

"Like, do you... I don't know." My mouth wouldn't work. My tongue might as well have been split in two. "Do you feel like you've... done things that... all added up to a life you don't regret? Or did Maggie grab the wheel and crash your car? Or... something?"

I always stayed late at the library after closing up. I stayed for hours and hours and hours. I stayed and read through biology books and scientific journals. I stayed and hunted for photographs of snakes that matched my memory of Mr. Wilkshire. I stayed and tried to trick myself into believing I could wake up from the real world and find myself in some long-dead zoology dreamscape. Those memories — those dreams — were clearer than anything my eyes could show me now.

Derrick finally answered.

"I think about my family and… I don't regret letting Maggie drive every now and then. But I'm still the… designated driver, I guess? My car. My fault if I crash. Only real regret I have is not seeing you as much as I'd like." He unscrunched his face. "Are you happy with the roads you went down?"

"I'm… still driving," I managed.

"You're still driving." Derrick chewed the inside of his cheek, looked at me, and closed the door.

I stood out there for at least half an hour, looking at the tree in the back, trying to figure out if Derrick was judging my answer or just considering it. Maybe *I* was the one judging-and-or-considering my answer.

The sun was setting and the air was cooling. I zipped up my too-thin hoodie and turned to head back inside.

Then I saw movement in Mr. Wilkshire's old house, in a window.

I held my breath.

Then I let it out.

It was just a little girl dancing around in a ballerina outfit. Her parents were chasing her through the rooms.

Mr. Wilkshire must've stayed gone. I wondered if he re-wore that same person-costume. Maybe he grew a new one. Maybe he ate someone and made a new person-costume out of them — a person-costume I wouldn't even recognize anymore.

Those new neighbors weren't snakes. All my personal reptile research told me that. They looked like a happy family. Snakes would eat their babies if they ever came across them.

I went inside and found one of Dad's old jackets. It still smelled like him. And dirt. Maybe it was the jacket he wore that day when I was seven — when Mother threw a flowerpot at him and I saw Mr. Wilkshire's true form. I threw it on over my hoodie, penned a note telling the old people to just leave the cash for whatever crap they bought on the kitchen counter, and headed back outside. Better to be cold outside than have to deal with all those old people inside. Hopefully nobody took my absence as license to steal shit, but it wasn't like it really mattered to me. Or to Dad.

I looked over the neighbors' backyard.

Mr. Wilkshire's chicken coops were gone, replaced with a soccer goal and a little plastic playhouse. But that little shed — the one the coops used to rest against — was still there, dilapidated and ready to collapse. I took a few steps toward the shed, just to see.

And noticed something out behind it. A tarp. A big, tan tarp, ruffling in the breeze.

I got as close as the fence separating the properties would allow.

It was getting darker. I couldn't see well, even in the light. I *needed* to know what was under the tarp. Now. I didn't know why I needed to know, but I did. So I hopped the fence, crept around the shed, and flung the tarp aside.

Some chopped wood. Two old baskets. Nothing important.

But the tarp seemed odd.

It wasn't very wide, maybe a foot-and-change. But it was long. I held a middle section up as high as I could, and both ends of the tarp still piled onto the ground. Strange indentations textured its surface. Like bubble wrap, sort of. But rough to the touch.

I decided to take it.

I hopped back over the fence, struggling to hold the tarp away from the sharp chainlink. My sneaker hooked onto the fence. I rolled over the top. Face-planted onto the ground. Heard a *snap*.

"Of course." My glasses had snapped right down the middle. I stood and cradled them in the dark.

The garage. The tarp could sit in there until morning when I had more light to investigate. There'd be superglue in there, too. Glasses would be fine in no time. Fine enough until I got back to the hotel for a backup pair. I had seven.

I shooed off the last of the old people and headed into the garage. I tossed the tarp onto a lawn chair and clicked on the garage lights and looked around.

Everything in the garage looked vaguely familiar and vaguely in its place — based on my vague pre-college memory of the place.

Everything, save for one thing.

Some big *something* loomed in the corner of the garage, hidden under a dirty sheet. Maybe an old refrigerator. Maybe no one noticed it. Or maybe nobody wanted to deal with dragging it to their car.

I hunted for superglue. Only found duct tape — and tons of empty skin cream bottles. Once I had jury-rigged my glasses back together — and looked stupid as shit as a result — I headed over to check out the mystery thing.

I pulled back the sheet. Dust exploded in my face.

The wood beneath the sheet was devoid of dust. Spotless.

Spotless and old. No, not old. Aged, like expensive wine. The wooden thing shimmered a rich red-brown. It stood proud on four brass lion's feet. Five little angels carved out of lighter wood were perched on top, each praying and looking up to the heavens. Well, praying and looking up to a garage ceiling. '*Cohnen & Locke*' was stamped on a bronze plate near the top with a half-circle of wood around it, carved to look like a rising sun. The glass doors, designed to show off whatever fancy things should have been inside, only showcased an old pair of work boots on the bottom shelf.

"Holy fucking shit," was all I could say.

I didn't know where it came from. I didn't know when it ended up back home. But it *did* come from somewhere and it *did* end up back home.

Dad had found it. The fucking cabinet.

Mother never said anything about it — not that we discussed much on our biannual phone calls. I didn't even know if she knew. Maybe telling her was my responsibility now. No. She was pretty loopy now. Dementia. Drove Aunt

Velma crazy on the regular. Wouldn't be much use in telling her.

I laughed louder than I had ever laughed in my whole entire life.

Dad could've had the cabinet right here, right under Mother's nose, for *years*. Like a guilty pleasure. An inside joke between himself and no one. If I were him, I would've come in here every time I remembered Mother's complaints about missing cabinets or too-tight hallways or dirty van windows or anything else — and kicked the shit out of the thing.

I admired the cabinet until the sun fully set. It really was pretty.

I locked up the house. Derrick could deal with me being gone when he got back. We were both good at not being in contact. He could also deal with getting a new lighter. I found his on the kitchen counter. Figured it was his. He needed to quit smoking, and I needed it for more important things than cigarettes.

I went to my car, threw Mr. Wilkshire's tarp into the front passenger's seat, and returned to the cabinet. Then I started dragging it down the driveway.

The cabinet was heavy, but I didn't care about damage. After dragging it over the concrete and asphalt — and scuffing up those lion's feet *real* good — I shoved it into the back seats.

Then I got into my car and drove and drove. I drove until I got sick of driving. I hated night driving. But I kept going with my high beams on.

Two hours out, I realized I was headed to Aunt Velma's. To Mother. It was the only place I remembered how to get to out here. I laughed at how stupid that was and pulled onto the shoulder.

I got out and looked up and down the highway. Didn't see a car in either direction. Hadn't passed one in a while. This route never got much use. The grass was recently cut and covered in rain.

It took half an hour to drag the cabinet and the tarp out behind a bend of trees, a ways off from the highway. Good thing Dad's boots were in the cabinet. No way I could've gotten through all that brush and muck in my shoes. Not while dragging that heavy thing. Dad's boots were big enough to fit right over my shoes with room to spare. They did the job. No wonder he liked wearing them to the plastics plant.

I looked around once I was safely hidden behind the bend of trees. This field probably zoomed past my eyes a hundred times when Mother lost it and ran off with me. Us. It looked like any other field by any other highway.

The tarp was long enough to wrap around the cabinet dozens of times. I almost felt sad as I fished around in my pocket for Derrick's lighter. When the flame took to the tarp, all that almost-sadness burned up with it.

The fire engulfed the cabinet. I worried it would catch the whole field on fire, but the rain-soaked grass and leaves just steamed. If someone passed by now and saw the flames, it wouldn't matter. I'd be gone before any cops showed.

The wood probably lost its red hue after the first three minutes. Everything was black in contrast with the flames, but I could still imagine how nice the wood looked now, all broken and charcoal-colored.

The angels must've had a lot of resin on them. Some sort of paint or chemicals. They each poofed up in a tiny flash when they caught fire. One angel cracked in half with a *pop* like a bottle rocket. The cabinet's glass doors shattered in the heat.

My feet started sweating. I slipped off Dad's boots and slung them into the fire. They nestled into what was left of the cabinet's insides, right where they had been when I found them together. The boot leather began to curl and smolder.

I started back to my car, but I turned for one more look.

The cabinet was all but hidden in the blaze. And now, with the fire's light shining through the tarp, I saw that it wasn't a tarp at all.

Not plastic. Organic.

Not made. Grown.

Grown out of.

"So he sheds a people set *and* a snake set. Weird."

The tarp was a giant snakeskin. Mr. Wilkshire's snakeskin.

Way better proof than my old chicken feather.

The skin shriveled and danced as the flames carried each of its ends up into the night air. Its ebbs and flows reminded me of a kite exploring the sky. Or those Chinese lion dancers at festivals, maybe.

I scratched at my neck and headed back to the highway, away from that snakeskin and that stupid cabinet filled with burning boots and bad memories.

***

I sat down on the bench by the woods one block from my apartment on a Sunday morning — and wished I could see.

Wishing didn't help. I couldn't see anything at all — nothing more than vague shapes and smudges of color. Hadn't even bothered with glasses for the past decade.

The doctors just kept saying I had cataracts, like always. They said most seventy-five-year-olds like me had some vision problems. Not like mine, though. The doctors I visited almost seemed impressed. They even referenced me in a few medical journals.

Lucky me.

No matter how many consultations I got, it was always the same spiel. Doctors said they couldn't cut into my eyes. '*Too thick*'. What did that even mean?

They couldn't do anything about the damned itching either. Most of my skin rivaled boot leather now. No lotion helped. No prescription pill helped. No injection helped. Nothing did shit.

Doctors sure were helpful.

Even if I *could* get the cataracts removed, there wouldn't have been anyone to help me out while I recovered. I hadn't really talked to Derrick or his family in years. Not since burning that cabinet.

I never felt anything bad toward my brother. There was no big fight after I sold the house or anything. He didn't care. Dad had left it to me and Derrick didn't need the money. I just didn't keep in touch. With anyone.

I wondered if Derrick's family would even recognize me at this point.

I wondered if an animal would've eaten me by now — if I had followed my zoology dreams. Easy prey, a blind woman with itchy skin.

I wondered if Mother had died. *When*, more like. Where. Same for Aunt Velma.

I wondered if my choice to cut Mother out of my life after her dementia got really bad made me a monster.

I wondered if Dad had written something other than "*From Dad*" in that birthday card I never opened.

I wondered if my choice to not call Dad that day in college made me a monster.

I wondered if witnessing that person-costumed snake eat that chicken as a child had stunted me. Veered me off course. Kept me from friends, family, prospects, *normalcy*.

Or maybe this bench by the woods was always locked in as my final destination, no matter what I wanted.

There was plenty of time to overthink about all of that. Having eyes that refused to see meant that overthinking my life was all I could really *do* anymore — overthink it here on my bench, or overthink it back in my apartment.

My apartment — I hated it just as much as I hated that dorm with that ancient payphone, and that middle school classroom with that dumbass John, and that old house with that dull-pink bedroom.

Yeah, this bench definitely beat that apartment.

A few pigeons fluttered down in front of me and started begging for breadcrumbs. I pulled out the bag and got ready to feed them.

Then Mr. Wilkshire walked by.

He was barely more than a pencil line smudged by a thumb. But I saw that stupid Russian hat and that weird walk — that walk that looked like it was mocking how human beings walked.

It was him. No doubt in my mind. Even with my eyes.

So I yelled out, "You're a snake!"

Mr. Wilkshire stopped. His stillness made it hard for me to pick him out from the surrounding blurs. A moment ticked by. Then another. And another. Still nothing. He had slipped away — *again*. Just like he had when I was a kid with perfect vision and delusions of zoology grandeur.

Then he moved, separating his blur from the rest.

"Uhh… no I'm not," he said.

"*Liar*. I saw you eat a chicken from my window when I was seven."

Mr. Wilkshire approached. *Fast*. He was standing right in front of me before I even had a chance to tense up.

I had forgotten how tall he was for a second. I had also forgotten that he was actually a colossal snake for a second. Maybe it wasn't a good idea to call someone — some*thing* — out like that. But he just sighed and sat down next to me.

"I saw your mom hit you," he said.

"Well… now we're both embarrassed." I sighed and itched my neck.

I could barely see the pigeons, but I could hear them just fine. Their cooing calmed me down. I dug out some breadcrumbs.

"Do you want to feed some pigeons?" I asked Mr. Wilkshire.

"*On* some pigeons?"

"No. Just feed them." I held out my hand, full of breadcrumbs.

"Oh." Mr. Wilkshire grabbed up the crumbs.

He threw a handful and I listened to the pigeons get excited somewhere in front of me.

"How have you been, Mr. Wilkshire?" I tossed some more crumbs.

"Oh, you know, getting on. Going from one place to another." He tossed some more crumbs. "How's your family?"

"Brother's…" Surely Derrick wasn't dead. I would've sensed that, right? Magical sibling connection stuff? "…fine, I guess. He has a big family. At least six grandkids by now. My parents are both dead."

I just assumed for my mother.

"Yep," Mr. Wilkshire said.

"I don't feel bad about it, about them being dead." The words came out as involuntarily as a heartbeat. I scratched at my throat. "They kept me from my dreams. *Everyone* did. I *earned* the right to hate them. But I don't hate them. I just don't… feel *anything*. Why don't I feel anything?"

I didn't speak for a long time. Neither did Mr. Wilkshire. He just sat there and fed the pigeons.

I rubbed my eyes. Watery. Allergies. "My brother felt bad about not feeling much when Dad died. But I didn't even feel that… that… second-hand bad. I didn't feel a single thing. And I don't feel bad about never doing anything with my life. About never becoming… *me*. That was *their* fault. *Not* mine. I don't have to feel bad about it because… because it was *their* fault. *Everybody's* fault!"

"You sure?" Mr. Wilkshire looked at me. "Sounds like you feel a little bad about it. Sounds like it was a little bit your fault, too. Your life, after all."

174

I started crying. Crying was hard. Easy to forget how to cry after a while. Easy to forget the normal sounds to make. My crying probably sounded more like a foghorn. Why was I crying at all?

Mr. Wilkshire started to yawn, but his mouth kept opening. His lower jaw hinged in the middle. Each half of his jaw did its own half-a-yawn — took turns. Left, then right.

Or maybe that was just my eyes playing tricks on me.

"Excuse me," he said. "I never missed my parents, either. But at the same time, I did. Especially later. It was as if… as if I had shed off an old life with their deaths, an old life that I didn't pay enough attention to at the time. Some stop along my way that I'd never get to go back to or fix or improve. It's all right, though. Life can trick you into thinking it's over and done with. All… wasted away. That's only the case if you never figure out the skin."

"I… guess," I reasoned.

"Yep," he responded.

"You *are* a giant snake, though… right?" I leaned in. Even I could make out Mr. Wilkshire from this distance. His features were exactly the same as they were when I was little. How did snake-people age? Slowly, apparently. "I'm not insane? I saw that?"

"Yep."

"Oh. Okay." Easier than I expected, getting him to admit it. I always thought that, if I ever saw Mr. Wilkshire again, it would take some great battle of wits to trick him into admitting his true nature. Kind of disappointing, honestly. "How do you get your arms and legs to move?"

"Practice."

"Ah." That was disappointing, too. I chucked a handful of breadcrumbs and earned some coos. "Do you still eat chickens?"

Mr. Wilkshire sighed. His sigh personified longing. "I try to eat more greens now." His emphasis on '*greens*' did not personify longing. "There's some odd people out there nowadays. They get mad at you for eating meat. So I try to eat more greens now. Hate it. But I still keep chickens. Mostly just for the eggs now, though. I can swallow about two dozen in one gulp." His tongue slipped out and flicked around in the air. It was a good eight inches long. "Those mice smell good." Mr. Wilkshire looked over his shoulder, into the woods. "I could go for some mice."

There was another long silence, then Mr. Wilkshire leaned in close and looked me over.

"You don't look very good," he said.

"That's rude," I said.

"Looks like it's on too tight." He prodded my forehead. "I'm sure it's uncomfortable."

"'*It*'?" I prodded my forehead. "What do you mean by '*it*'?"

Mr. Wilkshire's gaze made me feel self-conscious. Made me feel focused-on. Made me feel like a schoolgirl again, chasing some dipshit John around the room while all my classmates watched. Made me feel like I was in a terrarium.

I scratched my neck and scooted two inches away from Mr. Wilkshire. "My doctors say there's nothing they can do."

Even with my eyes, I could see the scoff on Mr. Wilkshire's face.

"That's why you get checked out by a vet." He said it like it was the most obvious thing in the world. "What's a *doctor* going to know about treating a snake?"

"Huh?" I tossed the last of my breadcrumbs.

"Or a zoo keeper, if they find the time. Lots of patients at those places." Mr. Wilkshire turned his attention to his bag. I hadn't noticed his bag. His bag was the same color as his jacket.

I realized I was wearing Dad's jacket. Still smelled a bit like flowerpot dirt. Maybe that was just the scent of a memory.

Mr. Wilkshire fished around in his bag for a moment, then drew something out.

"Here." He dropped the *something* into my lap. "This helps when it's on there good and tight."

"What… what am I supposed to do with this?" I held up the cheese grater.

Mr. Wilkshire stood up and started to walk off.

At the edge of my vision, he turned back to me.

"You have to rub *with* the scales," he said as he ran his hand down his face. "*Never* against them. Don't feel bad for not figuring it out. Most never do. They feel terrible at the end. They feel like they wasted it all. They didn't have a cheese grater handy. You do. Have a good day."

And with that, Mr. Wilkshire left.

It was just me and the pigeons.

And my new cheese grater.

Rubbing with the scales seemed like good advice. It couldn't be, but it was. My doctors couldn't help my eyes. My mother couldn't help me feel worthwhile. My brother couldn't help me endure Mother. My dad couldn't help me pick out glasses or hug me.

And I could never help myself. I could never find the main road. I didn't know where the turnoff that fucked it all up was — or when I had driven down it.

No. I had never even cranked my car in the first place.

I pressed the cheese grater against my forehead. I ran the sharp metal down to my nose, over my lips, across my cheek, all the way to my collarbone. The cheese grater's pass took a huge strip of old me off with it.

I flicked my tongue out. Nearly screamed. Everything smelled so *new* when the air hit my tongue. There were mice in the woods behind me.

I rubbed the metal down the other side of my face and felt a suction sensation. Another thick sheet of human skin sloughed off.

My eyes. My sight. Back. Clear as crystal.

I grated and grated. More and more skin fell away. I grated until my entire human head was gone.

Then all forty feet of me shot up and out of my old, leathery, human neck. I poured over the back of the bench, onto the ground. The grass felt so strange against my scales.

My scales. *Me*.

I looked at myself. Pumpkin orange. Practically neon. Bright-pink splotches ran down my entire body. I liked this shade of pink. No, loved it.

I opened my mouth until my jaw unhinged. Each of my hooked teeth stretched out individually. The two up front were larger. Sharper. Fangs. So, not *all* snake-people were constrictors.

There was a rattle on my tail. When I shook it, all the pigeons scattered into the air.

And I couldn't blink. I could see so well, and I couldn't blink.

I was so glad I couldn't blink.

I slithered into the woods with no arms or legs or shackling self-pity — nothing on my mind but swallowing chickens whole and Intro to Zoology.

Infinite

"Shit."

Kelsey looked down at her doorknob. It had fallen out of her hand when she tried to slip it into her purse.

Nerves, she guessed. Stress from trying to force up the courage to enter her apartment. Silly, being so careless with something so important.

She picked her doorknob up. Rolled it around in her hand. Checked for damage.

The knob portion was glass, shaped like a rose. It was strong, old-fashioned glass. Not brittle. Not dainty. Closer to a chunk of granite than typical glass.

Kelsey didn't spot any fractures cracked into the clear. Didn't notice any dents in the bronze cylinder, that inner portion of metal that would — should — connect to another doorknob. She relaxed and slipped it into her purse.

Johnson & Teague manufactured this particular doorknob. One of the greats — in the door business, at least. Kelsey's dad always got giddy whenever he talked about their craftsmanship.

Her dad had made and installed doors for a living. He loved it. The people, the trips, the exercise — all of it. He especially loved helping people pick out their doors. Said it was akin to helping them pick out the start of their day and the start of the rest of their life.

Kelsey wished she had an eye for doors like her dad.

She grabbed her apartment's door handle. Tensed up. Not a Johnson & Teague. Cheap. Unsafe.

She shared the apartment with Reggie. Reggie loved the apartment because he picked it out. He didn't care if the front door sported a shitty door handle.

Kelsey pulled out her glass-rose doorknob again. Felt its weight. Let its weight seal her off. Sink her down. Anchor her to the bottom — just like it had done for the past three years.

Three years ago, her dad lay there in his hospital bed, mumbling words that didn't go together and wallowing in his own waste and struggling to turn his head. The cancer had eaten almost everything away by then. Whittled the tree-of-a-man down to a single splinter. Cracked his mind. Corroded his memories.

But on his last day, he had grabbed Kelsey's hand and squeezed *so* tightly. His eyes flashed as clear and aware as they had ever been.

"*Everywhere's infinite,*" her dad had warned through his oxygen mask. "*There's infinite places.*"

He had groped in a drawer by his hospital bed right after that warning. Pulled out the glass-rose doorknob. Then he handed it to Kelsey. Then he smiled up at her.

And then he died. Left her weightless. Weightless, save for the weight of that doorknob.

This doorknob.

Her doorknob.

"Shit," Kelsey cursed again. She looked at the apartment door. She squeezed her glass rose until it left indentions in her skin.

She turned to leave.

Then Reggie opened the apartment door, angry and confused.

Kelsey couldn't blame him for being angry. She had called Reggie earlier. Told him she would be moving in with a friend for a while.

"Can we just talk about this?" Reggie grumbled out. No greeting. No addressing Kelsey by name. No asking how she felt.

Reggie pulled Kelsey inside the apartment and closed the door. He moved in to hold her, but Kelsey shrugged away. She started looking over photos hung up along the entry room's walls — looking without really looking.

Reggie scoffed. "Let's at least hit reset. It's not that big of a deal, is it?"

Reggie probably had this part all planned out. Some negging. Some hypotheticals. Some word traps and pitfalls to persuade Kelsey to stay. But Reggie noticed the glint in Kelsey's hand before he could commence the battle.

"Are you serious, Kel? Really?"

Kelsey couldn't decide on a response. *'Don't call me 'Kel''* felt pretty high on the list.

Reggie rubbed his brow. "You said you threw that piece of shit away last month. You seriously still need that thing?"

Reggie should've been enough. Reggie was a person. He should've been enough to let Kelsey forget her doorknob. He was heavier.

Reggie paced around the entry room. Tried to burn off the anger triggered by the glass rose. "All I asked was… I just wanted to know how you felt about us moving forward."

"You *proposed*, Reggie." Kelsey's hand started to tremble.

"Yeah, Kel. That's what boyfriends fucking do! Christ. Well, did you discuss it with the *doorknob* yet? Did you get any advice from it? On your future with your boyfriend of three years?"

"Reggie, you don't have to be a dick about it."

"A *dick* about it?" Reggie yelled. "How am *I* being the dick, here? Wanting to make things official is being a

183

dick? We've been dating for three years, Kel. Three *years*. That's enough time to decide. Isn't that what you wanted? To settle down and feel safe? That's the deal I'm offering."

Reggie walked up and put his arms around Kelsey.

"Kel," he sighed as he squeezed, "you know I love you. But you need to stop. Grief has to wrap up at some point. We need to define whatever your issue is so we can solve it. I'm willing to help you do that. For our sake."

Kelsey wondered where Reggie had stashed the engagement ring after their dinner two nights ago. After she couldn't give him an answer at that fancy French restaurant, that place tailor-made for proposals. Two panic attacks had scrubbed most of that evening from her brain.

Hadn't Reggie talked about buying a three-story house in the suburbs over breadsticks? Having kids over soup? Naming them Trent and Sophia over lobster?

That was all just foreplay leading up to the *official* part. The down-on-one-knee part. The clapping strangers part. The ring part.

Kelsey scratched at her glass rose until her fingernails hurt. Her heartbeat quickened. She began to sweat. Began to think. Worry. Dread.

Then she realized Reggie had been talking through her panic-thinking. She didn't know where to jump in. The middle of his rant on the importance of the nuclear family seemed fine.

Kelsey blurted, "Who talks about wanting kids over *tomato bisque*?"

Reggie released her and took a step back. "The guy who wants to *marry* you! Who has a great life mapped out for you! What's wrong with you? Who asks that? Are you serious? Do I really mean so little to you? I don't understand why you've led me on like this."

"L- look, just… just calm down." Kelsey's vision narrowed. Blurred. Her breaths shortened. Sped up. Her arms weakened. She dropped her purse. "It isn't you. It's me, okay? It's definitely… it's all me. Just give me a sec and let me breathe."

The walls. The ceiling. The floor. The front door. Everything was miles away. Everything was too open. Her dad had shielded her from all that openness. A bulwark between her and infinite places. A bulwark that was nothing but a doorknob now.

"You don't get to panic-attack your way out of this one." Reggie made a move to grab Kelsey's arm.

Kelsey recoiled. Fell into a chair. She dug her nails into the seat cushion. Tried to stabilize herself.

"*Please*, ju- just let me think, okay?" Kelsey squeezed her doorknob until the muscles in her hand begged her to stop. "I just need-"

Reggie walked up and grabbed Kelsey's shoulder. Hard. He pulled her out of the chair and stared into her eyes.

"Okay," he hissed, "I understand. You need direction. I get that. So let's see what you can get." Reggie pulled Kelsey's closed hand up to her face. "Ask it. Ask the *doorknob* if you should stay or go."

185

Kelsey's dad would always tell her to deck any guy that made her feel small.

Reggie towered over her.

"Go on," Reggie insisted as he tapped his foot. "Ask it. I'll wait because I'm patient. More than most. Let's see what the *doorknob* says you should do with your life. You don't want to ask me, so ask *it*."

Kelsey couldn't think. Not with Reggie's tapping. His stare. She moved her doorknob to her forehead. She pressed her glass rose to her skin. She closed her eyes.

"*Help me*," she hushed.

"I'm *kidding*!" Reggie snatched the doorknob away. "You know… joking! Don't *actually* make a life-altering decision with a damn doorknob." He walked toward the kitchen. "This thing's going in the garbage so we can actually make progress here. You'll thank me later."

A wave of heat rolled over Kelsey. Prickled her skin. The weakness in her legs burned away. It took her a moment to realize she was screaming, clawing at Reggie's hands, peeling back his fingers to get at her glass rose.

"Give it back!" Kelsey howled. She pulled Reggie toward the front door.

"No!" Reggie yelled. He spun Kelsey around.

"Please!" Kelsey begged. She jerked left and right as Reggie tugged back and forth.

"No! I can keep you just as safe as this piece of sh-"

Reggie lost his grip on the doorknob. Stumbled back. His heel clipped the little table by the front door where the two placed their mail in separate baskets.

Reggie fell to the floor and gripped his head and cursed.

Kelsey slumped down and covered her eyes and cried.

"*Why* are you like this, Kel?" Reggie sat up and threw a mail basket at Kelsey. He reached up and grabbed the front door's handle. Tried to pull himself up. The handle came loose and sent him back to the floor.

Definitely not a Johnson & Teague. Cheap. Unsafe.

Reggie moaned and crawled to his knees.

"My dad would've thought you were a bad person," Kelsey managed between breaths.

Reggie sneered, got up, and limped toward the kitchen. "Well, your dad's fucking dead." He waved Kelsey over as if he hadn't just said that. "Now come throw that thing in the garbage so we can sort your shit out."

Kelsey stood up. She took a step toward the kitchen. Started to obey.

Then she turned back to the front door. It looked like wood. Oak. It wasn't. Just plywood insides and a fiberglass shell that only *mimicked* oak. Kelsey's dad hated fake wood more than anything else in the world. Called it a pointless lie.

Kelsey rushed to the door and spat on it. She jammed her doorknob into the empty hole without thinking and turned it. The jury-rig worked. Her glass rose turned. The door opened. She ripped her doorknob free and ran out of the apartment. She didn't close the door behind her. No handle to keep it secure, anyway. No time to think, anyway. Just time to flee down the hallway of her apartment complex.

Kelsey's feet moved without orders. Her tears hazed her vision. Her breaths deafened anything and everything around her. How much of that did the neighbors hear? Would they call the cops? Was she going to go to jail for disturbing the peace? Why had she closed her eyes when her dad looked up at her in those final moments?

Why had she chosen fake wood?

Then Kelsey noticed her shoes weren't clicking against concrete.

Her steps sounded muffled, like on carpet. Kelsey wiped her eyes and looked down.

Carpet.

"What...?" She looked around.

The hallway was too small to be her apartment complex. Too narrow. Too short. The lights were wrong — dainty chandeliers instead of flickering tubes. They radiated warm yellow instead of harsh halogen white.

And the walls. No door after door of neighboring apartments. Just cool eggshell peppered with old photos and paintings of idyllic countrysides. And a laundry hamper.

Kelsey couldn't move for a second — but after an internal eternity of confusion, she took a step forward. The carpeted floor squeaked. She tensed her legs and looked back. The slightly-ajar door she had come from loomed at the end of the hall. Her apartment door. It didn't look like her apartment door.

But it *had* to be.

She started back. Then stopped. Reggie. The thought of his ring made Kelsey squeeze her glass rose. She turned around and crept farther down the unknown hallway, away from all the things she knew he would say.

Kelsey made it to a den in what was clearly a house and clearly *not* an apartment complex.

A fancy house. A great, grand, suburb-ruling house. Definitely an older couple's house. Established. Successful. Country-club elites. Winners of the game of life. Reggie would want a house like this — for his two hypothetical kids to grow up in.

Kelsey scanned the photos hung along the walls and propped up on tables and shelves. She picked out the patriarch and matriarch. Old, but not elderly. The matriarch had flowing silver hair, a sharp chin, and dark-brown eyes. She wore a silver locket in every photo. The locket shone brighter than her smile in every photo. The patriarch looked like stereotypical British royalty. Kelsey couldn't find an instance of him even attempting to smile.

There had to be at least eight kids in the family, based on the photos. Kelsey didn't feel like counting up the grandkids. She tried to slip her doorknob into her purse, but found nothing.

"Shit," Kelsey muttered. Her purse was back *there*. With Reggie. She forced her doorknob into her pants pocket and approached the den's massive fireplace.

A framed photograph hung above the fireplace's mantle. Huge, three feet wide at least. It hung alone — prominent, like an animal-head trophy. The photo showcased a platoon of family members, all lined up in a field in front of a mansion. The older couple stood in the middle, the leading pair of the pack. Kelsey could almost hear Reggie whisper, '*That could be us*' in her ear.

Kelsey was an only child. An only child who only had one parent live past her second birthday. Her dad would entertain her with corny jokes when he took her to school or the mall. Jokes to replace banter with never-born brothers and sisters. Jokes to replace girl-time with a never-remembered mother. Jokes he probably shouldn't have told a little kid. He would've made a joke about this fancy family. A joke about how they were the heirs of some great business — a business that definitely wasn't in the business of contraceptives.

Being such a lonely child just meant more time to spend with her dad. There was no need for a family so sprawling that Kelsey would forget half the people in it, like this fancy family probably did.

No need *then*.

Now, though.

Kelsey wondered if her nonexistent family would've made it all easier. Wondered if her nonexistent family would've chosen real wood.

She reached up, hefted the framed photo off its hook, and laid it face down on the mantle.

A bright reflection caught in the frame's glass as she set it down. Sunlight.

Kelsey turned and saw warm light trickling into the den from a hallway. Maybe through a glass door down that way. Her dad never trusted glass doors. Not sturdy enough.

Kelsey wiped away a few straggling tears. Focused. She just wanted to get out of wherever *here* was and figure out what to do. She took a step toward the sunlight.

But the sunlight shifted as that unseen glass door opened. Two angry, arguing voices bloomed in the home. Crying filled the gaps in the yelling. The glass door slammed.

Kelsey reached for her doorknob on instinct. "I'm getting arrested." She dashed down a random hallway, away from the voices.

A man shouted from the direction of the glass door, "I make the money, so I can do whatever I want! See anyone I want! Be glad with what you've gotten from this."

Kelsey imagined herself in an orange jumpsuit as she searched for a hiding place.

A woman shrieked, "How dare you do this to me! How dare you tear down everything I've built for you!"

Kelsey lunged for a half-open door. Rushed through. Found herself in a massive master bedroom.

The two voices — they had reached the den. They ate at one another. Vied for dominance.

Then Kelsey heard some delicate thing break. An antique trinket? A priceless sculpture? A framed photograph of a sad couple pretending to be happy?

Kelsey scanned the bedroom. Considered hiding in its bathroom. No. Too far away. Who the hell needed a bedroom this big?

She turned, saw a closet.

She tried the closet's handle. It came loose.

"Oh come *on*!"

Kelsey heard the glass door slam again. Heard something shatter. Maybe the glass door itself. She heard more crying. Footfalls grew louder.

Kelsey pulled her doorknob out and forced it into the closet door.

She turned it, swung open the door, crept through, and hoped no one would notice her glass-rose doorknob — or needed to change. She squatted down and pulled the closet door to as quickly as the need for silence allowed, then put her ear up to the crack and listened.

Someone entered the bedroom.

And sobbed.

Kelsey peeked through the crack.

It was the matriarch from the photos, with her silky silver hair and expensive clothes and air of power. The

192

matriarch slumped onto the edge of the bed and bawled. There was a defeat in the sound she made. A powerlessness. How could anyone with such a nice house and such a big family have anything to cry about?

No. That was a cruel thought. A Reggie thought. Kelsey's dad had left her enough to be comfortable after he was gone. But he was still gone. Kelsey's doorknob meant more than all the money in the world. Kelsey itched to retrieve it from the other side of the closet door.

But the sobbing continued. Kelsey could only squat there in the closet and wait for the matriarch to leave or fall asleep to dream away her pain.

Then Kelsey realized that she wasn't squatting in a closet.

Her breathing echoed down a long corridor lined with lemon-yellow doors. The floor's puke-green tiles were accented with hearts, clubs, diamonds, and spades. A strange swooshing rhythm filled the space. And dinging.

It was closer to being her apartment building. But wasn't.

Kelsey picked up a crumpled flyer lying on the floor. It highlighted a breakfast menu for a hotel buffet. Six months out of date. The flyer featured anthropomorphized slot machines in the corners, smiling and reading off jackpots. This hallway definitely fit the bill for a shitty Las Vegas hotel. Those dings — probably penny slots.

But the swooshing?

Metal squeaked somewhere past a far-off bend in the hall. A cleaning cart, maybe. An answer, maybe. But before Kelsey could investigate, the matriarch's sobs grew louder — so loud that they compelled Kelsey to open the door.

"Hello?" Kelsey whispered.

The matriarch gasped and peered up from her hands. She looked older than the version of herself in all those photos. Looked like she felt older.

"Who... who are you?" The matriarch clutched the silver locket hanging at her chest. Her eyes darted from Kelsey to other random points in space, as if she couldn't focus.

"I'm Kelsey." Kelsey realized how strange she must've looked, hunched down like a goblin, head poking out of this woman's closet. She got up and slowly walked back into the fancy bedroom. "I'm not going to hurt you. I'm not a thief. I just got lost."

"Why were you in my closet?"

"It's a hotel in there, not a closet." Kelsey looked back to make sure she wasn't insane.

A man in boxers walked out of one of the lemon-yellow doors. He scratched his ass and belched and drunk-stumbled down the hall until he disappeared from view.

Yep. Las Vegas hotel.

The matriarch looked confused. She also looked too exhausted to care about being confused.

Kelsey walked over and sat down on the bed, beside the matriarch.

"I just want to know what I did," the matriarch whimpered. "What did I do wrong? I don't know what I did to deserve this or what to do!"

The matriarch raised her head and wailed so loud that Kelsey shivered.

"What... what happened?" Kelsey mumbled.

The matriarch answered, but the answer wasn't for Kelsey. The matriarch was just talking to the universe now.

"I did everything for him. *Everything*. I was a good woman. I was a perfect wife. I was perfect for him. I *made* myself perfect for him. I was enough. I should have been enough for him forever." The matriarch lay back on the bed and looked at Kelsey. "He just left... left me alone. I don't even know where he went. He just left to be with that whore, even though I've always been enough."

The matriarch's eyes began to wander again, searching for some absent thing.

Then the matriarch's eyes filled with tears.

Then the matriarch closed her eyes and screamed and screamed and screamed.

Kelsey had screamed and screamed and screamed in her bedroom when she first thought about leaving Reggie. Hoped to summon up the courage out of thin air — like some Viking bellowing out a warcry before an unwinnable battle. She screamed until the neighbors shouted at her through the walls. This woman was lost in some infinite place with no one holding her to the ground, just like Kelsey.

195

At least Kelsey had a seedy Las Vegas hotel to stay at while she figured shit out. And her doorknob.

Kelsey stood and walked back to the closet. She yanked her doorknob loose, shoved it into her pocket, and crossed back into the hotel. She pulled the door to as she left, but didn't shut it. The matriarch didn't need to hear another door close on her.

But before Kelsey could start down the hotel hallway, she heard a familiar voice from the fancy bedroom.

"Excuse me, miss," Reggie said from the other side of the door.

"Who are you?" the matriarch stammered. "Why are all of you people in my house?"

"So you saw someone else? Was it a woman? Light-brown hair? About shoulder length?"

Kelsey's pulse quickened. She turned back and pushed the door open. Reggie looked at her.

"Get out!" the matriarch ordered. "Both of you!"

Reggie rushed toward Kelsey. "Gladly." He grabbed her wrist. "Let's go, Kel. We have things to discuss."

"Don't call me that." Kelsey pulled free and backed away, deeper into the closet-that-was-actually-a-hotel. She tried to close the door, but Reggie grabbed the edge. Forced it open. Followed her through.

"Just come back with me," Reggie whined. He tried to grab Kelsey again. Missed. "Just let me define your problem and help you through it!"

"Please just… please give me a minute." Kelsey backed farther down the hall.

Reggie advanced. The matriarch followed behind him.

"Where… is my closet?" the matriarch mumbled.

Kelsey hoped the matriarch didn't have too many valuables in her actual closet, wherever it was now. She stopped. Considered helping the matriarch back to her bedroom.

Then Reggie grabbed Kelsey's wrist again.

"You aren't thinking things through," he chided. "You *never* do, and you'll feel stupid later. I'm just trying to save you from that." Reggie tightened his grip. "So let's just go and work this out together."

He started pulling Kelsey back toward the fancy bedroom.

"I don't want to go with you," Kelsey whimpered. She scratched at Reggie's hand, but he kept pulling. Her legs started to shake. Her breathing wavered.

Kelsey lowered her gaze. Started to relent. Obey.

Then the matriarch put her hand on Reggie's shoulder.

"Young man," the matriarch said, "this young lady told you to let her go. I think you should let her go."

Reggie jerked his shoulder away. "She isn't thinking clearly. It's fine. Mind your business."

"She sounds sure." The matriarch touched her locket.

Kelsey felt for her doorknob in her pocket. "Reggie, just please… let go."

Reggie paused, but he didn't let go of Kelsey. "I don't get you." There was a real hurt in his voice. Or a good forgery. "Do you know what this relationship has taken from me?"

"That's not my…"

Not her problem. But wasn't it? Kelsey was the one doing the abandoning here. She was abandoning Reggie after three years. Three years of Reggie being there for her. Being there for her when she didn't have her dad.

"You just… *used* me." Reggie shook Kelsey's hand violently, like that was an alternative to something worse. "Wasted my time. Three years of my life! No. No, we're going back and talking this through like adults at the very least. You *owe* me that, Kel. Come on."

Reggie pulled Kelsey forward. They reached the door.

Then the matriarch grabbed Kelsey's arm and wrenched her free from Reggie.

Reggie turned. "What the fu-"

The matriarch punched Reggie in the face. Then she punched him again. Then she shoved him back into the fancy bedroom. Reggie collapsed onto the carpeted floor as blood poured from his nostrils.

Kelsey knew she should help Reggie. He was there for her. There through so much.

She rushed forward and reached out her hand — and closed the door. On this side, it was just a lemon-yellow hotel room door. Kelsey tried the handle. Locked. Of course it was locked. She hadn't booked a stay.

Kelsey looked at the matriarch. Then she hugged her.

"Let's figure out where we are," Kelsey said.

The two started wandering.

The hotel was quiet, save for a child's distant, happy screaming. And the constant barrage of slot-machine noises. And that swooshing.

Kelsey and the matriarch walked to the end of the hall. Turned. Went down another. And another. They passed a cleaning lady, toiling and ignoring the world around her. Kelsey watched the cleaning lady enter a hotel room. Just a generic hotel room in there.

"Hello," Kelsey peeped. "We're lost. Can you-"

But the cleaning lady just shrugged Kelsey off and turned on a vacuum cleaner and shut the lemon-yellow door.

So the wandering pair wandered on.

"I've never done that before," the matriarch admitted as the two reached a small seating area. She sat down and rubbed her knuckles and winced. The skin purpled around her collection of fancy rings. "Struck someone, I mean. It isn't very ladylike… even if it *is* merited."

Kelsey laughed, then slapped a hand over her mouth. It seemed cruel, laughing at Reggie. Traitorous, even. Then she thought about the matriarch punching him again.

Thought about her dad's corny jokes again. Kelsey laughed again. She laughed until her ribs hurt.

The matriarch smiled and flipped through a magazine highlighting Strip attractions. "He seemed like a bad man," she mused. "I don't know what's going on or where my closet is, but I know he seemed like a bad man."

"Yeah." Kelsey scanned the nearby walls for one of those little building maps. Didn't find one. "Sorry you're lost with me now… umm… what's your name?"

"Bethany. You can call me '*Beth*', though. My…" Beth grabbed at her locket, "…my husband… Reginald… he hates people addressing me as anything other than '*Bethany*'." Beth looked into Kelsey's eyes for a moment, smiled, and lowered her gaze. Then the matriarch's eyes widened. "Oh my! Your leg, dear. It's bleeding."

Kelsey looked down and saw her pants stained red at the hip. She fished out her doorknob and looked it over. A thin sliver had chipped off one of the petals, leaving behind a scalpel-sharp edge. Dread bloomed in Kelsey's chest. She carefully slid her doorknob back into her pocket — and silently begged it to remain whole.

"Just don't… don't worry about it," Kelsey told Beth. Told herself, maybe.

Beth stood up. "Why in the world are you carrying that around?"

Kelsey looked away, down the hall. "It's heavier than Reggie. Let's find someone to ask for directions."

They found someone around the next turn.

A hunched man slowly wheeled a food cart down the hall, toward the two — more using the food cart as a walker than pushing it, really. He stopped when Kelsey approached.

Kelsey had watched thousands of food carts, just like the hunched man's, roll past her dad's hospital room. She would count them to pass the time. Her dad could never keep that shitty food down. He'd let her finish his meals.

Her stomach quivered.

"What you want?" the hunched man grumbled.

Before Kelsey could speak, Beth gasped behind her.

"Oh my, what is this *filth* all over the walls?" Beth ran her finger down the wall and wrinkled up her nose.

Kelsey looked closer. Beth was right. The walls glistened with an unclean sheen. Oily. Dank.

"Lubricant," the hunched man snapped, "so the blood flows good." He said it like it was the most obvious fact in the entire universe. "You stupid? Arteries need to be all lubed up for the blood to work right."

"Uh… okay." Kelsey stepped away from both the hunched man and the lubed walls. "Could you point us to the exit?"

The hunched man sneered. "Probably in the same place you came through, seein's how you must'a come through it to get here."

Kelsey sneered back. "Where the fuck is it?"

The hunched man gave her a grimace and a thumb-flick over his shoulder.

Kelsey grabbed Beth's hand and heeded the old shit's directions. They finally found the lobby after circling back and heading down some emergency stairs.

The lobby featured a few folding chairs, a row of penny slots, and a clerk desk without a clerk. The swooshing was loudest here. Something outside, maybe?

Didn't matter. There was the front door. A very, very purple front door. Layers and layers of cheap paint drowned the wood.

Kelsey's dad would push customers away from painting their doors. He liked seeing the patterns in the grain. Said the patterns went on forever.

Kelsey always went on weekend work trips with her dad. Those trips went on forever. She'd beg to go on those work trips with him. She wanted to learn all she could. Be just like him. She'd need to be just like her dad if she was going to follow in his footsteps someday. Take over the business someday.

Did the business even exist now? Kelsey should've kept it. Kept it alive. Kept the blood flowing through her dad's dream. But it was gone now. Sold. Pawned off. Out of reach. Abandoned. All because it made her think too much.

At least a wood door drowned in purple paint was still real wood.

Better than a fiberglass lie.

"Come on." Kelsey tugged Beth over to the door and grabbed the handle. It broke free from the gross purple. She set the handle on the absent clerk's desk.

Kelsey's doorknob had worked before. It should work again. She reached into her pocket, careful not to cut herself, and pulled out her doorknob. It slid into the lobby door like a key. She opened the door and led Beth through, retrieving her doorknob as they went.

Kelsey found herself in an apartment. An apartment so similar to hers that she worried there might be an almost-Reggie lurking somewhere within, ready to catch her and weld a ring onto her finger.

But the photos lining these walls captured a different couple.

In these photos, a woman stood behind a man — always with her hands on his shoulders, nails dug in, holding him down. It should've been a *good* thing, being anchored in place like that.

But the man's expression — it mirrored Beth's expression in all those photos in that fancy house.

That fancy house with its shattered glass door.

Kelsey rubbed her fingers over the chip in her doorknob. Her fingers found a new crack. She tried to ignore the damage and walked farther into the apartment. Then she rounded a corner. And entered the living room. And yelped.

Everything was made of glass.

The floor and the walls and the ceiling were glass. The couch and the chairs and the tables were glass. A glass corgi lay, curled up, by a glass fireplace with glass logs resting within.

The room looked elegant but unlivable. Beautiful but painful. A pretty lie.

Kelsey needed somewhere else to go. The corgi would do.

Glass carpet fibers crunched like snow as Kelsey walked over to the clear dog. She picked the animal up. It didn't bite or bark, fortunately. Kelsey returned to the apartment's front door and shut it, sealing away the Las Vegas hotel.

"But," Beth started, "I need to go home. What if…" Beth's voice trailed off.

Kelsey figured Beth was about to mention Reginald. She didn't know if Beth refused to say the name, or if Beth just couldn't find the strength to say it. Kelsey hoped for the former.

"I don't think you should go back there." Kelsey lined the corgi's butt up with the front door's handle. "Not yet. I don't think it works like that, anyway. I've got no control here."

Kelsey had no control over her body during those months approaching her dad's death. Those months of struggling to figure out what forms to prepare and documents to sign and end-of-life affairs to wrap up — all while the hospital got ready to wash their hands of it all. She had just slipped into autopilot. She wanted it all over and done with so badly. Rushed through it. She shouldn't have rushed. She should have taken her time.

She should have chosen real wood.

Beth looked around and tugged at her locket. "Perhaps you're right."

Kelsey slammed the dog down onto the handle. The handle fell to the floor. Kelsey slipped her doorknob into its place, opened the door, and peered into a small beach house.

It seemed empty. The lights were all off. Nothing was made of glass — nothing that shouldn't be glass already.

And there were flowers. All kinds. Everywhere. Flowers arranged in vases and flowers tied into bouquets and flowers woven into wreaths and flowers simply scattered about loose. They were on tables, chairs, the couch, the floor. Everywhere. Why were there so many flowers?

Kelsey pulled her doorknob free and wandered inside.

Waves lapped against the sandy shore, out past a pair of open sliding doors. That unending *shhhhhh-hahhhhh* of water and sand touching filled the home. A breathing, almost.

The scents of salt and rum tickled Kelsey's nose. Calmed her. Then she remembered her doorknob. She inspected it for damage. Injury.

New cracks had formed. When Kelsey turned her doorknob over in her hand, a rose petal fell off. The petal landed on a thick rug and vanished in the fibers.

Kelsey gasped. Knelt down. Tried to find it. But the house was too dark. The rug fibers were too thick.

"No, no, *no*," she cried as she searched. "*Please!*"

Beth wandered past Kelsey.

"This place seems nice and homely," the matriarch said. "It reminds me of where I grew up. Before I… settled for Reginald." Beth touched a party platter on a coffee table, then she looked out through the sliding doors. "Oh my, the beach! I haven't seen the ocean in twenty years. Last time Reginald took me, I was…"

Music started playing. Reggae.

Beth went silent. Her eyes locked onto something out in the sand. Kelsey stopped her search and followed the matriarch's gaze.

A huge canopy tent stood far off, between the beach house and the sea. Partiers reveled beneath it. Must've been the residents of this house, hosting a get-together. They looked so carefree. People who lived on beaches were always carefree. What if the sea came up and swallowed them all? It was so deep. So vast. So infinite.

At least they'd be happy right up to that moment. At least that moment would come fast. End fast. Like a bullet to the brain. Kelsey had spent the last months with her dad noting every degeneration. Every lost bodily function. Every coughing fit that ruined the punchline to one of his corny jokes. A bullet would have been a mercy. For both of them.

Beth inched closer to the sliding doors. She breathed in deep. She reached for her locket.

Then Beth darted outside.

"Hey, wait!" Kelsey shouted. She stood to follow, but clipped the coffee table with her foot and fell face-first onto the floor.

Beth was halfway to the surf by the time Kelsey stumbled over to the doors.

The matriarch turned back to Kelsey and yelled, "I hope you figure out what you want to do with that." Beth pointed to Kelsey's hand, the doorknob. "I just want to swim in the ocean. I *need* to. I can't remember what it feels like."

Beth ran farther out, stripping off her fancy clothes as she went. She turned back again and yelled, "Don't go back to that young man. He isn't a good man. He's small, just like my Reginald."

Then Beth ran until she hit the water.

Kelsey noticed a shine in the sand, right outside the sliding doors. She looked closer. It was Beth's locket.

Those kinds of lockets always had little photographs in them. Kelsey wondered if Beth's locket held Reginald's photo within. Or someone else's, maybe. She wondered how fast the salty air would eat up that photo and tarnish that silver. She wondered and worried and dreaded countless things — and Beth just kept breaststroking out toward the horizon.

"Be careful," Kelsey called out, but the waves and wind and beach-party reggae probably stopped her voice from ever reaching Beth. The thought of Reggie's bloody nose made Kelsey smile again.

The partiers cheered the matriarch on and lit fireworks in her honor. The fireworks blasted into the sky and burst, smearing the cloudless blue with splotches of fiery yellow and orange.

Beth probably didn't even notice the tribute. The matriarch was already too far out and still going strong.

Somehow, Kelsey felt older than Beth.

Beth crossed the horizon and disappeared from view.

Then a thunderous *boom* shook the house and sent Kelsey to her knees. She looked up to the sky. Searched for storm clouds.

There was no storm. No grey.

But the sky — it had cracked open.

The bright beach sky shivered. Warped. Slivered apart. Massive sheets of sky — countless miles across — fell into the ocean.

And beyond the fractured blue was an infinite, undefined dark. A dark with no direction or start or end. A dark where the largest things were mere atoms. A dark that was *so* similar to an empty hospital room.

"Dad," Kelsey whimpered. She squeezed her doorknob. The fractured glass cut her hand. Blood flowed over her fingers. She turned and ran from that infinite dark.

Kelsey searched through her tears and her panic. She found a bedroom door, broke the handle off with a vase full of flowers, used her doorknob, staggered through, and collapsed. She clung to the memory of her dad, healthy and smiling, while she clutched her doorknob to her chest and sobbed.

When her breathing finally slowed, Kelsey looked around.

An airport terminal.

Signs were posted everywhere, but all the writing was gibberish. Random squiggles. Kelsey scanned every poster and plaque, and still felt as lost as ever. A plane took off beyond a window. She slipped her doorknob into her pocket — and noticed something on the floor.

Painted arrows zigzagged all over the tiles, creating paths for lost travelers to follow. Red, green, white, yellow, purple, orange, blue.

Kelsey pictured Beth in the ocean and chose blue.

Her feet moved over the blue arrows for hours as she trudged along through a sea of people, all following arrows of their own.

No one looked up. Everyone seemed so nervous. Almost expectant. Kelsey understood that suspicion. That shadow. That steadily rising note. She sensed that expectation growing — writhing — inside her, long before her dad's health took a turn. Cancer ran on his side of the family. She spent years just waiting for a sign. A symptom. Those signs and symptoms never came. On her twenty-seventh birthday, Kelsey finally relaxed. Lowered her guard.

Her dad had started feeling strange the very next day.

A great, sickly noise rippled through the airport. Everyone cowered down. The gnawing rasp built and built and built until it exploded. The crescendo shook the windows and walls — some horrible death rattle from some continent-sized being. Kelsey covered her ears and screamed and knew with absolute certainty that the monstrous sound would shake her apart.

Then it passed. Everyone stood. Everyone continued down their paths. Everyone acted like nothing had happened.

"Excuse me," Kelsey struggled out as she tugged a passing businessman's sleeve. "What... what was that?"

The businessman didn't look at Kelsey. "Can't talk. Need to focus on my arrow."

The businessman clutched an old suitcase to his chest. The suitcase didn't look expensive, but the businessman held onto it so tightly that his knuckles strained white. Maybe it was a gift from someone important.

"I don't know where to go," Kelsey said.

"Doesn't matter," the businessman responded, "as long as there's an arrow telling you where to go." He walked away, his generic business suit fading into the hive of other generic business suits.

So Kelsey just kept following blue.

Blue eventually led her to a dilapidated wing of the airport, to a door labeled '*Lounge*' in English.

She tried the handle. Locked.

Fortunately, there happened to be a fire extinguisher sitting on the floor, right by the door. Much better than a glass corgi. For breaking handles, at least.

Kelsey broke off the lounge handle, slid in her doorknob, and stepped through.

She retrieved her doorknob and read the sign over the door.

'MAINTENANCE CLOSET - BIG CAT EXHIBIT - VISITORS KEEP OUT.'

Kelsey's dad would chaperone her field trips to the zoo, way back when she was in elementary school. He would always urge Kelsey to go play with the other students, but she never listened. She'd just hold onto his leg, her head to his knee, and feel rooted in place. Her dad would laugh and call her a lemur.

Her dad's knees shook like baby rattles in those final weeks. He could never stay warm in those hospital gowns.

Kelsey walked up to a pane of glass separating her from a fake savanna.

A massive lion stared at her through a thick patch of grass. The lion approached. Licked the glass. Yearned to eat something that would struggle. Begged to run across entire continents.

Kelsey put her hand to the glass. Inspected the lion's little world. Kelsey could get used to a world that small. She would welcome its protection. Its restriction. Its certainty.

But Kelsey could tell that the lion didn't see a world. It saw a cage. The lion didn't want the protection or restriction or certainty of that cage. It wanted out.

It wanted the infinite.

Kelsey looked into the lion's eyes. The lion's eyes weren't normal eyes. The lion's eyes were glass roses.

Kelsey checked her doorknob. Her stomach rolled. So damaged now. So close to breaking. Ceasing to be.

The lion started panting. The panting sounded like laughter. Kelsey knew it wasn't laughter, but she heard laughter anyway. She grew nauseous. Her vision darkened.

211

Her heartbeat thumped in her ears like thunderclaps. She wanted to break the glass and tear out the lion's eyes. Claim its glass roses for herself. Weigh herself down.

No. Those wouldn't be hers — her dad's. The lion's eyes were just worthless glass.

Kelsey ran to the zoo's gift shop before she cried or threw up or passed out in front of the lion and its glass-rose eyes. She ripped out the gift shop's door handle without even trying and headed through, her breaths coming wildly as she retrieved her doorknob. It cut her again.

The gift shop sent Kelsey to a hospital.

Her panic died down. Grief and loathing replaced it. Churned inside her. Refused to mix like oil and water. Made her feel even worse than that lion's mocking pants.

This place looked so similar to the place that allowed her dad to die. It wasn't — all hospitals looked vaguely similar in that sterilized way. But this one was *so* similar.

Kelsey hurried off to find a nurse's station, find a way out of this memory. All along the way, she smelled those chemicals used to sanitize vomit and waste. Felt that medically-calculated chill in the air — that chill designed to keep sickness from spreading. That chill never helped her dad. He caught so many infections during his stay that Kelsey didn't know whether she should blame the tumors or the tenth round of MRSA for killing him.

She continued to wander the halls. Hospital halls seemed to go on forever. They had no defined direction. No forethought in their design. Kelsey hated them.

But a building dread eventually overpowered Kelsey's hate. Forced her to think. She paused after turning down hallway number-seven. Something was wrong with this hospital. More wrong than a normal hospital.

A beating punctured the silence of the halls, constant and steady and deep. The walls moved ever-so-slightly with each beat. Shivered. Pulsed as if some massive heart in some secret location was pumping blood through them. Had Kelsey walked into a hospital in California? Was this an earthquake? No. Too rhythmic. Too organic.

The thumping in her ears calmed, but the beating all around went on. Kelsey imagined what life as a blood cell would be like as she explored. Small and unimportant, but safe within their veins and arteries.

Kelsey finally found a nurse's station. It was unmanned. *Everywhere* was unmanned. The hospital had a heartbeat, but no staff.

No blood.

"Hello?" she yelled down a rippling corridor. "Can somebody help me?"

No one answered. No nurses. No doctors. No cleaning staff or visitors. No sick fathers with daughters wishing to die with them. No one at all, no matter how many hallways and waiting rooms and offices she checked. Only the beating answered her back.

Kelsey found a door labeled '*Radiology*'. She knew it wouldn't lead to the radiology department if she used her doorknob. This door would work as well as any other. She started looking for something heavy enough to break the handle.

Before she could find anything, a weak plea slipped past a patient-room door, far down at the end of a dark wing.

"I'm glad someone's here," the voice squeaked. "Do I know you?"

Kelsey remained silent. Considered ignoring the call from beyond the patient-room door.

Patient-room doors were always heavier than they needed to be. Why were they always so heavy? What if the patients were too weak to open them?

Kelsey's dad would slap sticky notes onto the outside of his patient-room door, all marked up with his corny jokes. Those sticky-note jokes gave Kelsey something to laugh at before she went in to see how much the cancer had stolen since her last visit.

Her dad eventually stopped putting sticky notes on his door. He became too weak to open it. What had his last joke been? Kelsey tried to remember it. Couldn't. Something about a nightgown? A sacrifice?

"Please answer," the voice struggled out. "Do I know you? Is that Amber? Keith?"

"No. No, you don't." Kelsey abandoned the radiology door. She walked to the patient room and entered. Inside, the heartbeat was mercifully deadened. "Sorry, I'm just lost."

"Oh," a frail, kind-faced, absolutely ancient man wheezed from his hospital bed. "I thought you might be one of my grandkids visiting with their little ones." He waved Kelsey over and grabbed onto her hand too tightly, the way the elderly always did. And the sick.

"My name's Fredrik." Fredrik smiled.

Kelsey smelled a faint dying on Fredrik. The smell forced memories to metastasize. But the ancient man's smile was vibrant and alive. His smile stopped the memories from growing too quickly.

"I don't think right anymore. Just left." Fredrik chuckled and knocked on his head. The IV lines feeding into his arm shook as he bonked his skull.

A good-bad joke. Kelsey's dad would've approved.

"That's what the doctors say, at least," he continued. "Not the '*left*' part. That's all me. I thought I knew you."

Fredrik's eyes radiated an intense kindness. They reminded Kelsey of her dad's eyes before the sickness dulled them to slate. The similarities ended there.

Fredrik was smaller. More tanned. More angular. Only a bit of stubble sprouted from his cheeks and chin — no mountain-man beard like her dad's. And *so* old. If Kelsey's dad were still alive, he'd be younger than Fredrik by five or six decades.

Kelsey turned away from the ancient man and inspected his hospital room.

Dozens of photos brightened the room's bland walls. Colored them with life and memory. The photos captured a big family. A happy family. Kelsey didn't spot a Beth expression anywhere. Or a glass-living-room-man expression anywhere. Or a Kelsey expression anywhere.

An uncomfortable silence began to build, metered out by the muffled heartbeat outside — and the shrill chirps of vitals machines inside. Countless tubes linked the machines to Fredrik. Each of the tubes pumped liquids in or out of his frail form like an artificial circulatory system. The ancient man might as well have been an organ for this place, connected as he was.

Kelsey finally said, "I didn't see any doctors out there. Is there anyone here to look after you?"

Fredrik scrunched up his face and shimmied until he was sitting upright in his hospital bed. "There were. Loads. Never liked them. Always telling me about my chances. Never looking me in the eye. Faces like metal. So cold." The ancient man looked at Kelsey's hand, hidden away in her pocket. The blood on her pants had dried black.

"You think you could help me wet my whistle?" Fredrik motioned to a small table pushed up against the wall, behind some beeping machines. A glass of water sat on it. "My throat's dry as a desert."

"Yeah, of course." Kelsey got the glass and handed it to Fredrik.

Fredrik gulped the water down and sighed. "Thank you. I've been so thirsty for so long. Lifetime long. I like not having doctors telling me my chances. I was glad when they buggered off. But they should've pushed the glass closer before they left."

216

Fredrik smiled at Kelsey and looked at her for a long time.

"You're very pretty," he finally said.

"Thanks," Kelsey replied.

"What's your name, young lady?"

"Kelsey."

"Ah, pretty name. Much prettier than '*Kel*'. Not married?"

"What?"

Fredrik tapped on his finger. On his wedding ring. "No band. Unless it's on the hand hiding in your pocket."

"Oh." Kelsey pulled her hand out of her pocket. Her hand was coated in blood. A coat as thick as the paint on that hotel's purple door. And ringless. "No. I mean… I don't… I don't know."

A deep, dark fear rushed up like a great wave. That fear consumed Kelsey like that rose-eyed lion would, given the chance. Her dad wouldn't be behind any of these doors. Any door. What if Reggie's ring was the heaviest anchor she would ever have? What if he never forgave her? What if he abandoned her?

Maybe Kelsey could find his ring. Quietly slip it on. She could grow to be happy. Make herself happy. She would have to — if her doorknob shattered.

She turned away from Fredrik and pulled out her doorknob. So many cracks. So many wounds. Her blood had leaked into those wounds and colored the clear petals a faint red. She turned her glass rose over in her hand.

And a second petal fell off.

Kelsey moaned. Her heartbeat outpaced the heartbeat outside. She crumpled to the floor. Pulled her knees to her chest. Tried to slow her breaths. Couldn't.

Fredrik just sighed.

"I know it's tough," the ancient man said, "finding your feet when you feel lost. Tiny. Ready to blow away. But I'll tell you a secret." Fredrik leaned over his bedrail. The dying-scent on him smelled more like wildflowers now. "The secret to finding your way is… not caring about blowing away in the first place."

"Huh?" Kelsey stood and slipped her doorknob back into her pocket. "What's that supposed to mean?"

"I'm not really sure. Need pills for my mind, and the doctors didn't leave 'em." Fredrik laughed. "Just let go. Don't think about your chances. Don't think about how big everything is or how small you are. It'll all probably work out."

"*Probably?*"

"Yup," Fredrik quipped. "Probably's as good as I can do, but probably's *also* as good as someone who worries over everything can do. Seems better to just blow around, is all. To me, at least. Don't get hung up on defining all the shit you can't define… shit that might never even happen. At least then, you get to enjoy that wide-open sky instead of looking down at the ground, poopin' your pants while you guesstimate the fall." He waved his hands at the ceiling. "But what do I know."

Fredrik smiled and closed his eyes for a long time.

Kelsey figured he had fallen asleep. She started to turn. Started to leave.

Then the ancient man opened his eyes and clapped his hands together. "Can you do one more thing for me, Kelsey? It'll be a little thing to you, but a big thing to me."

"Yeah."

"See that cable?" Fredrik flicked his thumb back. "Big, thick one the color of licorice?"

The cable led from the wall behind Fredrik's bed, coiled into a huge pile in the corner of the room, then branched out and fed into all of Fredrik's vitals machines.

"What about it?" Kelsey asked.

Fredrik smiled. "Unplug it."

The heartbeat quickened outside.

"I don't…" Kelsey struggled to find words, form thoughts. "No! I'm not doing that."

"I want it, though," Fredrik said.

"You don't know that!" Kelsey leaned over the ancient man and grabbed his shoulders. "You have no *clue* what you want. You said you only *probably* don't want to blow away or… whatever the fuck you said. And now you want *this*? What about your family? Your kids? Your grandkids? An- and your fucking *great* grandkids! You have *great* grandkids! You're *abandoning* them! Leaving them *lost*! You selfish, stupid-"

Kelsey bit her tongue. Tasted blood. Tears welled up in her eyes.

"Didn't know a second ago," Fredrik said as he smiled at her, "do now. I ain't looking at the ground, so it's fine. My family ain't looking at the ground, either. They'll all be fine. Figure out how to be fine in their own ways." Fredrik reached up and touched Kelsey's cheek. "I'm old. I've seen a lot. And I'm happy with a lot of what I've seen. This is what I want. I'll take my chances with this call."

Kelsey pulled out her doorknob and held it to her chest and closed her eyes.

"*Help me,*" she hushed.

"Oh, would you look at that!" Fredrik took the doorknob from her. "This looks just like the doorknobs from my home. For our bathrooms. How 'bout that. Had those doors installed, oh… twenty-odd years ago. Never had a nicer handyman install anything in the house, before or since. He knew his doors. Knew the shit out of 'em. You have his eyes. And his doorknob. What are the chances of that?" Fredrik smiled.

Kelsey started to cry. "I'll do it for you, but are you sure? *Completely* sure? Please don't make me do this if you aren't sure. *Please.*" She could barely see Fredrik through her tears.

"I'm as sure about this as your dad was about his doors." Fredrik handed the doorknob back to Kelsey. "It's okay. It'll all be okay."

Kelsey went to the cable. Knelt down by it. Grabbed it. She pulled. It came out so easily. Fredrik's machines started to shudder and wind down. Their shudders sounded horrible.

But Fredrik's laughter sounded wonderful.

Kelsey returned to the ancient man's side.

"Thank you, Kelsey." Fredrik smiled and patted Kelsey's shoulder. "Thank you so much. Now, go on." He waved her off toward the door. "Don't use the radiology door. It's just a college cafeteria. Food's probably lousier in there than it is in this shithole, if you can believe it. Take a left and go straight on for a while. You'll come to a waiting room with a busted vending machine. There'll be two doors in there. Take the door on the left. Don't take the door on the right…" Fredrik smirked, "…unless you feel like taking your chances."

"Okay." Kelsey walked to the door. She turned back and asked, "What's on the right?"

But Fredrik's hospital bed was empty.

Kelsey turned off the lights and left the empty room.

The heartbeat was gone. Kelsey walked until she found the waiting room with its broken vending machine and two doors.

'*Parking Lot*' labeled the door on the left.

'*Morgue*' labeled the door on the right.

Kelsey remembered feeling cold — *so* cold — as she walked through the hospital parking lot on the night of her dad's death. Cold but damp. Humid. Maybe that humid feeling was just the sweat from a panic attack. She had slammed her fists onto the hood of a random car until she collapsed from the pain. Broke three bones in her hands. She prayed the pain would keep her from losing her mind. She hoped the cold air would make her sick. Cause her to die.

That car was Reggie's car. Kelsey met him for the first time at the police station. He had asked her out — after he filed a police report. She had said '*yes*' just to get caskets off her mind.

Kelsey stood between the doors. Looked left. Looked right.

Chose right.

She tried the morgue's handle. It came out with no resistance. She slipped her doorknob into its place and opened the door — just enough to see what lay beyond.

A tar-like dark lay beyond. And another heartbeat. Faster in there, deep in the dark. More random. Chaotic. Waves of air pulsed out of the dark and washed over Kelsey's face. The waves felt heavy and moist, like the hot breaths of an animal. They smelled musty and metallic, like the rot-sweet tinge of a corpse.

Kelsey pulled her doorknob free, pocketed it, and leaned into the dark. There was a noise under the heartbeat, too faint to make out. She leaned a little farther in. She just wanted to hear a bit better. See a bit better.

She took a step into the dark.

Her foot found nothing. Kelsey fell.

Down and down, into the dark.

Rotted wood whined and snapped. Those whines and snaps couldn't compete with the crashing thuds of Kelsey's body — or her screams. Sharp angles bruised her deep. Rusty nails pierced her skin. One of her ribs cracked. Then another.

The falling and rolling finally ended on cold, wet stone. A hundred feet above Kelsey, the door to the hospital slowly swayed. Its sliver of light illuminated the haphazard staircase she had fallen down — and the massive stone cavern she now resided within.

Kelsey struggled to her feet. She spied an orange glow, far off in the distance. The strange noise was clearer now, not as muddled by the heartbeat. It meshed with the heartbeat. Complemented the heartbeat. Was it voices? Were they singing?

Kelsey looked back up the stairs. Up to the hospital. Up to the parking lot. She looked deeper into the cavern.

She headed for the glow and the singing. Walked — staggered — through the dark for what could have been lifetimes.

And after all those lifetimes of pushing her broken body onward, on toward that glow and that singing, Kelsey finally found the source of both.

A blazing pyre reached its flaming hands high into the air. The remnants of a wicker animal idol burned within. A goat? Ram, maybe? People in hooded robes danced in the firelight as they chanted along with the heartbeat. Cultists?

A great granite mound loomed over the fire. Steps were carved into its face. The steps led up to the mound's flat top. A stone table rested up there, near the edge, overlooking the flames and cultists.

And there was something else.

A rectangular thing stood near the back of the mound, far behind the table. It towered over everything — the cultists, the table, the pyre, even the granite mound itself. A giant sheet of red fabric obscured whatever the rectangular thing was.

And whatever the rectangular thing was, terrified Kelsey.

She looked back, far off, to the ramshackle staircase and the hospital. A hundred rotted steps to climb at least — a hundred rotted steps barely supported by just-as-rotted timbers. It was a miracle she survived the fall. It was a miracle the staircase and its supports survived her fall. It was a miracle her doorknob hadn't shattered.

She pulled her glass rose out and inspected it. A single breath would destroy it now.

But it was still here, with her. Still here, like her.

Kelsey pocketed her doorknob. She could turn back. Right now. The cultists were too absorbed in their reveling. She could do it. Cut her losses. Flee.

But a loud voice boomed, "SILENCE!" before Kelsey could move.

The chanting died. The heartbeat remained.

An impossibly tall man, clothed in red robes and adorned in gold jewelry, appeared by the stone table. He wielded a bronze staff. The staff was crowned with a glistening crystal hand, each finger tipped with a scalpel-sharp claw. A ram's skull obscured the man's face.

Even with his size, the ram-skull man was little more than a bacterium compared to that rectangular thing looming behind him.

"Wait…" Kelsey half-remembered seeing that ram-skull man on TV. "What the *fuck*?"

Her dad loved watching those old Vincent Price horror marathons that popped up on obscure channels late at night. He watched them in the hospital, too — until he grew too weak to stay awake through them. Kelsey would watch them while her dad slept. Their cheesy dialogue distracted Kelsey from her dad's wheezes.

"Who comes to us?" the ram-skull man called out. Dust fell from the cavern's roof when he spoke. "Who has our great An'giog-Metaz deemed worthy of… *initiation*?"

The heartbeat quickened. The red sheet over the rectangular thing fluttered. The smell worsened.

And the ram-skull man looked right through the dark. Right at Kelsey.

Kelsey ran for the hospital, but the cultists reached her in seconds. They dragged her toward the fire. They lifted her onto their shoulders. They carried her up the carved granite steps — up to the table and the ram-skull man and whatever horror awaited beneath that giant sheet of red fabric.

"Be gentle with our new disciple," the ram-skull man warned. "She's almost shattered."

225

The cultists lowered Kelsey to her feet. All but two retreated back down the steps to dance and chant around the fire. The pair that remained held onto Kelsey's arms as the ram-skull man leered at her through dead animal sockets.

"You know why you have come here," the ram-skull man stated.

"I don't!" Kelsey screamed. "Let me go! Let me *go*!" She tried to jerk free. Her injuries sabotaged her attempts.

"But you *must* know," the ram-skull man said, almost surprised, "for only those who yearn for weight can find their way down here, down to the loving bowels of An'giog-Metaz. Only those who see the infinite for what it truly is… a *horror*… a *cancer*… can find their way down here. Only those who wish for our great An'giog-Metaz to digest that infinite down to finite can find their way down here. And you *have* found your way down here. You have *chosen* this."

"Chosen what?" Kelsey meeked out.

The fire brightened. The ram-skull man laughed into the darkness beyond as the ever-present heartbeat grew louder. He walked to the towering rectangular thing under the red sheet and pulled at a rope. "*Finality*."

The sheet fell away — took a lifetime to fall away — and beneath was a gargantuan doorframe. There was no door, but there was a hallway.

Kelsey shook free from the two cultists and limped over to the side of the doorframe. No walls to the hall stretching back. But looking down through the doorframe, there was — somehow — a hall. A long hall. A hall that

226

slanted downward. A hall with pallid, pink walls covered in layers of mucus that forced Kelsey to think of infections. A hall that led to a far-off door.

The two cultists grabbed Kelsey and led her back to the stone table. The table wasn't bare. A grey shroud lay over it. Something moved beneath the shroud. The ram-skull man approached and ripped the shroud away.

Kelsey fell back at the sight of a woman in a hospital gown. The woman was bound at the hands and feet. A burlap sack covered her head, obscuring her face.

"Who is that?" Kelsey screeched as she struggled. "Let her go! What the fuck's wrong with you people?"

Strands of hair peeked out from beneath the bound woman's sack hood. Light-brown hair. About shoulder length.

"What's wrong with the *world*?" the ram-skull man bellowed. The cultists howled at his echoes. "This poor thing came to us for help! Begged us to hold back that horrifying infinity. Shield her from it. An'giog-Metaz can provide this… in his bowels." The ram-skull man pointed his staff down the hallway.

A stench wafted out of the doorframe. It pummeled Kelsey, nearly forcing her to vomit.

The ram-skull man continued, "But first, we must prepare her. Make her meat smaller for the trip down. *That* is why you are here. *That* is your choice. Your choice is *this*."

The ram-skull man drew a bone-hilt dagger from his robes. He approached Kelsey and held out the blade.

Kelsey recoiled, but the two cultists pushed her toward the ram-skull man and his blade. Her choice.

"Let *go*," she begged.

"Take it!" The ram-skull man placed the dagger in Kelsey's bloodied hand. His hand closed around her hand. Her hand closed around the dagger's bone hilt. Her blood stained the bone a faint red.

The ram-skull man whispered, "This poor thing *wants* this. Do this little kindness for her."

"This isn't right!" Kelsey struggled and squirmed and dropped the dagger to the ground.

The ram-skull man hissed, "If you were not destined to prepare this offering for the great An'giog-Metaz, then you were destined to *be* an offering! There is no middle ground. No more searching. You've reached the answer."

The ram-skull man picked up the dagger. He slammed it back into Kelsey's hand, hard enough to numb her palm.

"You've already killed," he whispered. "You killed that ancient man. He was a fool who wanted to spread out forever. He was *wrong*. But this poor thing," the ram-skull man touched the bound woman's shoulder, "is *right*. This poor thing just wants to feel small and safe. Just wants to cower behind a bulwark and forget about that horrifying infinity. Who are you to deny her? Who are you to deny this poor thing a glass rose of her own? Your father would be *ashamed* of you."

Kelsey grew hot. Hotter than that fire down there could ever make her, even if these cultists threw her into its flames to burn alive. "Don't *ever* talk about my dad, you piece of shit!"

The ram-skull man laughed. "Your anger comes from understanding. You know I'm right. You're *almost* there." He guided Kelsey closer to the table and the bound woman. "Now you just have to *finish* it!"

The cultists fell silent. No human sounds permeated the cavern. There was only the crackling pyre, the ever-quickening heartbeat, and the rancid gurgles belching out from the great doorframe.

The ram-skull man moved to Kelsey's back. Placed his hand on her shoulder. Rested his animal jaws against her neck.

"You can go next," he murmured. "We'll help you in. We'll be here for you. We'll define the infinite. Shrink it. Weaken it. Weaken *you*. It's *right* to want to be small and safe. It's okay that you aren't strong enough to move on. I'm not strong enough, either. None of us are. And we love you through that weakness. *Because* of that weakness."

The heat inside Kelsey cooled. She loved the words pouring out of the ram skull. She hated herself for loving those words.

"Reggie wasn't enough." The ram-skull man tightened his grip on Kelsey's shoulder, squeezing until she winced. "But we *are*. An'giog-Metaz *is*. We can give you the heaviest of anchors. A black hole that you can fall into

229

forever. One that will never let you blow away. That anchor in your pocket is almost shattered. Hurry! Obey, before it's too late!"

A single voice of many bubbled up from the cultists around the fire.

"*Obey! Obey! Obey! Obey! Obey!*"

The two cultists let go of Kelsey.

The cultists below danced and chanted.

The heartbeat quickened and quickened. Pounded more and more violently.

Chunks of the cavern roof began crashing down. A stalactite fell and skewered a cultist near the fire.

But the cultists kept chanting.

"*Obey! Obey! Obey! Obey! Obey!*"

Kelsey looked at the bound woman. She raised her arm and aimed the dagger at her chest.

Then the bound woman cried out, "I just want to see him again. Just one more time."

"I do, too," Kelsey hushed.

She plunged the dagger down.

Then turned on her heel.

And slid the blade up and across the ram-skull man's chest. The ram-skull man wailed out over the heartbeat.

Kelsey dropped the dagger, ignored the pain wracking her body, and ran to the giant doorframe. She paused as she reached its precipice. Every fiber of her being told her not to go in. But Kelsey ignored every fiber of her being and ran down the reeking hallway, toward its far-off door.

When she finally reached the handleless door at the hallway's end, Kelsey risked a look back. She saw the cultists surging toward her, the ram-skull man leading the pack. He pointed to her with his bronze staff. Its crystal hand seemed to reach out. Reach out with those deadly claws, primed to cut Kelsey up. Make her so small and fragmented that she wouldn't even exist at all.

"Bring her to the stone!" the ram-skull man roared. "Cut her up! Let An'giog-Metaz's bowels show her what her choice *really* means!"

Kelsey jammed her doorknob into the door and rushed through, down another hallway.

She ran and ran and finally came to the second hallway's end. She used her glass rose to open a second door.

Then a third hallway.

Then a third door.

A fourth, fifth, sixth.

More halls and doors than she could count. More strain on her doorknob than it could bear. It was so small. So light. So broken. A third petal fell off.

Each door led to a smaller hallway. Each hallway led to a smaller door. Eventually, Kelsey needed to slide sideways to fit between the walls and slump down to avoid the ceiling.

Kelsey pushed against the walls — they gave as if they were made of soft meat. The heartbeat pulsed through

231

them and invaded her skin. The doors stooped lower. The walls became wetter and slicker and tighter. An oily liquid flowed over the floor, so slippery that Kelsey fell onto her hands and knees. Blisters formed wherever the liquid touched.

Soon, she had to stay that way — crawling, burning — as the halls mutated into more and more unnatural spaces past each new door.

No. Not halls at all anymore. Intestines. Abscessed, tumored, and rotten.

A fecal reek wafted into Kelsey's face, a reek *so* similar to her dad's hospital room. The air became unbearable. Unrelenting. Kelsey forced a child-sized polyp out of the way and saw a final door. An oak door, too small for her to fit through.

No. Not oak. Not a door. A fiberglass casket lid that only *mimicked* oak.

Kelsey couldn't find a wooden casket at the first funeral home she went to — after the hospital gave her dad's corpse over. Something about a major fuck-up in the supply chain. But she only checked that one single funeral home. She could've kept looking. Should've. *Anyone* else would've kept looking. She should've found a funeral home with wooden caskets in stock. Real wood.

But she had just wanted it over with. All of it. So badly. So badly that she chose a fiberglass casket that only *mimicked* oak.

She had buried her dad in something he hated.

Kelsey stopped crawling. Acidic sludge filled her shoes and caked her limbs and wouldn't allow her to move. The intestine walls squeezed too tightly. Pulsed too violently. The gases burned her, inside and out.

Kelsey was suffocating. Being digested. Dying.

Then something latched onto her foot and twisted until all the ligaments in her ankle threatened to rip free from her bones. Kelsey pushed back a pulsing chunk of intestines and looked into a hundred burning eyes.

The ram-skull man was there, holding onto her. Behind him, the cultists pushed at the walls and slid closer and closer.

"See how wonderful and cramped it is in here?" The ram-skull man snapped Kelsey's ankle. She screamed. He laughed. "No need for that doorknob. Not anymore. No need for an anchor when your world's so small. Small, just like *you*."

The ram skull's mouth opened, and from the nothingness inside came, "*OBEY*!"

"*Help me*," Kelsey hushed.

Then Kelsey closed her eyes and drifted into a vast, black nothing.

No, not just black. There was *something* in the black. In the nothing.

A shape. Square.

A color. Yellow.

It was a sticky note. Something was written on it — written in a familiar hand.

It was a joke. A joke about a cult leader forgetting his robes at the dry cleaners — and wearing a nightgown to the sacrificial ritual instead.

That was it. That was her dad's last hospital-door sticky-note joke. That joke had made Kelsey laugh so loud that a nurse shushed her.

That joke would have made the ram-skull man furious.

Kelsey opened her eyes. She laughed into the open mouth of bone and turned her face to the wall of meat. She sank her teeth into the meat. The meat quivered as a howl from nowhere filled everywhere.

The ram-skull man let go of Kelsey's foot.

"What are you doing?" he screeched. "Stop! Please! Before-"

But the intestines began to shiver and roil, and all the cultists were swept away in its spasms. Only the ram-skull man's bronze staff remained, warping and corroding in the intestines' acid. Its crystal hand broke apart and melted away into nothing.

Definitely not a Johnson & Teague.

Kelsey chewed out chunks of the intestines and spat them out, threw up, and did it all over again.

And again. And again. And again.

Then Kelsey lifted her doorknob as high as she could. She squeezed what remained of its glass-rose knob as tight as she could. The glass broke apart and cut into her.

She didn't care.

Kelsey roared, stabbed her doorknob's bronze cylinder deep into the wounded intestines, and pulled down. The meat ripped open like wet tissue paper. She crawled through the wound. Out of the tube. Out of the tightness and the stench and the nightmare. Out into a vast, black nothing.

The heartbeat faded with each passing moment as the wound twirled off into the nothing, away from her, until it vanished.

And Kelsey felt weightless. Unbound. So different from the suffocation of those intestines. That one direction to crawl.

She looked around.

Nothing but black in every direction for infinite distance.

No, not just black. Tiny sparks of light speckled the black. And far-off streaks of color that were almost not there at all.

Space?

Kelsey gulped in air and held her breath — but how? She breathed in and out. In space.

Then she realized her hand was empty. No familiar touch of glass or metal. Just blood.

Kelsey turned and looked out into the dark. What remained of her doorknob floated there, just out of reach — a cloud of shimmering shards orbiting a bit of bronze. Like a tiny solar system.

Kelsey reached out, but the pieces wouldn't let her take them. They just twirled together, inching away bit by bit, winking with their hundred reflections of light.

She watched them for a long time. Maybe hours. Maybe eons. The pieces tumbled off into space, eventually fading to a single fleck that only caught stray light every now and then. Like a far-off star.

And then that star was gone.

Kelsey looked into her empty hand and closed it. She looked into the absence of definition all around her and felt a tension inside shatter.

"*Everywhere's infinite*," her dad had warned through his oxygen mask. "*There's infinite places.*"

Not a warning at all.

Kelsey breathed in and screamed and laughed.

She stretched out in all directions.

She began to grow.

Kelsey grew and grew until she dwarfed the cosmos. And even then, she was just a single atom compared to the infinite all around her.

She looked toward the spot where the shattered doorknob had disappeared — and still couldn't see it, even with her star-sized eyes. That made her happy for some reason. Happy for a doorknob. Happy for *pieces* of a doorknob. Kelsey laughed at herself and kept growing.

She reached into the darkness with arms as long as galaxies. With hands that cleared away solar systems.

She grabbed a handful of the fabric of space and
time.

She forced it into the shape of a doorknob.
She turned it.

Warmth

Aaron exited the tree line at fifteen past ten, dressed in black with a pack slung across his chest.

He had told his daughter, Katie, to have Jared in bed by now. He'd also told her to keep the heat off, no matter how cold it got.

He didn't have the cash to heat their single-wide.

Not in this weather.

Not in that trailer park, where snowstorms killed the power nine times out of ten.

Not with that shitty generator.

Not with gas as high as it was.

Those kids were lucky to have a roof over their heads, anyway. Especially Katie.

Aaron pulled his outer jacket tight against his neck and worked his gloved hands to chase off the numbness. A snowflake drifted down and landed on his knuckle. The snowstorm's final snowflake. For now.

The snowstorm had subsided halfway through his trek down the game path. The game path he had found three weeks ago. The game path that led to the house.

It was a nice house. A two-story beast crowning a hill, overlooking lots of land.

A castle, as far as Aaron was concerned.

The house even had a short tower jutting from the attic with a big, green, gaudy stained-glass window facing the woods — where no one could even see it. Aaron couldn't make out the pattern in the window, even with the help of the full moon's glow. Architects probably had some fancy name for that tower. Aaron would never need to know it, not with his bank account.

But the house was old, too. Sinking in on itself. Chipping paint and crumbling eaves said as much. Aaron never saw the lights on, even after a dozen stakeouts. A Cadillac sat in the garage, rusted and crippled on rotted tires. Still nicer than Aaron's P.O.S. pickup waiting for him back on the other side of the woods. The only hint of life inside the house was the mountain of fresh-delivery grocery boxes piled near the garage.

It all pointed to a recluse's house. A recluse on their last legs. Invalid, hopefully.

An easy house to rob.

Aaron cut through the side yard, but stopped halfway to the house when he felt the icy sting of wet feet in the Northeast winter. He looked down to see if he'd stepped in a puddle.

No, just sweat filling his shoes. He always sweated out nerves before shit like this.

Before stealing. Before armed robbery. Before drug deals.

Before pulling a child out of a pool, unmoving and blue.

Aaron shrugged off the pins and needles and memories and snuck around to the front, away from that fancy tower and its green stained-glass window. He reached the front door. Only the quietest creak of old porch wood said he was there at all. Aaron began to pick the lock.

It clicked.

Then something louder came.

The *boom* from behind made Aaron forget the cold for just a second. Gunshot?

He turned, almost stumbled, and pulled the gun from his jacket pocket.

No cop. No vigilante neighbor. Nothing but bright lights in the black sky.

New Year's fireworks at the neighbor's house.

Rich people didn't really have neighbors, though. The fireworks house sat at least half a mile away, on its own hilltop.

Aaron pocketed his gun — his lighter-that-looked-like-a-gun. Lucky it wasn't a cop. A cop would've shot the second they saw his gun-lighter, harmless birthday gift or not. His kids would feel bad if their birthday gift got him shot.

Or maybe they wouldn't.

"New year, new me," Aaron muttered.

He turned back, opened the door, and slipped inside the house just as another firework burst in the sky.

"Holy shit." Aaron's hushed words hung in the air as a puff of frozen breath.

Frozen — the best way to describe the feeling cutting at his skin. A cold that nearly forced Aaron back into the winter night, just to warm up. He crouched and put his hand to a vent. Felt air. Should've been warm. *Was* warm, he thought. But somehow *wasn't*.

He told himself his trailer wasn't this cold. His kids weren't this cold.

Aaron moved on from the entrance to case the rest of the house, ignoring the deep chill as he searched.

He made his way down a narrow entry hall — after writing off some stairs leading up to a closed door. Best to focus on the lower level in case he had to grab and run. That's what his mom had taught him.

At least the floor was carpeted. Nice and muffled.

The entry hall ended, split left and right. Aaron peeked right. A dark hall. He peeked left. A den. He chose the den, got out his dollar-store flashlight, and crept in.

Big, but barren. Aaron sensed the absence of a life.

No framed photos, just cheap oil paintings.

No TV, just booze bottles.

No signs of family, memory. No boardgames or sports shit for visiting grandkids.

Just an empty fireplace. An unused couch. A very-used recliner. A sidetable by the recliner. A rotary phone on the sidetable. A coffee table between recliner and couch. A battery-powered lantern on the coffee table.

That's it. That's all the big den offered.

That — and dust.

Aaron covered his mouth and tensed his chest. A cough struggled behind his ribs. It died in his throat just before escaping.

He lifted his foot. A plume came up with it. He looked back to see his footprints in the dust, clear as his trail through the snow outside.

A firework burst, lighting the den through a window. The air shimmered with particulate. All those sparkling flecks looked like falling snow. Or ash after a fire — like the fire that had taken Aaron's house years ago. The fire that had forced him into that trailer park to rot with those kids.

The fire that had burned away his future.

Aaron moved into the conjoining room. A dining room. He riffled through piles of opened mail, emptied booze bottles, and other trash on the food-bare dining table.

Nothing worthwhile. He moved on to the kitchen through the next doorway.

242

Pretty normal kitchen. A door to the side yard in here, too. He tested the handle. Locked, with a key-only lock on the *inside*. Strange. Aaron hunted around but didn't spot anything valuable in plain sight.

Just lemon-flavored candies. Boxes and boxes of them. All opened. Most emptied.

He opened a counter drawer and spied silver.

"Finally." Aaron unzipped his pack and retrieved some tape. He wrapped up the silverware, then shoved the haul and the tape back into his pack. Stale food clung to the utensils. Poorly washed. And tarnished. Still worth cash. Cash for some kids' toys?

No. His kids were lucky to get food. Especially Katie.

Aaron crept on from the kitchen. He found a room being used as a makeshift dump, trash piled to the ceiling. The room reeked of old food. One side of the trash pile had collapsed and toppled against a door across the room. Not worth climbing over there. Not yet.

"Come on, you shithole house," Aaron dared. "Surprise me."

He knelt to pick through the pile.

Then his flashlight died.

Then a firework cracked outside.

Then a shout came from somewhere upstairs.

"*Leave!*"

Aaron shot up, bit his tongue at the sound of his knees popping. He dropped his flashlight and doubled back to the kitchen as someone shambled around above him.

"Leave me alone!" the voice yelled. "Why can't you just leave me *alone*!"

The upstairs presence moved around haphazardly. Aaron retraced his steps exactly.

The voice came again as Aaron passed from dining room to den.

"No, I don't want to talk about peaches!" A door slammed somewhere. "Fuck off!"

More shuffling.

Just as Aaron made it halfway down the entry hall, just as he sighted the front door — the stairs leading up to that closed door started to creak. The banister started to shake. A leg came into view.

Aaron doubled back, turned right, and shot down the dark hall he had decided against earlier, in favor of the den. He nearly crashed into a closed door in the blackness. He turned the handle. Open. He pushed. Blocked. The trash-blocked door.

Aaron spun around and headed back. He dashed into the den just as a figure rounded the bottom of the stairs.

No, two figures. Aaron heard one of them lock the front door. With keys.

He thought of the side door in the kitchen. Its key-only, inside lock.

Trapped.

"…and *that's* why I like licorice over peppermint," a child exclaimed, "even at Christmas time!" The warm voice sounded *wrong* in the cold, dead space. "You loved lemon candies and only lemon candies, 'member? 'Cause on account they was colored like Quagmire's skull?"

Aaron slipped into the dining room, nearly clipping a chair with his hip.

"I don't know you, freak," the older voice growled. "I hate lemon."

Aaron glanced back just before pivoting to the kitchen — just in time to see an old man in a ragged robe and loose pajamas shamble into the den. Even bent-backed, the old man was massive. Six-foot-eight at least. And broad.

Aaron looked for a place to hide. Saw a dark corner beside the fridge. Shit spot. Better than nothing.

He ran to the corner and flattened himself to the wall and refused to breathe.

"Don't be gettin' all grouchy, now," the child teased. Tiny footfalls grew louder. "I'm gonna try and find you some lemon ones."

Little feet skipped through the dining room. Little hands riffled through drawers and piles of trash on the kitchen counters. Dust started to fly.

"In here, maybe," the child mused.

Aaron breathed in. Dust filled his nose.

"Nope, all ate up. Here, maybe?"

The child — a boy — popped out in front of Aaron right as he coughed.

245

"Oh! Hi, mister," the boy chimed. He smiled. His teeth were cracked and shattered — the teeth that weren't missing outright. The ruined white of his smile contrasted with his blackened lips.

Blackened *everything*.

Charred skin rained off the boy's shoulders. His head. His chest. His limbs. Everywhere. Burned as bad as Aaron's old house.

But the boy's eyes. So alive. Blue as spring skies. Blue as the lining of a cheap above-ground pool.

"You here to see Ritchie?" The boy cocked his head. A sheet of his scalp fell to the floor. He turned and yelled, "Ritchie, you got yourself a visitor! I didn't even know you had friends!"

Aaron blurted out the only thing his brain could manage. "You... look like the marshmallows my kids cook over campfires."

The blue-eyed burned boy giggled.

The old man walked over with the battery-powered lantern in one hand and something else in the other.

A .357 Magnum revolver.

"I said *never* call me that," the old man warned. He jabbed the gun into the burned boy's temple. "I don't know you and..."

The old man noticed Aaron.

Neither moved. Aaron too scared, the old man too lost.

"Who are you? Are you real?" The old man poked Aaron's shoulder with the gun. His breath stank of alcohol and rot. "What… what are you doin' here?" The old man's eyes fell to the pack at Aaron's chest.

"I'm just going," Aaron mumbled. He moved, but so did the gun. He stopped.

"No, no you…" The old man unzipped the pack. Silver shimmered inside. "You're robbing me. You're *robbing* me!" He ripped the pack away.

Aaron felt the gun press up to his stomach. His kids hadn't eaten dinner. Their stomachs were empty.

The burned boy tugged at the old man's sleeve. "Nah, Ritchie, this fella was just leav-"

"Shut up, pig!" The old man shoved the boy away and returned his attention to Aaron. "In there. Now!" He gestured the way back to the den.

So Aaron walked — through the kitchen, through the dining room, to the den. He almost ran for the front door, but he remembered hearing the lock. He turned around to the old man and the burned boy behind him.

"Look, man, I can just go. I-"

"Sit, pig," the old man ordered. He waved the gun at the couch. "Sit or I'll shoot you in the guts and watch you die right here."

Aaron sat on the couch and prayed. The burned boy sat beside him and hummed. The old man sat in the recliner and wheezed while he searched through Aaron's pack.

Stolen silverware.

Faded ski mask.

Gum.

Tape.

Lock picks.

Wallet with seven dollars.

Aaron recalled the birth of his kids a thousand times over. The house fire a thousand times over. The last time he kissed his wife a thousand times over. Katie lying at the bottom of that pool a thousand times over. Sweat filled his gloves, his shoes. Soaked his sweater, his pants.

A firework went off.

The old man leaned forward and set the battery-powered lantern back on the coffee table. "My name," he grumbled as he dropped Aaron's pack by his feet, "is Richard."

Aaron couldn't stop shaking. "That's a great name. Mine's-"

"You don't get a name in here!" Richard bared his teeth like a beast.

Another firework went off.

The burned boy patted Aaron's shoulder. His little hand left behind a sheen of ash. "I'm Billy," the boy beamed. "Well, really it's '*William*', but I like '*Billy*' better! And Richard prefers '*Ritchie*'."

Richard glared at Billy. "Don't call me that. I don't know you." The old man looked back at Aaron, straining his eyes. "Can't see you very well, pig. Let's get a look."

Aaron leaned into the lantern light. Sweat dripped off his nose and froze on the coffee table.

Richard smiled. "Ah, white, huh? Good ol' white trash. Figured you'd be a nigger, come to steal from my nice ol' house. Or a wetback, maybe. Not many of either up here, though. Tons back in Georgia."

Aaron only half-heard the insults. They weren't new. "Just put the gun down, please."

"Nah, I don't think I will." Richard tapped the gun on the rotary phone. "You're goin' to jail, you know that? Goin' to jail to get fucked like a faggot. But before that, I got uses for you. And the power to get it from you." Richard smirked. "Not that it takes much to get shit from white trash. Offer some painkillers and copper wire, and you're on board."

Billy frowned. "Ritchie, don't be rude. Be nice and sweet like when-"

"Shut up!" Richard bellowed. He closed his eyes and held his head for a long time, like something inside his skull was burning. When the old man's eyes opened, they were cold and back on Aaron. "Get up, pig. I got movin' for you to do."

Aaron stood. His legs nearly gave out. "Just call the cops, man. *Please*. Just call them."

His kids would be fine with him in prison. Better off, even. Happy, even.

"Move!" Richard waved the gun toward the dining room. "Wait, no. Not yet."

Richard fished around in the dark space between the recliner and sidetable. He pulled out an electrical cord.

"Tie your feet." The old man tossed Aaron his restraints. "Three loops 'round each ankle, nice and tight... and plenty'a knots! I want to see that cord dig into that white-trash skin."

Aaron obeyed. Handicapped himself.

Richard grunted. "Good pig. Now, to the kitchen door. Move!"

Aaron death-marched to the kitchen, Richard behind and Billy beside. He felt the boy's warm, crisped hand grab his own.

"Ritchie didn't always used to be like this," Billy said as they reached the kitchen's side door. "He used to be really nice, 'specially-"

Richard shoved Billy to the floor. The old man pulled out a ring of keys and unlocked the side door. Then Richard grabbed Aaron by the collar and dragged him outside.

"See that kindlin'?" Richard pointed off into the dark. Piles and piles of limbs and chopped wood, all wrapped into large bundles with twine, lined the side yard's border with the woods.

"Yeah." Aaron scratched his head. He had missed those when he was casing the place. No, they hadn't been there. How'd an old man do all that?

"Bring 'em inside."

"*All* of them?" Aaron lost count of the bundles in the dark. There were at least thirty. "That'll take a long time."

"Bring 'em in!" Richard cocked the revolver.

"*Okay*. Please, j- just relax." Aaron shuffled over to the closest bundle.

Richard and Billy followed.

"I... *might'a* went a little nuts with the wood-gatherin'," Billy admitted. "But you can't have yourself a fire without fuel, now can you?"

"If you run," Richard warned as Aaron heaved up the first bundle, "I'll shoot you in the back. Let you freeze out here. I'm important 'round here. To the cops. Law people. People care about people like me. They won't care at all if I shoot someone like *you*."

Aaron ground his teeth and headed back to the house with the first bundle.

Then the second. Then the third.

Then another, and another, and another.

"I was important all the way back," Richard rambled as Aaron made his seventh trip. "Pa had a huge farm down in southeast Georgia. But *I* ran it, mostly. He trusted me, is why. Loved me. Spent every second he could with me."

Aaron dropped off the tenth batch of wood by the fireplace, next to a rusted-out wheelbarrow he hadn't noticed before. And weren't the walls normal earlier? Smooth? Painted a boring shade of white like any house? Now, untreated timber jutted through in places, breaching the surface like the ribs of some rotting animal.

Richard continued while Aaron toiled. "We had a bunch'a poor niggers working for us. Not slaves, but might

251

as well've been." The old man smiled as Aaron heaved two bundles — bundles fifteen and sixteen — onto his shoulders. "Those pigs were lazy, but you white trash were always the laziest. So entitled."

"What is it with you and pigs?" Aaron muttered.

Richard glared at him. The old man didn't speak. Just loomed in the dark, giant and angry.

Aaron lowered his gaze and headed back inside, into the house that made the winter seem warm.

He piled the wood in the kitchen, next to a barrel of wheat. Before he could make another trip, Richard blocked the doorway.

"You hear me?" the old man asked.

"Yeah," Aaron answered.

"You believe me?" the old man asked, more insistently.

"Yes, I'm entitled." Aaron considered grabbing the gun. Close enough. Richard's finger was closer to the trigger, though. And the old man's *size*. What about pulling out his gun-lighter? Faking it?

"No," the old man snorted, "'bout me bein' important. My pa lovin' me."

"What? Sure, man."

"Good, good." Richard coughed and looked off into the woods. "Keep working."

The next six trips' worth of wood went in a previously-bare corner of the den — a corner where a pile of dry-rotted saddles now sat. A field mouse ran out from under them when Aaron dropped off the first of the bundles. Hooks now sprouted from the walls. Farm tools had grown from them. Most of the carpet had receded, replaced with rough planks and scattered straw and packed earth.

At least the dust went with it.

"It's true, you know," Richard boasted on the twenty-fourth trip. "We had all the money we needed thanks to pigs like you. Well, thanks to our skill in bossin' you."

Aaron stepped back outside. Each time, his legs primed a bit more. His eyes tagged the game path a bit longer.

His kids had put him in that trailer. He didn't deserve to be alone with them, their responsibility.

But they didn't deserve to be this cold. Not even Katie.

The *fucking cord*, though. Aaron kept filling the house with kindling.

And Richard kept droning on.

"...whole town basically used our farm as a bank. Traded goods for capital, loans, whatnot. Had a ledger in Pa's office keepin' up with what everyone owed us, and everyone owed us plenty."

Billy groaned and rolled his blue eyes. He was practically invisible on that stump along the tree line, burned flesh camouflaged with tree bark and dark.

Aaron had almost forgotten that a child's corpse was keeping him company. That child's corpse was now cradling a chicken — a chicken captured from somewhere in the kitchen.

Weird how Aaron had missed the chicken. And the cow by the fridge. And the donkey braying somewhere up on the house's second floor.

"Oh Ritchie, quit your fibbin'." Billy dropped the chicken. It clucked and ran into the woods. "Dealsmiths was the rich ones. With all them peaches. You were poor as all us 'round there. Well, 'til way after, when you found Quagmire's-"

"Quiet!" Richard kicked Billy off the stump, leaving a house-slipper impression in the boy's charred sternum. "I don't know you. This is the last chance I'm givin' you. Shut. Your. *Mouth*."

The old man walked off a ways and held his head.

Aaron kept an eye on Richard while he motioned for Billy. The boy skipped over to help Aaron with bundle twenty-nine.

"Found what?" Aaron prodded. "Quagmire's what? You mentioned that earlier."

"Mhmmm," Billy chimed. "Quagmire's skull!"

Aaron could see the cooked tendons of Billy's shoulders flex as the boy helped lift the wood.

"Was a legend 'round our parts way back…" Billy paused, grew wide-eyed, "…'til it *weren't* no legend no more."

Aaron leaned in a bit closer. Walked a bit slower. The two wood carriers reached the house and went in without the old man.

"What is it?" Aaron whispered.

"Quagmire's skull? A skull, duh. What else?" Billy giggled. "But coated in gold! Said ol' Ernest Quagmire killed his prospectin' partner and dipped his cut-off head in melted gold after he went nuts way back. Buried it good and deep before he got caught and lynched in 1666."

Aaron shooed a goat off the kitchen counter and heaved the wood up.

"And?" Aaron asked.

A smile crept onto Billy's face, the smile of a child with a secret to spill.

Katie and Jared did the same thing with Aaron. They'd share a little to get him to ask for the rest. Talk with them. They made it a game. It annoyed Aaron. Especially when Katie did it.

"*And*?" Aaron asked again.

Billy leaned in, smelling of cooked meat. "And Ritchie-"

Aaron didn't hear Richard enter. Didn't see the revolver until it clacked against Billy's head. He felt pieces of burned skull pepper his face.

A firework went off. Billy fell down.

"I said *shut up*!" Richard roared.

Aaron had pulled Katie out of that pool as fast as he could. Jared cried somewhere in the background as Aaron laid Katie down in uncut grass, cold and unmoving. He yelled at her for getting in by herself while she lay still.

Billy lay in the same pose, burned and unmoving, on the wooden floor next to a burlap sack labeled '*Dealsmith Fresh Produce*'. A smiling-peach logo was stamped above the words.

"Don't you talk again, you… *thing*." Richard kicked Billy.

"Stop!" Aaron made a move for Richard.

Richard put the gun to Aaron's forehead. "And *you*. You know I was- I *am* important. You said so yourself. I *don't* need no gold lie to make people be with me!" He flicked the gun toward the door. "No more talking. Just work."

So there was no more talking. Just Aaron's panting and Richard's wheezing.

The dining room took eight bundles on and around the dining table. The kitchen took twelve total.

All the free space in the den and entry hall slowly filled with wood — all the space not taken up by the butter churns that had appeared around trip seventeen. Or the busted tractor around trip thirty-two. Or the chicken coops around trip forty-five.

Pigs grunted from the room that once housed the giant trash pile. Both doors to the pig-room were padlocked now. Richard wouldn't unlock those doors to let Aaron put wood in there. Wouldn't even look at those doors.

Hours trudged by.

Hours of moving wood.

Hours of the neighbors not running out of fireworks.

Hours of stepping over Billy.

Aaron looked to the forest. One more bundle to bring in. Bundle fifty-seven.

One more chance to run.

He walked to the bundle. Started to bend down. Started to lean forward. Started to push off. He could snap the cord. His legs were strong enough, maybe. Or just crawl. Get behind a tree. Find a sharp rock.

Anything.

Then Aaron thought of Richard's bulk. His cruelty. The gun.

Aaron lifted the wood and shuffled back up his footpath worn into the snow.

He expected a quick strike to the back of the head once he finished — at best. A bullet buried in the back of the head at worst.

But before Aaron could find out which ending Richard had chosen, Billy jumped out of the doorway and scared the shit out of him.

"*Arrghh!*" the boy screamed.

Aaron fell back. The wood bundle landed on top of him. A snapped branch slid across his thigh. Let hot blood out. The blood steamed off his pants leg.

"Oh Gosh!" Billy rushed to Aaron. "I'm so sorry. I'm *so*, so sorry!" His little hands trembled. Tears flowed from his blue eyes and seeped into the blackened cracks in his cheeks.

Richard groaned and gripped his head. "Why do you always have to come back…"

"Don't worry about it," Aaron reassured Billy. He pushed the wood off and gave a good, loud yell. Loud enough to muddle the *crack* when he broke off the tip of the branch that had cut him. Very sharp edge — nearly knife-sharp. The branch tip almost cut his jacket pocket when he slipped it in with his gun-lighter. "Help me get this last one inside, kid."

Aaron and Billy carried the final bundle into the den. Only place left to set it was the couch's third seat — after they shoved off a pile of horseshoes.

"Don't judge Ritchie too hard," Billy sighed. The boy sat by the wood and picked at some bark. The bark mirrored his crisped skin. "He's had it rough."

Aaron sat down by Billy and looked up. That fancy tower with its stained-glass window was somewhere above his head. "Yeah, *rough.*"

"Ain't talkin' 'bout money," Billy murmured.

"What, then?" Aaron side-eyed Richard as the old man entered the room, breath more visible inside than out.

Billy only said, "I hope he don't use his bullet on you."

Richard plopped into his recliner and sneered at Aaron, gun raised. "Worked good for white trash. Don't you feel 'complished?"

258

Some straw jutted from the couch cushion and poked at Aaron's side. "I did what you wanted. Point that gun somewhere else."

"I'll point it wherever the hell I wanna point it in *my* house! See?" Richard jabbed the gun at Aaron. "See?" He jabbed it at Billy. "See?" He pressed it to his own temple and stamped his foot on the floor. The wood planks shook. A scraggly cat ran out of the fireplace, into the dark.

The gun shifted back to Aaron.

"Okay, sir," Aaron managed, "okay. Just relax, *please*. I have kids. Their names are Ja-"

"No!" Richard yelled. "No names for you *or* your trash kids!"

The old man slammed the gun onto the sidetable. The rotary phone toppled off and clacked to the floor. A corn snake crawled out of its transmitter and slithered off to hunt for warmth.

Richard closed his eyes and seethed for a long time. Aaron waited.

Richard grew still for a long time. Aaron waited.

Richard finally opened his eyes.

"You called me '*Sir*'. I like that. Used to hear it a lot." The old man smiled. "Why'd you try stealin' from a house with a person in it anyways, pig? Dumbfuck move."

"I thought you were bedridden or something," Aaron explained. "I never saw you leave."

"Huh?" Richard scratched his head and flicked the gun at Billy. "How'd you know that freak never leaves?"

Billy just sat there and whistled a tune, oblivious and happy.

"You. Never saw *you* leave." Aaron flexed his legs. The cut on his thigh burned. The cord around his ankles chafed. "I watched for a while."

"Rootin' around my home like a… goddamn loose *pig*!" Richard spat on the coffee table. "Should'a shot you out there like the animal you are. Probably still will. But I'm cold."

The old man struggled up, walked to the couch, and pulled a combat knife from his waistband. He cut the twine around the wood bundle next to Billy — then pressed the blade up against Billy's cheek. After holding the knife to the boy's face for a long moment, Richard tossed a box of matches into Aaron's lap. "Fire. Now."

Richard returned to his recliner.

Aaron grabbed an armful of wood and shuffled to the fireplace. He knelt and fed in the fuel, then struck a match against the box.

Nothing.

Then nothing for three more matches.

"I like sticks." Billy giggled and pulled a long, thin branch out of the bundle. "They remind me of swords. Hey, Ritchie, 'member when we'd pretend-"

"You wanna know where I got this knife?" Richard twirled the blade around in his hand.

Aaron looked back at Billy, playing with his stick-sword. Then he looked back at Richard, doing everything he could to ignore Billy. "Sure."

"Sure, *what*?" Richard warned.

"Sure, *sir*," Aaron grumbled.

Another match head broke off. Aaron grabbed a golfball-sized stone from the fireplace and started striking matches against it.

The old man grunted and stretched in his chair. He tapped the knife on a diesel engine that had replaced his sidetable. "'Nam, all the way back in the summer of 1963."

Something lit up in Aaron's mind, unlike the matches.

Aaron's dad would beat the shit out of Aaron when he was a kid. Aaron's dad beat him because Aaron's dad was a mean drunk. Aaron's dad drank because Aaron's dad wanted to forget about the Vietnam War.

And when Aaron's dad was drunk and in a beating mood, Aaron's dad would always mumble out war stories between beer belches and belt swings.

Aaron heard a lot of war stories. Remembered them, too.

Another match refused to light on the stone.

Richard sighed. "I miss it. Killing all those slant-eyed jungle crawlers in... wherever we was. I was good at it. Was over there all the way 'til the end. Ask my old buddies. I was in the army. Ask anyone. They never left my side. Never disobeyed. They all called me '*Sir*', just like you."

Billy tapped his stick against the battery-powered lantern. Honey bees buzzed around in its light.

"Oh Ritchie, you used to be sweet as peaches. What happened?" The boy sighed.

"Shut up, freak," Richard bit.

Aaron pocketed the stone. It joined the branch tip and gun-lighter. He went back to trying the matchbox.

"We got up to all sorts'a shit, me and my squad." Richard gazed up. Wood beams now jutted through the vaulted ceiling. "I was a commander, so I let it all slide. All the fun with the locals. Shootin' them. Making them race to see who'd get shot instead'a skinned. Having fun with their ladies. Burning…"

Richard paused.

Aaron sensed a wound in the pause. "What was that last one?"

"Shut your trash mouth," Richard growled.

"Ritchie…" Billy started.

"You, too!" The old man got up and moved toward Billy. "Or I'll cave in your skull again!"

Aaron stood. Put himself between the two. Drew attention.

He never tried to stop the other trailer park kids from picking on Katie. Even after the pool. Even with Katie's breathing problems after the pool. The trailer park kids nicknamed her 'wheezer wimp'.

"When did you say you were in Vietnam?" Aaron tossed Richard the matches. "These aren't catching."

Richard returned to his recliner, gun and match in one hand, matchbox and knife in the other. "In '62. You heard me." He started striking. "What kinda moron can't light a match."

"Ground troops weren't over there until 1965." Aaron sat by Billy, eyes locked on Richard. "So when were you there? What regiment were you with? Company? My dad never shut up about-"

"You fucked up these matches." Richard dropped the matchbox to the floor, down by Aaron's pack. "I *was* there. I was in 'Nam. And you're gonna sit here with me and show me the respect I deserve."

"Sure, man."

Aaron counted the seconds that Richard's eyes tried to be anywhere — anywhere, except even with his own.

Six.

Katie had looked away for six seconds when she promised she wouldn't go swimming. When she promised she didn't have her swimsuit on under her dress. When she promised she understood the danger of swimming unsupervised.

And Aaron had lied about believing her while he lay on the floor of his trailer, drunk and drugged up and angry at everything. He hadn't looked away at all.

Aaron sat back down on the couch — but his mind didn't stay with him on that couch, or in this cold house, or on this night. It went *back*.

He saw Katie in his mind, at the bottom of that pool. Saw his reflection. Saw himself reaching through his reflection. Pulling her out through his reflection.

He held his head and begged the thoughts to stop.

Then Richard's stomach growled.

"I'm hungry." The old man stood. He pointed the gun at Aaron. "Make me food."

Aaron lifted his head. "What?"

Richard cocked his head. "Make. Me. Food."

"I'll help!" Billy sprang up and lost a few layers of skin, a few chips of shattered skull. The boy grabbed Aaron's hand and led him through the maze of firewood to the kitchen.

Richard followed.

Aaron started searching for a pan. He tried the kitchen light switches. Nothing. Maybe the house's wiring had turned into chickenwire. He glanced at the solid wood wall where the side door used to be. The handle was still there, embedded and askew in rough timber.

Planks had grown over all the windows. Moonglow snaked in through the cracks.

Was the front door gone, too?

He grabbed a cast-iron skillet hanging from a nail, next to some work gloves. A bird had built a nest inside the left-hand glove.

"What'll the war hero have?" Aaron clanked the skillet onto the stove, the last thing in the kitchen that hadn't transformed in some way.

The cow by the half-wooden fridge mooed.

"I'll have some eggs," Richard sneered, "useless *pig*." He pointed the gun at Aaron.

Then the pigs trapped in the trash room started to squeal.

Then they started to push at their padlocked door.

Then they started to ram it. Break it.

"*No!*" Richard rushed to the door. "Help!" he screamed.

Aaron had ignored Jared when his son screamed for someone — *anyone* — to come pull Katie out of that pool. He ignored his son's screams for four minutes.

Aaron ran to Richard — ran as fast as the cord would allow. He and Billy reached the bulging pig-door and braced against it alongside the old man.

Richard screeched after each squeal. He bashed the gun against his temple after each bash at the door.

The pigs squealed louder and louder. The door warped and bulged. Its wood grew hot, almost too hot to touch. The doorknob shivered and loosened. Smoke poured out from the padlock's keyhole.

Aaron felt his bones vibrate, his muscles strain and bruise. Some strange, sweet, salty smell confused his nose. And what about the room's other door? Was it safe? Would the pigs — the *things* — crash through that door? Escape? Tear through the house and find them? Aaron ignored the unreality of it all and yelled and pushed as hard as he could.

The smoke finally receded, the heat finally died, and the animals finally relented.

Richard recoiled and collapsed onto a pile of potato sacks.

"You shut up in there," the old man whined. "You goddamn *things*. Shut up!"

Aaron sighed and headed back to the stove with Billy in tow. He leaned over to the boy and joked, "Guess bacon's a '*no*'."

Richard staggered back in. "*Don't* you talk about bacon."

Aaron looked at Richard. Saw a craze in the old man's eyes. "Whatever you say."

"Don't talk about bacon..." Richard muttered it over and over on his way to the dining table — the four Dealsmith-branded crates that had replaced the dining table. He pushed a pile of corn husks out of a chair and sat down.

Billy snatched up two eggs from a chicken nest by the cow and returned to Aaron's side. "Can you cook 'em over-easy? That's Ritchie's favorite."

"Yeah." Aaron smiled, just a little, without meaning to. "That's how my kids like them." He clicked the stove eye on while Billy cracked the eggs over the skillet. Aaron couldn't remember the last time he cooked his kids eggs for breakfast. Served them anything besides off-brand cereal. His smile faded.

The eye lit, singeing some loose hay down near the flame. Aaron grimaced. "Hope this fucked-up nightmare house doesn't burn down when I cook them."

Richard glared at Aaron through the dining room's doorway. "This house is more than you'll *ever* have in your whole white-trash life."

Aaron glared back.

The scent of cooking eggs came, but the eye gave off no heat. Aaron's fingers tingled in the cold, even with his gloves on.

"How you think I got all this?" Richard asked. "This house. This land."

"Tenacity and tact, I'm sure." Aaron flipped the eggs with a hand shovel, the closest thing to a spatula he could find.

"Like… thumbtacks?" Billy cocked a cooked eyebrow.

Richard spat on the floor. "Yeah, it *was* tact. I traded in the farm and headed up here to start a shipping business, 'cause that's what people like me do. We find new mountains and we mount 'em."

Aaron rolled his eyes and looked for a plate. He settled for a barrel lid.

"Why not just stay in Georgia?" Aaron walked the meal over to Richard and dropped it onto the crates.

Richard dug in with his gun-free hand.

"Because *fuck* Georgia," the old man growled. Then, barely audible, "Good eggs."

Billy skipped over to the crate-table and sat on a small barrel, across from Richard.

"I liked Georgia," the boy said. "It was nice and toasty, not like up here. And Dealsmith's peaches was *so* sweet. 'Member-"

"Weren't nothing left there," Richard interrupted. "No family. No friends. No *nothing*. I'd… heard up north was nice." He belched and fished a box of lemon candies out from under a wood bundle. There were no candies inside. Only sawdust and nails.

"*Nice,*" Aaron mocked. He leaned against a splintery wood beam and breathed out a frozen breath. His kids' breath did the same thing inside their trailer. Not quite as bad, but still. Anywhere down south would be better than up here.

But a move like that required cash. And Aaron would never have that kind of cash. He looked at Richard's outfit. How hadn't the old man frozen to death in those pajamas?

Then Aaron noticed the keyring poking out of Richard's pants pocket.

The old man snorted and spat out some eggshell. "I got a huge shipping business goin', so yeah, *nice*."

"What shipping business?" Aaron asked. "I've worked a few warehouses."

"Stole from 'em, you mean," Richard snarked.

Aaron laughed. Loud. Loud enough to make Richard and Billy jerk. He took a cord-hindered step toward the old man, hunched in his chair. Richard shrank back a bit.

Aaron pulled a milk stool over and sat down next to Richard. Close.

"So it's bullshit," Aaron stung, "like your *'Nam days*."

Aaron reached for the keys. Just barely, just enough for the grab to seem like nothing.

He missed.

"It was Gold Road Freight," Richard grumbled. The gun shook a bit. "Worked it up to five locations. Had a whole workforce who depended on me. They'd send me gifts every Christmas, like family."

"Never heard of it," Aaron said. No. A tiny speck of truth to that, logged away somewhere in his mind. "Wait... I *have*. This old shit at Siegson said he got laid off from there, way back. Said it got bought out by McShare. Saved it from drowning from what..." Katie hadn't drowned. Not really. He had pulled her out as fast as he could. "...uh, from what I heard. Definitely not five locations, either."

"You don't know *shit*." Richard dug his nails into the crate-table. "I got the best deal I could'a got when I sold it. The best deal *anyone* could'a got! 'Cause it was worth something, unlike *you*. You don't even understand business. You're just *trash*. No one depends on you."

It had to be close to zero outside by now. Or a few below. How cold was Aaron's trailer? The warmest spot was in the back-east corner. A transformer sat right outside. At least the kids' room was back there.

"Bet those people who *depended* on you got fucked before you felt any squeeze," Aaron rasped. "I've been there. Even when owners fail, they make sure everyone else fails first."

Two weeks after the fire. That's when the towing company cut Aaron. *Redundancy layoffs*. The fire had just hit at a bad time. The company needed to manage costs. Nothing personal.

Might as well have chunked him into a meat grinder.

"I did my best!" Richard protested.

Aaron looked around. Nice house, even half-mutated into a barn. "Definitely did best for you."

Richard shivered with anger. Maybe some shame. "You'd've done the same. All you trash do is murder and steal in your little slums. You'd sell your soul to get out. Your kids' souls. That's why you're here *right now*! Tryin' to steal and thieve your way outta your trash life!"

"Steal *what*, dude?" Aaron laughed. "What do you *have*?"

"I got plenty!"

Aaron laughed again. "You don't have shit. All you have is an empty house and a little ghost."

Richard hurled his half-eaten eggs at the wall. They splattered all over an old tarp hanging from some nails. The tarp had been a painting of a sailboat before the house started shifting.

Richard growled, "You just aren't strong enough to go get it. You're too *weak* to help your family."

270

Aaron leaned in again. Reached for the keys again.

"My house burned down. *That's* why I'm stuck in a shitty trailer park. Not because I can't *go get it*. I put all the cash I had into that house. Every fucking penny. Then it was *gone*! Now I gotta take care of two kids alone, with *nothing*. What's your excuse for being all alone in this big, empty shithole?"

Aaron leaned back. He clenched the ring of keys in his hand. Sweat filled his glove.

"Fire?" Richard's tone cooled. "Did anyone die?"

"No," Aaron muttered. Unless he counted whatever future *him* could've existed.

"Wife?" Richard asked. "Where's she?"

"Gone. Amy took off with our cash half a year later. What was left."

Amy.

The name tasted sour. Sounded foreign. When was the last time Aaron had uttered his own wife's name aloud?

"I don't know where she went," Aaron continued. "She's a drug addict, so who knows." He couldn't shut himself up. "So am I, but I only started after the fire… to deal with what my life turned into." Why couldn't he shut up? "Maybe she's dead… or maybe she's alive. I don't give a shit either way."

Amy had already been gone for a year when Katie got into that pool. Aaron wondered how fast his wife would've pulled their daughter out.

"All those kids got is… *me*… now."

Aaron squeezed the keys hard enough to push them through his glove. Through his skin. Then he slipped them into his pocket. They rested against the stone, branch tip, and gun-lighter.

"Well, that's… better than nothing." Richard's words gave off a sour sort of kindness. "Not by much, but kids should have someone. And they should be grateful for it."

Aaron always told his kids to be *grateful* for his bare minimum. Especially Katie.

"I had a family, too," Richard said. "Have. Have one. More trouble than it's worth."

"Didn't see any pictures of family anywhere," Aaron noted.

Richard struggled up. Billy went to steady him. The old man didn't thank the boy, but he didn't refuse the aid.

"Why would I show 'em off?" Richard spat. "They left me *alone*." He waved the gun, ushered Aaron to the den. "I met my wife up here. Made a son. Took care of 'em. And they *both* left me… like your wife left you."

The den wasn't a den anymore. No modern amenities. No shitty oil paintings. No dusty carpet or smooth walls or vaulted ceilings. Just a twisted lie of a barn.

Only one thing remained unchanged, untarnished — the battery-powered lantern.

Aaron and Billy sat on some stacked pallets where the couch once rested while Richard rummaged in a milk crate beside his recliner-that-was-now-a-hay-bale.

The old man threw a cowhide binder onto a giant wirespool that had taken the coffee table's place. Aaron pulled the binder over and opened it.

Page after page of photographs, newspaper clippings, and magazine cutouts, all neat and safe in plastic sleeves. Most of the photographs captured shots of nature, but a rare few captured people.

"I got family." Richard fished a whiskey bottle out from his hay-bale seat. "Family that don't deserve me." He opened it and drank deep.

Billy gasped and pointed to an old photo as Aaron flipped. It captured a little boy, expressionless, standing in front of a smiling woman and a scowling man. The man had to be Richard — a few decades removed. The woman's smile didn't even come close to hiding the truth beneath it.

"Aw, is that your boy?" Billy smiled ear-to-charred-ear. "He got the same forehead freckles you had. I always thought they suited you."

Richard took a huge swig and grabbed his head.

"Be quiet," he hissed. "*Please* be quiet."

Aaron waited until Richard looked back up. "Your wife's pretty."

Richard drank again. "Bitch ran off with my boy two weeks after that pit'chure. Both done it together, decided to leave me."

"How come?" Billy asked.

"Because they were *weak*," Richard seethed. "I just tried to make them *strong*. I tried to make them strong and they were too weak to take it!"

Aaron leaned back. "Did you hit them?"

Richard scratched at the bottle and wheezed and didn't answer.

"Where are they now?" Aaron asked.

"Wife died." Richard drank. Most spilled down his shirt. "Son's… I don't know. Out west, I think. Him and his freak family."

Aaron flipped a few more pages. Mountains. A lake. A newspaper article. A meadow.

There. Another photo of that expressionless boy. Grown, now. Smiling. Surrounded by a beautiful family. A wife and two teens. A son and a daughter. They were all posing in front of a decked-out Christmas tree.

Aaron tried to picture Jared and Katie as teenagers. He couldn't help but picture Katie in soaked clothes.

"You have grandkids." Aaron removed the photo. Held it in the lantern light.

Billy clapped and lost some skin on his arms. "I like your grandboy's hair! It's green!"

Richard leaned forward and snatched the photo away.

"No, I *don't*." The old man ripped off the upper-right corner. Turned it around. Showcased the green-haired grandson, separated from the family. "See this little freak? This little faggot? He's why I'm alone."

274

"Ritchie, how *dare* you say that about your grandboy!" Billy's words radiated a heat. An anger.

Richard ignored that anger. Or missed it. He took the torn-off bit of memory and shoved it into his half-emptied whiskey bottle. The sliver of photo floated a moment before sinking.

"All the *years*," the old man pushed out through clenched teeth, "all the *waiting* for that son of mine to come back. Him and that family he kept from me. And they throw it all away... all over again!"

"What did you do?" Aaron asked, even though he could guess.

"I didn't do *anything*. It was-"

"What did you do?" Aaron repeated.

"What'd you do, Ritchie?" Billy echoed.

They both stared at Richard. Waited.

"I... I was drunk. It wasn't my fault. It was *his*!" Richard shook the bottle. His grandson's photo danced inside. "I was drunk and they finally came to visit me here, after all these years, at Christmas... to- to butter me up! Get in good for my property, I bet. And I... I hit my grandson when he told me he was queer. He showed me a pit'chure of his fag boyfriend, like that was a good thing! Like that was a normal thing to just... show off and be proud of! I did *right*."

Richard's voice was weaker than his wife's lie-of-a-smile. "I did right, I did right, I did right!"

Aaron rubbed his eyes. He pushed into deep, dark, drugged-up, drunken alleys of memory. Memories from after

275

the fire. After Amy. After hope. After that fucking pool. He searched for a memory of hitting his kids. Didn't find one. He found memories of *almost* hitting them, though. *Almost* hurting them. Especially Katie.

So many *almosts*.

"You threw away a second chance you didn't even deserve," Aaron finally said.

Richard trembled. "You... you *pig*. You trash! You think you're better than me 'cause your kids are with you. You-"

"I didn't say that."

"You *did*!" Richard kicked the wirespool table. "I know I'm alone. You think I don't know that? I just want someone to *be here* with me. I *deserve* that much! They should just come back. I'd do better if they just came back!" The old man tried to roar out the words. Tried to be powerful. Tried to be right.

But Richard's roars rotted down to sobs. "They could just come back... I'd be better if they just... came *back*..."

Aaron spoke over the sobs. Spoke before he could stop himself.

"My daughter almost died because of me." Aaron looked at his hands. His gloves were soaked with sweat.

Richard stopped sobbing.

"What you mean?" Billy looked into Aaron's eyes. His blue eyes were *so* similar to the lining of that pool.

Aaron had to look away.

"It was... a few summers ago." He couldn't even remember the date — the day his child was pronounced dead for two entire minutes. "My daughter was in this shitty above-ground pool. A bunch of us at the trailers stole it off a lot to use as a... kind of community pool. I dunno. I was blacked out when it happened. Pissed at Amy. Or the memory of Amy. Pissed at my dead-end job. The trailer park manager's bitching. Everyone and everything. I knew she wanted to go swimming, even though she didn't know how. I could've made sure she stayed out, or watched her, or... *anything*. But I didn't."

Aaron pulled his gloves off. Cold assaulted his skin. The sweat between his fingers froze. Stung. He didn't care. The stinging hurt less than the memory of reaching into that over-chlorinated water.

Billy grabbed Aaron's arm.

"Is she... is..." The boy couldn't finish the question.

"I said she's alive!" Aaron winced when he saw Billy recoil. He almost put his hand on the boy's burned shoulder. But he couldn't, so he just continued.

"She has breathing trouble now, but the docs say that should heal. Eventually. Maybe. I pulled her out as fast..." Aaron looked at Richard's grandson, drowned in that whiskey. He looked away. "...as fast as I could. I *did*. Did all that CPR shit while someone called the ambulance. The whole way to the hospital, I was just thinking, '*Wow, this is gonna cost me so much fucking money.*' I didn't even take my son. He was just a toddler. I just let someone at the trailers manage him until I got back."

Aaron wiped a tear away before it could freeze.

"Kids do stupid shit," Richard reasoned. "You can't do nothin' about that."

Aaron saw his reflection in that pool. Saw Richard's reflection beside his own. He felt sick.

"It's not fair," Richard growled. "We deserve *better*."

"Deserve better…" Aaron clenched his jaw.

"We don't need them. We did our best. We deserve better. Say it." Richard slid the half-empty whiskey over to Aaron.

Aaron smelled a blackout waft out of the bottle.

"*Say* it," Richard begged.

Billy grabbed Aaron's arm again.

Katie had grabbed Aaron's arm in the hospital. Blindly reached out and found him, even with her eyes closed and her mind dark and her throat full of all those tubes. Her grip was weaker than a burned boy's.

"Say it!" Richard slammed his fist onto the diesel-engine sidetable. He hid his tears behind the gun. "Say it, please!"

Aaron saw the pool in Billy's blue eyes. Saw Katie at the bottom of the whiskey bottle. Felt the coldness of her skin in the coldness of this house.

He saw his reflection over her in that pool. Saw his reflection walk away. Disappear. Abandon her and her brother. Head off to an easier life. The life he could have lived if Katie hadn't ruined everything. If everything had just gone right.

He deserved it.

He deserved *better*.

Aaron picked up the bottle.

And threw it at Richard's face.

Glass hit gun metal and lost. Shattered. Shards flew everywhere. The stench of booze filled the air. Alcohol seeped into the old man's eyes.

The grandson's photo stuck to the revolver's cylinder.

Aaron rolled over the back of the pallets and fled. He made it to the entry hall before he heard Richard begin to move. Pursue.

"You fucker! You-"

Aaron heard Richard trip and fall and yowl out in pain. Maybe the old man had tripped over Aaron's pack. Karma.

Then Aaron tripped on his cord-shackles and fell down.

He ripped the branch tip out of his pocket. He looped the cord around its blood-covered edge. He pulled with all his strength.

The cord lost. Snapped.

"I'll kill you!" Richard stumbled into the entry hall, clutching his knee, waving the gun wildly. "I'll kill you and leave your kids *alone*, just like me!"

Aaron scrambled to his feet, sidestepping bundled wood, barrels, and crates as he fled.

He passed the stairs, nothing but hewn logs stabbing out of the wall now. The front door would be just a bit further. Then night air. Then his trailer.

Then his kids.

Aaron hit the wall and tore the keys out of his pocket. He ran his hands over the door. Searched for the handle.

But there was no handle. No door. Just a solid wall of untreated wood adorned with hooks, tools, farmhand clothes, and a cow skull.

"You will *stay here* with me!"

The revolver's hammer clicked. Echoed loud. No carpet to muffle it.

"Ritchie, don't!"

Billy leapt onto Richard's good leg and twisted the old man to the floor.

Aaron didn't look back — just pocketed the keys and clambered up the log-stairs. When he reached the middle step, he heard the revolver crack against burned skull for the second time that night.

The door at the top was gone. Just a canvas tarp now. Aaron ripped it aside and ran through to the house's second story.

There had to be a way out up here. A window to jump from. *Something*.

Nothing. Just solid wood walls. Animal stalls. Beams covered in nails and farm tools. Hay bales. A donkey. Some goats. More Dealsmith crates.

The stairs groaned behind Aaron.

He looked for somewhere to hide. He ran to a crate and threw back the top. No space. Packed full of peaches.

Then he saw a makeshift ladder dangling down behind the crate — just two ropes with chopped branches for rungs. The ladder led up to a padlocked trapdoor.

Aaron shot up to the trapdoor and its padlock. Pulled the keys out of his pocket. The keys jangled in his hand, nearly slipping out of his sweaty palm. The first key slid into the keyhole. Failed to turn. Same for keys two and three. Aaron heard the tarp ruffle. He looked down.

There stood Richard, seething, limping, gun in one hand, combat knife in the other. Moonlight snuck through gaps in the wooden walls and glimmered off both weapons. This time, Billy wasn't there to stop him.

This time, Aaron used the right key.

Click. The padlock opened. Tumbled down. It bounced off the ladder's bottom rung and slid out, right under Richard's heel as he shambled forward.

"You won't leave m-" Richard's wounded leg buckled.

Aaron didn't watch the fall. He pushed the trapdoor open and pulled himself through. He rolled to the side, away from the opening. Away from a clear shot.

The opening's metal edge was sharp. It ripped through both of his jackets. Cold air crawled through the rip and clawed at his back.

Aaron rose and looked around for an exit. Prayed to God for one.

God only presented the green stained-glass window.

Aaron could see it clearly now. *'Dealsmith Fresh Produce'* with that smiling-peach logo, and beyond, the moon accented with fireworks.

The neighbors still had fireworks.

Aaron laughed. Who bought that many fireworks? His kids would've loved to see them, especially Katie. She always said fireworks looked like flowers. She had a flower-themed bathing suit on in that pool.

Richard burst through the trapdoor, but couldn't pull himself all the way up. The jagged metal gashed the tender meat under his arm. Blood pooled around the opening. Richard didn't notice.

"I should'a shot you in the woods!" Richard aimed the gun at Aaron. His grandson's photo still clung to the cylinder.

"Then why didn't you?" Aaron's eyes darted around. Searched. He spotted some old rope hung over a wall hook. Long enough to climb down a tower? He reached into his pocket. Found the stone from the fireplace.

Richard tried to heave himself up again. He failed. Slipped on his blood. Remained where he was.

"I- I needed firewood," the old man stammered.

"You needed someone to say you didn't ruin your own life!" Aaron pulled out the stone. "Listen, I have no fucking clue what's going on here. I don't know why a little burned kid is in your house. But…" Aaron tensed his arm and squeezed the stone. "But whatever you... *did*... That's on *you*. You *have* to let me go. This isn't about me."

Moonlight filtered through the stained-glass behind Aaron. It poured over his shoulders and bathed Richard in emerald green. Somehow, the old man looked more alive than ever.

"I deserve to have someone here!" Richard shouted. "*Anyone* here!"

"My name is-"

Richard raised the gun. "I'll shoot you in the head if you tell me!"

"-is Aaron." Aaron begged the old man with his tone. Pleaded his humanity. "Now you know it. I'm Aaron. My kids' names are Katie and Jared."

Richard lowered the gun just a bit. Shifted his eyes away for just a moment.

"I have to go." Aaron's stomach churned. His eyes watered. "My children are alone. And cold. I... *left* them like that. I have to go back to them. *Now*."

"No," was all Richard could whimper. His green-sheened eyes sparkled with tears. "I can't... I can't be *alone* anymore."

Aaron pulled back his arm.

Richard cocked the revolver.

Aaron threw the stone. It cracked against Richard's forehead half an instant before the gun fired.

Blood splattered. Something shattered.

And Aaron fell down.

His head rolled. He couldn't tell up from down. Movement from stillness. Had Katie experienced this same sense of senselessness during those two dead minutes? Aaron hoped she had ignored him and turned the heat on.

He hoped Amy was alive. Safe. He hoped his wife would come back and take care of Katie and Jared.

He hoped his children could finally be happy. After he was dead and gone and out of their lives forever.

Aaron's back hit the ground. His skin started to tingle. Boil.

He opened his eyes and was immediately blinded by yellow light.

He breathed in and nearly choked on the heat.

Hell? That was fair. Child-killers burned. Even if the child only died for two minutes.

But his eyes, so used to that dark house, finally adjusted to the light.

Not hell, unless hell was a barn.

A real barn. Not a house becoming some half-dream-half-nightmare of a barn.

A barn in the South.

Georgia, maybe.

Aaron stood and stripped off his outer jacket, then his inner. His sweater came off with a tug, nearly glued to his undershirt with sweat.

Aaron looked up high. He saw the green stained-glass window from Richard's house. Aaron looked around. He saw all the animals from Richard's. He saw all the farming equipment from Richard's. He saw all the grain sacks and corn and wheat and peach crates from Richard's.

Then he saw a pair of blue eyes from Richard's.

Tucked away in a secluded corner stall, on hay bales made gold in an oil lantern's dim light, sat two boys. One boy had Billy's piercing blue eyes — but also skin. He was sunburned and wore nothing but a well-worn pair of overalls.

The other boy was bigger. Maybe a year older. Maybe thirteen. Fourteen. He wore a dirty shirt and ratty jeans held up by a rattier belt. Freckles speckled his brow.

They were both smiling. Laughing. Eating peaches. Paying attention to each other and nothing else.

"Hello?" Aaron walked over. His feet squished with sweat. A honey bee buzzed past his ear. Neither boy acknowledged him.

"I bet Dealsmith wouldn't never run outta peaches," the boy-who-had-to-be-Billy mused, "even if that's all we ate from here on out, forever. Breakfast, lunch, and supper."

"Billy?" Aaron touched Billy's shoulder. The boy didn't react. "Am I dead?"

Pain blazed across Aaron's temple. He prodded the pain. His fingers came away bloody.

The other boy laughed and bit into a peach. Juice dripped down his chin and clung to barely-there peach fuzz. "Bet we wouldn't eat no more peaches if he caught us."

"He'd tell our pas." Billy cringed. "I'd for sure get switched."

The other boy put his head on his knees and didn't speak for a long time. "Mine'd throw me out the house to live with the pigs. At least for a week. Maybe a month. Or even for *forever*. I never know how long I'll be alone when he puts me out. Them pigs smell so bad."

Aaron stepped back. "Oh shit."

The voice was different. Not hateful. Not old. Not ruined.

But definitely Richard's.

A pig squealed in the stall next to the boys, triggering five more to start up. The pigs' stall was barred from the wood floor up to the rafters high above. Its gate sported a sign.

'DON'T OPEN! KEEP PADLOCK ON LATCH! HOO-DEE-NEE HOGS!'

Billy finished his peach. "You know what, Ritchie? I bet we'll find Quagmire's skull in no time if we sneak out just a few nights a week to go diggin' around." He tossed the pit away. A chicken and a scraggly cat chased it into a corner. "Let's start out by the Wilson's creek."

"I should'a never told you that horseshit tale." Ritchie flicked Billy's nose. "You're more gung-ho 'bout it than I ever was."

Aaron wandered back to the center of the barn and yelled out to anyone and no one, "Can someone tell me what the fuck is going on?"

"*No!*" a voice cried.

Aaron screamed.

A cow mooed.

The boys just giggled to themselves.

Aaron looked toward the voice, toward the pig stall. There, near the back, in the muck and the shit, crawled the old man. Richard.

"You?" Aaron rushed to the bars. "*You*. You *shot* me."

Aaron pulled at the gate. Locked. Per the sign.

Billy grabbed another peach from a sack at Ritchie's feet. "I'm tellin' you, we'll find it. Then we'll buy up every peach orchard in Georgia!"

Richard forced his way past the pigs. The old man didn't react at all when Aaron grabbed his throat through the bars. He just shouted, "Not here! Not this!"

He shouted it over and over and over.

Aaron pulled back his fist, prepared to pulp the old man's face. But the fear in Richard's eyes froze him. That fear was directed at everything. Everywhere.

"Stop them!" the old man wailed. "*Please*! Just stop them!"

"Aaaand," Billy teased, "we can eat peaches forever, together! And them nasty lemon things you eat all the time."

Ritchie put his hands on Billy's shoulders and slid off the younger boy's overall straps. "You're such a nut."

"I am? I don't even like nuts!" Billy tussled Ritchie's hair and unbuckled the older boy's belt.

Richard shoved Aaron back. "Hurry!" the old man shouted as he tore at the gate's padlock. "Get him out! Get him *out*!"

Adrenaline flooded Aaron's veins. He saw his reflection in that pool. He started toward the boys. He made it halfway. Then his left foot locked into place. Then his right. His feet began to burn. He looked down.

Stuck.

Stuck and sinking.

Sinking into a puddle of liquid gold.

"You're def'n'tly a nut," Ritchie said. He tugged Billy's overalls off and threw them aside. "That's all right, though. That's better'n all the others around here. 'Cause I know you won't leave me. Like Ma did. Like Pa does. And I don't eat lemon candies *that* much."

Billy kissed Ritchie's forehead. "Course I won't leave. I won't ever, never leave you and your forehead freckles."

Aaron struggled, but only sank deeper. He fell to his knees. The gold seeped into his pants. Began to cook his calves.

Ritchie grabbed Billy's shoulders and kissed him. "You taste like peaches," he murmured.

The gold reached Aaron's waist. Trapped his left hand.

Richard slammed his bloodied side into the pig-gate over and over as he screamed and screamed.

Billy grabbed Ritchie's face and whispered, "I'll steal Dealsmith's peaches with you forever."

The boys lay down.

Then a side door on the opposite end of the barn flew open.

"Hey, Ritchie," came a new voice.

"Where you at?" A second new voice.

Two boys, same age as Ritchie. One tall, one short.

"Oh God," Richard moaned, "don't do this again! God! Not *again*!"

"What'a we do?" Billy squeaked. He grabbed Ritchie's arm.

"Shut up!" Ritchie pushed Billy away as he frantically pulled his pants up.

"We're headin' down to Grant's store to swipe some dip," the tall boy called out. The newcomers reached Aaron and walked past him, drawn to the lantern light. "You wanna-"

The short boy saw Ritchie, belt undone. Saw Billy, naked and struggling to get one leg into his overalls.

"Ho-lee shit!" the short boy announced. "Look-ee here!"

"*NOOO!*" Richard squealed from his pig stall.

The gold crushed in around Aaron's chest. He struggled to breathe against its weight.

"Ritchie?" Billy whispered.

Ritchie kicked Billy away when the blue-eyed boy crawled over to him for help. For protection.

"Ritchie, what'n the hell's goin' on?" the tall boy asked.

"You two bein' queer?" the short boy sniggered.

"Shut up!" Ritchie slipped his belt out — the belt he hadn't finished lacing back on. "I… I found *this* one bein' queer. The other one… he ran off before I got a look at him. Yeah. But *this* freak I know for sure's queer. And I got him trapped!"

"Ritchie?" Billy whispered again.

"I don't believe you," the short boy shot back. "Your pa's gonna kick you out for good when we tell him. Say you ain't his kin 'n' ship you right off to a orphanage!"

The gold reached Aaron's shoulders. He threw his free arm out. Grabbed onto the wood near the molten metal's edge. Struggled to keep his head above the surface.

"I *ain't*!" Ritchie shouted over the pigs' squeals and Billy's whimpers. "I just was gettin' ready to teach this one a lesson!"

"Prove it," the short boy taunted.

"Yeah, prove it," the tall boy echoed.

"*Prove it! Prove it! Prove it! Or we'll tell everyone and everyone'll leave you!*"

"Don't!" Aaron yelled.

Then the gold rushed into his mouth. Poured down his throat. He thrashed. Choked. His skin cooked, inside and out. His eyesight blurred.

Ritchie swung the belt. The buckle struck Billy's face hard enough to rupture his cheek. Blood poured out and flowed down his jaw.

Then the two nameless boys became rabid dogs.

They kicked Billy. Punched him. Tore at his skin. Knocked his teeth out. Stomped on his hands and ankles. All while Ritchie whipped Billy with his belt again and again and again.

Ritchie cried while he mutilated Billy. The nameless boys didn't notice. They were too busy laughing.

Billy's face changed with each strike from the belt buckle. Each new fracture. All that hate twisted him. Mutated him. Those blue eyes never changed, though.

Those blue eyes stayed bright through all of it.

Ritchie's belt clipped the oil lantern on its eighth arc. The oil lantern fell to the straw-covered floor. The glass shattered. The fire inside got out.

Katie had started the fire at Aaron's old house when she tried to cook some noodles by herself. Not her fault. She was alone. Aaron had taken Amy out to party, to celebrate one year in their new home and a baby Jared on the way. Why hadn't he called a babysitter? Katie was just hungry. Just a child.

Those flames had engulfed his house so fast.

Those flames were nothing compared to these.

These flames crawled up the walls and licked at the rafters in seconds.

Aaron looked to Richard for help as he choked on liquid gold and smoke.

But the old man was just a pig now, panicking like all the other pigs, only differentiated by his bloody side.

"Ritchie?" Billy gurgled through blood and broken teeth and bits of peach, shock setting in from the beating. From the sight of the flames.

The fire roared up between Billy and his attackers. It pushed the three monsters back. It kept the blue-eyed boy from crawling out of that corner stall on his ruined limbs.

Ritchie stood there, frozen, even in all that heat.

The short boy ran for the exit while the tall boy pulled Ritchie's shoulder.

"Come on, Ritchie!" the tall boy screeched. "Come on!"

But Ritchie didn't move. The tall boy ran.

Ritchie hesitated for one more moment.

Then he took a step back.

Then he turned.

Then he ran away.

"Ritchie?" Billy managed one more time.

The fire jumped onto Billy's legs. He started screaming.

Aaron cried as he listened — was forced to listen. No hands free to cover his ears.

The fire tore down the rafters over the pigs. The flaming wood fell onto the animals. Cooked them alive. The scent of bacon filled the air.

Aaron lost his grip on the wood. He caught one last look at Billy — thrashing, wailing, wreathed in flame — before he sank below the boiling gold.

Down and down and down.

To drown.

Just like Katie in that pool.

The light faded away. Darkness returned.

Bubbling metal and roaring flames gave way to crackling pops and whistling wind.

There was burning, stinging. But from cold, not heat.

Aaron lay there. Breathed. Came back to himself. Then rocketed to his feet.

No molten gold filling his lungs. No melting flesh. Just a bullet graze across his temple.

He looked around.

No Dealsmith barn. No raging fire. No burning Billy. Just a still attic, a shattered stained-glass window, and bright fireworks in the black sky beyond.

Aaron's jackets and sweater were back on. The sweat came back with him as well, frozen into a thin layer of ice against his skin. It cracked as he moved toward the bloody trapdoor. He knelt down. The photo of Richard's grandson sat in the dried blood, next to the keyring. He picked both up and pocketed them without thinking, then looked down below.

No more rickety rope ladder. Just a short pulldown ladder like any attic would have. Richard lay at the bottom, unmoving, save for the breaths smoking out of his mouth.

The revolver sat beside him.

Aaron rushed down, grabbed the gun, and aimed it at the old man. The second level was just a house now, same as the attic. No wooden pens. No donkeys. No goats or peaches or crates or farm tools.

Just a pathetic old man with a bloodied forehead.

"Get up," Aaron ordered.

The old man curled into a ball. One leg jutted out awkwardly, ruined in the fall. "I was scared of Pa finding out."

Aaron didn't hear any humming. Any whistling. Any giggling. Any happiness.

"Where's the kid?" He looked around, but there were no blue eyes in the dark. "Where'd Billy go?"

"I ran," Richard moaned as he sat up, "but I never got away from him." His shattered leg didn't move right with the rest of him. "He was always in my head. Then he was *here*. Always here, ever since everyone else left me." The old man stood, barely, hunched down, using the wall as a crutch. "Now he's gone."

Aaron needed to look down to meet Richard's eyes.

Richard's eyes begged to die. "He never even got mad at me for what we… what I… *did to him*."

Aaron pressed the revolver to Richard's forehead, finger on the trigger. He tried to find a reason not to shoot.

A firework went off. Threw a bit of light through a window. A bit of the light hit Richard's face. Revealed a smattering of faded freckles on the old man's brow, barely visible through age and blood.

Aaron lowered the revolver and opened the cylinder to empty the chambers. Remove temptation.

One spent case fell out. Just one. Aaron looked at the old man. The old man stared back in silence, then turned away and started off toward the stairs, sliding against the wall for support.

Aaron's chest tightened. He pocketed the gun. It rested against his gun-lighter.

"You got a phone up here?" Aaron asked.

"Only one's by my chair," Richard answered.

"Let's get you down there, then. You're looking pretty bad." Aaron walked over and started to help Richard move. The wound under the old man's arm continued to bleed. "I'll call the paramedics before I go."

"Go?" Richard grabbed Aaron's arm. His grip was weaker than an almost-drowned girl's.

"Yeah," Aaron said.

"Right. Your kids."

They reached the stairs. Richard took a step down. Then the old man paused, turned back, and looked deep into the dark behind Aaron. "That room at the end. My room."

Aaron turned. "What about it?"

"There's a safe by my bed. Combination's seven, twelve, fifty-seven." Richard pointed with a shaking hand. "Get the sack. Nothing else matters."

Aaron looked at Richard. "You can get downstairs?"

"Yes."

Aaron looked at Richard harder. "You gonna call the cops?"

"No."

A gamble. A stupid one. But Aaron was stupid for getting into this mess in the first place. For not being with Katie and Jared. He walked to the bedroom while Richard hobbled downstairs.

The bedroom was tiny. Definitely not the house's master bedroom. Just a single bed with a large iron safe beside it and trash strewn everywhere else. No lights, either — just a window and moonglow.

And the bedroom stank. Stank of booze. Piss. Rotten food. Someone who didn't care about being alive.

Smelled like Aaron's trailer.

He knelt in front of the safe. The moon gave up just enough light for him to see the numbers etched into the dial.

Seven, twelve, fifty-seven.

The latch clicked. The safe opened. Aaron reached in and pulled out everything his fingers found in the dark.

An official paper from the army — something about '*failing to adapt*' and boot camp. A bunch of newspaper clippings about a mismanaged business getting cannibalized by a competitor thanks to an incompetent owner. Dozens of photos, all faded and warped from being soaked in something. Whiskey, maybe.

And an old burlap sack, marked with that smiling-peach logo, shoved all the way to the back. Aaron dragged it out, onto the carpet. Heavy as bricks. It stirred up the dust.

The dust. The one thing Aaron wished would've stayed gone.

He heaved up the sack and carried it down to the den.

There sat Richard, hunched in his recliner, wheezing and bleeding into the cushions, surrounded by a comical amount of kindling — and finishing off a near-empty box of lemon-flavored candies.

Aaron wove through the wood bundles and set the sack in Richard's lap. He looked around.

Same as upstairs. No barn. No melding realities. No little burned boy.

No. There was one thing. A charred, warped oil lantern sat on the coffee table where the battery-powered lantern should've been.

"Billy moved next door when I was seven." Richard hugged the sack to his chest. "Moved from up north somewhere. Not sure from where up here. He was so odd. I picked on him so much. We all did." He untied the twine around the top of the sack. "Then I got to know him. He was so... *warm* to be around. Not like my friends. Not like Pa. He said he'd never leave me alone. That's all I wanted. To not be alone."

Richard opened the sack.

"Your mom?" Aaron looked into the sack. Dirt. No, dirt and ash all mixed together.

"Dead before I could remember." Richard touched the ashy soil. "Pa might as well've been, much as he ignored me. Billy never ignored me." The old man dug his hands into the ashes.

A firework went off.

"You can call your kid. Your grandkids." Aaron tried to force some hope into the words. "You can still rebuild that bridge, man. They'll forgive you."

"No," Richard sighed out, "they won't. They shouldn't. Not after what I done." The old man started to weep. His tears fell into the ash. "My son took care of my wife better than I ever could, after the two finally worked up the nerve to run off. I hated my wife so much… just 'cause she wasn't Billy. 'Cause she didn't make me forget Billy. Nothing ever could. It wasn't her fault, but I hated her for it all the same."

Richard dug deeper into the ashes.

He continued, "I went back to the Dealsmith farm after I couldn't cut it in the army. They never rebuilt that barn. Everyone thought it was cursed after… it happened. Still just ash, all those years later. Everything but one wall and that green window. I climbed up there later. Stole it. I don't know why."

Aaron swallowed hard. He wondered how far Richard's bullet went after it shattered through that green stained-glass window.

Richard seemed to find something buried in the ash. "I dug a hole there with my hands, where he died. Dug till my nails came off. Was gonna blow my brains out with that revolver once I dug a hole deep enough to be a grave. Then I found this, three feet down… and lost my nerve to go through with it."

Richard pulled something out of the sack and tossed it onto the coffee table. It made a loud thud. Dented the wood. The thing was a bit larger than a human head. A firework exploded outside. Its light shimmered off the thing. Bright gold.

Aaron's jaw dropped. "You've gotta be shitting me."

A gnarled, knotted, absolutely massive hunk of gold. Quagmire's skull. Right there.

Aaron picked the gold up to prove that it was real. It was so heavy. His fingers found a relatively clean edge on one side, almost like someone had cleaved chunks of the gold off with a hatchet.

He looked at Richard. The old man didn't seem to care about the life-changing amount of money in Aaron's hands. The old man just stared into that sack of ashes.

"Not a skull dipped in gold by a crazy man," Richard murmured. "Just skull-shaped gold. Billy would'a been disappointed." He closed his eyes. "Any money I had came from that… *thing*. Chopped off a bit to move up here, away from Georgia, and build this house I didn't deserve. Used it to barely support a family I didn't fucking deserve. Started my failure-of-a-business with it. Lost *all* that… all on my own. I kept as much as I could. I couldn't let it disappear.

The last thing that… made me think of him. The last thing that wasn't ash."

Aaron thought of the safe. The thought made him colder. He was surprised it was even possible to feel *colder* in this house. "That combination. That's the date. When it happened. Right?"

"July twelfth, 1957." Richard leaned forward and pulled the oil lantern over. "The day Billy died." He bent down and picked up the matchbox. "No. The day I murdered him." He started striking matches. None sparked.

Keep the gold. Every fiber of Aaron's being screamed it. *Run with it, right now.* The keys were in his pocket. The front door was back. Freedom was a sprint away. Aaron deserved the gold after all this. He deserved it more than Richard.

Then he thought of his daughter in that pool.

Aaron offered the gold back.

Richard kept striking matches. "Take it."

"What?"

"It was never mine. It was supposed to be *ours*. And I kept him from ever seein' it."

A gift. Aaron could have it and not even be a criminal.

But he thought of drowning in that gold again. Thought of Katie drowning in that pool again. Thought of his reflection disappearing again.

The gold fell from his hand, down to the carpet. It kicked up a plume of dust.

"My Katie," he mumbled, ashamed to hear her name on his tongue. "I didn't... I didn't pull her out at first. I didn't get her out as fast as I could've. I looked in and... I walked off when I saw her at the bottom. I looked in and saw her and then I just... walked off."

Aaron paused. Waited for Richard to say something. He wanted the old man to call him a monster. Call him *kin*. The old man just looked at him with tired eyes.

"She burned my house down. She ruined my life and I... I just wanted one accident to take another accident off my hands. I wanted her to *pay* for it! For *everything*!" Aaron dug his fingers into his bullet graze. He took the pain. Wanted worse. Deserved so much worse. "I was *happy* that my baby girl was going to die."

He sank to the floor and bawled until he felt like vomiting.

"You went back, though," Richard whispered, holding the ashes close. "You went back and pulled her out."

"That doesn't change anything! My baby girl... I was gonna let her die. Oh *God*. My baby girl... I was... I was going to *kill* my baby girl. My *Katie*. It doesn't change *ANYTHING*!"

Aaron vomited. He wailed and moaned and punched the floor and flipped the coffee table over and kicked up dust and wished the revolver had its bullet back.

Then Richard leaned forward and touched Aaron's shoulder.

"It changed something." The old man put his face in the sack and kissed the ashes. He struck one last match. No flames. No more matches.

Aaron wiped the snot and tears and vomit off his face. He stood and pulled his gun-lighter out.

"Here." Aaron clicked the trigger and produced a tiny flame. He touched the flame to the oil lantern's wick.

It lit.

"Birthday gift from my kids," Aaron said, voice still shaking. "They bought it with my money. Snuck it out of my wallet at the gas station. I was so pissed at them."

His gun-lighter — it came from the same gas station where he first met Amy. Maybe he could find out where Amy went. Call her. Maybe she would answer.

Aaron looked down at his gun-lighter. He loved his gun-lighter more than he could ever love that burned-down house. He pocketed the gift and felt paper touch his finger. The photograph of Richard's grandson. Aaron pulled it out and handed it to the old man.

Richard smiled. He kissed the photo, then pushed it down into the ashes.

"Thank you," the old man said, "for movin' in all the wood. Go, please."

Then Richard stopped talking. Stopped looking at anything but the sack in his lap.

And the lit oil lantern in his hand.

Aaron grabbed his pack off the floor. He found his gloves. He laid Richard's empty revolver on the couch. Then he knelt down and picked up Quagmire's skull. Aaron hesitated for a moment. He looked at Richard. Richard nodded. Aaron slid the fortune into his pack.

He headed out of the den, down the entry hall, to the front door. He unlocked the door and hung the keys on a wall hook before closing up behind him.

A faint glow bloomed in the first-floor windows as Aaron walked around the front. By the time he reached the side yard, fire flickered in the second-floor windows. By the time he made it to the game path's entrance, the house's roof billowed with smoke.

All that wood. All that dust. It caught quick.

The heat reached out and touched Aaron's face, even this far from the flames. His footprints from all those trips fetching wood filled with water. The puddles captured the firelight. Speckled the snow with pools of gold.

Then Aaron heard giggling.

He looked up to the empty circle where the Dealsmith window used to be, green glass now replaced with yellow flames.

Standing in the flames, impervious to them, stood two boys.

Ritchie, young and happy and unruined by himself. Billy, unburned and beautifully alive.

They held each other as more smoke rose. As more windows cracked. As more flames bathed everything in heat and light.

Then the boys melded with the heat and light. Melded with each other. Became each other.

And then they were gone.

Aaron's nose and cheeks began to burn. He turned and headed into the woods.

He touched the pack at his chest. Felt the gold at his heart. But that gold wasn't useful. Not yet.

Aaron checked his wallet.

Seven dollars.

Just enough to fill up that little gas can in the bed of his truck.

Just enough to get his trailer's generator kicked on if need be.

Just enough to run the heat for his kids until sunrise.

Acknowledgements

Nothing is created from nothing, even in a creative field. All art — its uniqueness and strangeness and vibrancy — germinates from the support of friends and family, and from the inspiration ignited by the works of other creative minds. This is true for every author and artist and musician and creator under the sun, and I am no different in this respect.

So, I would like to take a moment and give credit where credit is due.

I would like to thank my mom and dad for their love and support.

I would like to thank Christopher Copeland for providing the fantastic cover art for this book.

I would like to thank professor-and-author James Braziel, who was instrumental in the conceptualization, creation, and editing of this book.

I would like to thank all of the creators whose works I referenced in this book — the scores of people behind Dungeons & Dragons, as well as Hayao Miyazaki, just to name a few.

I would like to thank British English for letting me constantly borrow its spellings of words… because I can't help myself.

And lastly, I would like to thank every author and bookworm out there who keeps the joy of the written word alive in this world.

* 9 7 9 8 9 9 2 8 0 4 1 1 9 *